THE Avant CHAMPION

~Ashes~

C. B. Samet

THE AVANT CHAMPION

ASHES

CB SAMET

NOVELS BY CB SAMET

For Mom

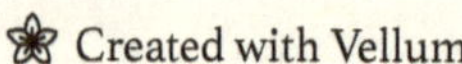 Created with Vellum

1
———

Fierce blasts of icy wind threatened to blow me off the mountainside. I closed my grip on the jutting rocks as tightly as my gloved fingers allowed. I pulled my head deeper into my leopard furs—the same way a turtle retracts into its shell.

Above me, even through the howl of the wind, I could hear the snarl of the wolves overhead. I wriggled the toe of my boot into a crevice of rock, securing my leverage, and then pushed up with my thigh muscles.

"*Mother Moon*," I swore.

Starving animals threatened to eat me. The wind threatened to freeze me. The looming gorge below threatened to break me. Death lurked in every direction. Yet I only had one direction to go in.

To the drooling anticipation of the beasts above, I clambered upward on the frigid mountainside.

"Sure, Dean Lariat," I cursed to myself, as I pushed up another half-meter. "I'll take the students on a mountain field trip. What could possibly go wrong?"

Pausing to take breath, I answered my own question: "Oh. Only a spontaneous blizzard, during an unprecedented season of wolf over-population."

I shook my head.

"'Why Abigail,'" I mocked Dean Lariat's voice, imagining what she might have said, "'you should have transported everyone home at the first sign of impending clouds.'"

Ha! I'd have been happy to—except that *some* of the students thought it would be fun to wander off.

After I rounded them up and corralled them in the safety of tightly-packed pines, I spent the next hour rescuing various other stray hikers.

A silken male voice suddenly sounded in my ears: "Some might question your sanity, Abigail, if you continue this conversation with yourself."

Fortunately, Mal didn't physically appear and only spoke to me audibly. An abrupt appearance might have distracted my climbing efforts—not that I'd have been able to see much of him through this storm anyway.

"So says my imaginary friend," I replied grimly.

"That I exist only in your mind doesn't make me imaginary."

I huffed and pushed myself further up the mountainside. "Not imaginary? Well, let's think about that. Only *I* can see you. Only *I* can hear you. The evidence supports my imagination."

Cold bursts of wind stung my cheeks.

"If I'm a figment of your imagination," Mal retorted, with that infuriating calmness of his, "would I be able to give you such valuable information about the future? Would I have led you to all those stranded hikers?"

I hoisted myself higher on the cliff face. "About that, Mal," I argued with the voice in my head. "It would have been immensely more valuable had you warned me further in advance about the storm—and mentioned the wolf infestation."

He scoffed. "I'm a powerful entity, but I'm not all omniscient—and you are being ungrateful."

"Deepest apologies, *prince of darkness*. My normal abundance of gratitude must have fallen off the edge of the cliff at the same time I tumbled down the embankment."

Mal remained silent for a moment, punishing me for my sarcasm.

He spoke at last, "Why aren't you simply transporting yourself back to flatter ground?"

My footing slipped slightly. I gasped, somehow caught myself, and then took a ragged moment to breathe and steady my shaking muscles.

Merciful monks.

Stiff, cold, and wrapped in twenty kilograms of fur, I felt rigid. "This blizzard has my star sense discombobulated," I snapped at Mal. "I can't get my bearings to transport."

My transporting ability originated from a blue star tattoo on my palm, gifted to me by a Blue Gypsy many years ago. With its power, I could transport myself—and other people or objects—anywhere I had been or seen; or to anywhere a person I touched had been and I could envision.

The star had saved many lives over the years—especially *mine*—but it did have limitations. For example, whatever speed I was traveling at when I transported, I'd continue at when I arrived at my destination. Therefore, if I fell off this cliff face right now, I *could* transport, but wherever I chose to appear, I'd be moving at the same speed and facing the same force of impact as where I'd left.

I had also discovered there were places on the planet I couldn't travel into or out of—such as the enchanted Black Stag Forest in the Southern marsh.

Lastly, I'd discovered in only the past half-hour the conundrum posed by severe weather: When I'd tried to envision where I wanted to transport—back to the flat mountain trail—I only saw a white haze of blinding snow.

If I transported under these conditions, would I land on sure footing? Or would I land on top of someone—perhaps even one of my students? Or, even worse, would I land right in the middle of a pack of wolves?

Such were the conditions and uncertainty that left me climbing this cliff, in the middle of a blizzard, while conversing with the evil entity residing within me—Mal.

Well, *partially* evil.

Mal mostly behaved himself, but I was never certain if his good behavior was the product of our friendship, or merely the limits of his confinement within me.

"You know, I could warm you up if you so desired." Mal's voice was a smooth purr, conjuring images of how he appeared in my dreams—a lean, dark-suited figure with long lashes around predatorial eyes, whose darkness was perpetually filled with a mixture of amusement and sensual hunger.

"No, thank you, Mal. Happily married. Three children. Remember?"

As I felt for the lip of the top ledge—finally reaching the peak of this gargantuan cliff—I heard the snapping and gnashing of teeth that sounded entirely too close.

"How many?"

"Four," Mal answered.

"Splendid."

Before I'd even clambered over the edge of the cliff, teeth clamped down on the sleeve of my furs. I yanked my hand back into the sleeve, as the hungry wolf looming above me snarled. He shook his head violently with a mouth of fur and no meat.

As I brought my torso up over the ridge, a second wolf snapped at my head. I jerked away from him, too, and he sank his teeth into my shoulder. Fortunately, the beast mostly chomped down on a mouthful of fur coat, but I still felt the pressure of his jaws. When he thrashed his head back-and-forth, pain shot through my shoulder.

I scrambled, desperately dragging the rest of my body up onto the top of the cliff. Crawling blindly, I kept my face down, buried in the snow, to avoid giving the wolves any further opportunity to snap or bite at my head.

As I crawled, I lashed out with my right hand, and my fingers clamped down around the wolf's throat. Using the strength of my Warrior Stone, I squeezed. The animal yelped, releasing his vice-like jaws from my shoulder. As he warily backed away, the pain eased. Even without looking, I knew the wolf hadn't broken skin, but his teeth would still leave wicked bruises.

The other wolf continued to snarl and shake his head, shredding my sleeve while unleashing ferocious growls.

I pushed myself up to my knees and blinked the snow from my eyes.

Almost as soon as I'd done so, a third wolf leapt onto my back, seizing my hood in his jaws. His weight almost sent me toppling face-first back into the snow. I reached back and grabbed one of the legs he had hooked around my shoulders. Again, using my Warrior Stone, I hurled the wolf from my back into the other wolf—the one determined to find my arm within my sleeve. The impact sent them both flying.

The fourth famished animal lunged for my face. I ducked, and a rapidly-fading howl of fear followed him as he plummeted off the edge of the cliff.

As I wiped the remaining snow from my face, I braced for yet another attack. Instead, squinting into the dense sheet of white, I saw the wolves retreating. One limped away, and I suspected his companions were hungry enough to turn on him in due time.

Now with a moment's respite, I rested on my knees, catching my breath and shivering in the frigid air. It constricted my lungs, stifling me even as it gave me life.

"*That* could have ended badly." Mal appeared and stood over me, the freezing wind and blinding snow whipping straight through his non corporeal body.

"It did ... for the wolves."

Thankfully, the Warrior Stone had given me the strength of a giant, otherwise I'd be sixty kilograms of wolf dinner right now.

"Are you injured?"

I shoved myself to my feet. "Awe, Mal. I didn't know you cared. Touching."

"Of course I care. If you die, my next source of entertainment doesn't arrive for almost a thousand years."

"Pity." I began to trudge through the snow away from the cliff.

"Did we get all the hikers?" I asked.

"Yes."

"You're certain?"

"Without a doubt."

Mal had been not only the one to alert me to the stranded hikers, but he also ensured I found each and every one of them.

"Can you lead me to the students?"

I'd left them safely under shelter, warmed by a fire, but I wasn't sure I could correctly transport myself there in this raging storm.

"One diversion first."

I brushed clumps of snow off my knees as I followed Mal's spectral form. We'd already had about ten diversions today, and the safety of the students was supposed to be my top priority.

"Nearly dying on a cliff's edge qualifies as a diversion."

"This one's better." Mal led me to a cluster of pine trees and rocks.

As he nonchalantly pretended to lean against a tree (since he couldn't *actually* touch anything), he nodded toward the rocks. They were slick with ice and snow.

"In there?" I glanced skeptically at him.

"Yes."

"Is what? A bear? Giant, blood-sucking spiders?" What scheming caused that ridiculous quirk of his lips?

A whimpering sound emitted from a crevice between the rocks. I looked down and saw a ball of hair with blue eyes staring up at me.

"Oh, Mal! What am I supposed to do with a wolf pup?"

I maneuvered onto the rock and ensured my feet were secured, before reaching down for the black furball. My gloved hands closed around him

"I've no idea," Mal scoffed. "You should've considered that before you made it an orphan. You could leave it there—a snack for another wolf."

I lifted up the shivering pup. "I have children, and horses, and chickens. I can't raise a wolf." I stuffed the pup into my coat, before pulling the thick fabric back around me.

Mal straightened, looking pleased with himself. "Yet, you saved him still. You have a horse seasoned in battle, a hawk capable of blinding a Black Marsh adder, and now you've added a wolf to your armament."

"I don't *need* an armament, remember? I'm only needed in times of crisis, and those crises have all been managed."

"Are you certain?"

I glared at him. "To my students, if you please."

"As you wish. They're dawdling in a dense cluster of trees north-east of here."

"Lead the way."

The sooner I returned the students to their cabins out of the storm, the sooner I could submerge into a delightfully warm bath.

By the time the sun had set, I'd finally returned all the students to their cabins, safe from wind and snow and warmed by a fire. We'd all travel back to the university tomorrow, where I'd be heralded as a hero for saving both students and hikers.

Not in this universe.

I'd likely face an inquisition about endangering the students during a blizzard.

I felt exhausted from the effort of star traveling, using my Warrior Stone to fight a pack of wolves, and trudging through thirty centimeters of dense snowfall.

The small creature still in my coat wriggled.

I pulled out the wolf cub and held him up. "You're a cute thing, aren't you?"

He licked my hands.

"If my children take one look at you, they'll want to keep you. But I can't have you eating my chickens—and no one has time to train you."

But somebody somewhere else does.

I transported, and immediately appeared in the Gunthi Monk sanctuary, outside the dining hall. The sound of clinking dishes and congenial conversation emerged from the large room, which was bathed in the soft glow of candlelight.

In the distance, the muffled sound of a waterfall gave a pleasant, ambient noise to the sanctuary, adding even more tranquility to the monks' secluded home.

Around me, tall cliffs of tan and red rock rose up from the valley. A rich, sapphire, star-lit sky twinkled above, and the two moons—mother and infant—cast a gentle glow on the grass and trees.

Zack walked by me at that moment and stopped at my abrupt appearance. His long, white hair danced softly in the gentle breeze as his blue cloak rustled around him.

"Abigail?" He stared at my heavy furs, still thick with ice. The sanctuary was far to the south of the present blizzard, and this cool, spring day required nothing more than a sweater.

"Zack, I'm sorry to drop in unannounced at meal time."

He looked around with a raised eyebrow. "At least I don't see any caged giants with you this time."

That had been an isolated event.

"Only this." I held up the puppy.

He smiled, the wrinkles around his eyes crinkling. "And what crime has this creature committed?"

I bit my lip. "I may have killed his parent—in self-defense, I might add. I was hoping Baird could take him."

"I'll go get him."

I took a step forward. "I'm late picking up Joshua. Do you think you could take the pup to Baird for me? I'll come back tomorrow to see him and explain."

Zack took the wolf cub and patted his head. "I'll take him to Baird."

"Thank you." I bowed.

Instantly, I transported myself to Joshua's clinic and found him scribing by candlelight. As I admired him quietly working, I recalled how Joshua had always preferred candlelight to bioluminescent lamps, which had a brighter glow but were tinted with an aqua hue emitting from the algae lining the glass.

Joshua's office was surrounded with shelves of books, herbs— both dried and packaged—, and varieties of liquid tinctures. One supply cabinet overflowed with dressings for various traumas, and numerous ointments for skin infections and burns. Joshua had spent a dozen years building this place, stocking everything he could for the many illnesses that arrived at his door.

He turned to me and stood. "Abbey! I thought you might eventually remember your husband." He gave me an affectionate kiss on the cheek.

"I'm so sorry. A snow storm hit us unexpectedly, and I've been rescuing people ever since."

"It's okay. Breathe." His golden-brown eyes twinkled as he placed his hands on my shoulders. "I know when you're late, it's always for a gallant reason—you're not gone at the marketplace to buy jewelry. Now, let's get us home and get you out of those wet furs."

I nodded and transported us home.

Together, we walked up the driveway, crunching across the snow still left from a light dusting several days ago. Tall oaks rose around us, canopying our walkway. As we approached our home, the blue-green glow of bioluminescent lanterns emitted from the main room. When we entered our house, the children flocked to Joshua, lavishing him with kisses.

Paul approached me. "Mama, you look like a bear!"

I growled playfully, making him giggle. As I peeled off my heavy furs, Natalie left her father's embrace and walked over to me, hands on her hips.

"You're late. *Again.*"

"Yes."

Her eyes narrowed. "You're *always* late."

"Not always." Twenty-five percent of the time was nowhere near 'always.'

Joshua placed a gentle hand on Natalie's shoulder. "Be easy on your mother. She does a lot of important work."

"We're important," she replied, her gaze dropping to the floor.

My heart felt an unpleasant surge of guilt. "Of course you are. That's why I'll always come back home—even if I'm late on occasion."

Natalie seemed to accept my statement, although she didn't soften enough to grant me a hug.

I slumped in the kitchen chair, numb to the screaming around me.

I had slain evil, mastered swordsmanship, fought giants, earned an advanced degree in chemistry, ended a civil war, freed an entombed wizard, and rescued an island of people from a harbor wave, but none of these feats prepared me for motherhood.

Rebekah screamed relentlessly. Squirming at the table, she refused her cabbage with a raging belligerence, as if I was trying to force boiling lava down her throat. Paul ran through the kitchen with a battle cry as he held his wooden sword high in the air. Natalie vied for my attention, all because a button was missing from her dress.

"Mama. Mama. Mama," she repeated.

I closed my eyes for a long moment, wishing Joshua was here rather than at work. It was a Saturday, after all—a family day, not a working day.

All of our weekday childcare had the day off, which left only the children and me. I was entirely outnumbered.

Opening my eyes, I looked at the toddler who'd strewn her food all across the table, her lap, and the floor.

"Rebekah," my calm, firm voice cut through her temper tantrum. "You may leave the table, but you're *not* eating again until supper."

She scowled. "Why?"

I lowered her out of her high chair. "It will take at least that long to clean up this mess."

She ran out the front door before I'd even finished answering her question.

"Paul, can you keep an eye on your sister?"

My son gave me a laborious sigh before following her out the door. I watched him go. He was growing so fast—already five-years-old. I needed to let the hem of his pants down two centimeters and sew the hole in the knee.

"Mama. Mama. Mama."

I turned my glaring look towards my oldest child—the one who was supposed to be at the age of reason. Natalie should recognize that I couldn't address her buttons while dealing with a mutinous toddler and Paul fighting forces of evil in the kitchen. "Natalie, perhaps your button could have waited a little longer, until Rebekah was calm."

Natalie shook her head, ringlets of soft brown hair dancing around her face. She put a hand on her hip. "Mama, she's never calm."

I couldn't argue the point. "What's this about your button?"

Natalie opened her palm to show me a blue, glass button.

"Oh. That's off your lovely green dress."

"Yes, and I'm wearing it next month to the spring ball, so we've got to fix it."

"Okay, okay."

Was the spring ball so near? I should have remembered. Natalie had spoken of little else since receiving the Queen's invitation. I'd been receiving various invitations and politely declining them for so long that I hadn't even considered that my children might have reached the age at which they'd want to go.

I knew Natalie had visions of ballrooms and fancy dresses dancing through her head. I blamed the princess children's books my in-laws had bought her. They were beautifully illustrated, and Natalie loved to read them, but they did nothing to represent reality. In reality, she needed an education and an occupation—not royal balls and fancy dresses.

I smiled at her, reminding myself to let children be children, as my mother had always reminded me. If one's imagination couldn't be let loose in childhood, when could it?

"Of course. We'll have it fixed before the ball. And you'll look beautiful."

"Will I talk with the Queen?"

"I'll do my best."

A procession of people would be waiting before the ball started to meet Queen Rebekah the Fourth. We'd have to arrive early and stand in line for close to an hour for little more than a brief introduction. Perhaps I could request more of an audience—not the day of the ball, obviously, but at some other time. I could ask for the Queen to spend a little time with my family.

What should I call my relationship with the Queen? Stronger than an acquaintance, but not *friendly*.

Yet, we had a bond and a mutual respect—enough that I suspected she'd grant us her company for a brunch or afternoon tea, despite her busy schedule.

"Why don't I deliver a request for all of us to visit her majesty?"

Natalie's face brightened before her brow crinkled. "Even Rebekah?"

I ran fingers through her soft hair. "Good point. Perhaps Rebekah's presence will depend upon the time of day and her mood." She might do well at a brunch, but as the day advanced, she became more of a tyrant.

"Thank you, Mama. That will be wonderful!" Natalie spun around the room.

"It may take some time to free her schedule," I warned, "so we must be patient."

Natalie nodded with an expression that suggested there'd be no element of patience.

2

———————

At last, the house relaxed in tranquil quiet. Messes from the day had been cleaned, the animals were fed, and the dry clothes pulled from the line. Rebekah slept soundly in her bed. Natalie was reading to Paul in his bed.

Joshua sat in his cushioned chair beside me in the den, staring at the flames in the fireplace. He'd propped his feet on a nearby stool.

I pulled thread through the fabric of Natalie's dress to secure the button. "How was your day?"

Joshua rubbed a hand across the back of his neck. "Busy. As a healer, I'm a bit out of my element—trying to pitch the need to build a hospital to investors and developers."

"You can be charming."

"I'm not sure charm is what they want."

"Well, you can be infuriatingly rational as well. I'm sure they'd listen to the volumes of patients you're seeing and know immediately that the right decision is more space."

Joshua had begun the clinic twelve years ago, and had grown it from three rooms to ten. He went from being the only healer to managing a staff of three more, with an additional apprentice in training. The clinic desperately needed to continue to expand. Although Joshua was the only one there who commanded the Healing Stone capable of curing people's maladies magically, he'd made such careful studies of ailments over the years that he and his team of healers now tried to seek practical remedies before ever resorting to magic. In addition, Joshua's research benefitted more than just the patients of his clinic. He'd added substantially to the general knowledge of treatments and medicine.

"I think the investors listened, Abbey. I hope they'll see the benefit."

I leaned over, gripped Joshua's hand and squeezed. I lifted it to my lips, kissing the back of it.

Joshua's eyes rose from the fire to meet mine. The light of the flames danced in his brown eyes, illuminated the flecks of gold within them. He leaned closer and cupped my chin. "My beautiful champion. I'm sorry I've neglected us with these Saturday meetings. It'll get better, I promise."

I mustered a weak smile, unsure the situation would ever change in the foreseeable future. Joshua had such dedicated passion for treating patients, but the escalation to building a hospital, followed by the work of maintaining it, suggested there would be many more six-day working weeks to come.

"As long as it continues to bring happiness and fulfillment, I can manage the children on my own for one day a week, at least."

Four days a week I worked at the university. I was home the other three days, but I still had help with the children for half a day on Fridays. The children had home tutors, sitters, planned meals, and playtime. We lived too far away from the nearest school to enroll them. While I could feasibly transport them to school daily, I'd become more cautious with those of whom I let know about my powers. I had children now, and I wouldn't want them receiving either favoritism—because their mother was the Avant Champion— or to be shunned by those who either feared magical ability or resented it.

"Thank you, Abbey."

I watched Joshua in the firelight. His square jaw was always clean-shaven and his broad shoulders reminded me of his college days, storming the Shullby field and winning the game. Since we'd wed, Joshua had given me everything I could have ever asked for—love, companionship, a home, and three beautiful, boisterous children.

"I can think of ways you might repay me, should you feel oblig-ated to do so." I winked at him.

His gaze grew heavy-lidded. "The children are in bed?"

"They'll be asleep by the time you've taken your bath."

He shoved to his feet, grinning. "Then I'll get to that bath."

The next morning, Paul bounded into the bedroom and shoved his way between Joshua and me. He burrowed his little body under the covers.

"Come here, my little rabbit." I wrapped my arms around him as he giggled.

"Not fair! His little feet are cold," Joshua protested playfully.

Paul deliberately walked his cold feet up and down Joshua's back.

He rolled over and seized one of his son's feet. "What've I got?" As Joshua tickled Paul's foot, the little boy thrashed wildly.

Gone was my moment of snuggling. I tossed aside the covers and reached for my robe. "I'll get breakfast started."

"I want to help cook!" Paul scrambled out of bed after me.

"Absolutely." I tussled his soft brown hair.

We whisked eggs, sizzled bacon, and baked biscuits. For the most part, Paul instructed me how to do each step properly—per his training from our house cook.

Within an hour, Paul and I had breakfast served. My family sat around the oval table in the center of the dining room. The morning sun radiated against the sheer white curtains, basking the room in soft, white light.

Joshua did his best to feed Rebekah, in between her flailing and knocking food to the floor. She didn't discriminate when it came to whom she'd torment at mealtime. Natalie, meanwhile, poked at her food, complaining about the consistency of her eggs. Paul ate three people's share of bacon.

I refilled water glasses and joined my family at the table. "So, family day. What's the plan?"

"Dad and I already decided. We're going to Mulan Island." Natalie pushed the eggs around her plate.

"Well, we should ask everyone," Joshua suggested.

"I want to go to the volcano," Paul said.

"Me! Me!" shouted Rebekah.

"Mulan it is." I took a bite of my eggs.

As we ate, we discussed plans for our excursion to the beach. The children then shared their weeks' activities with their father. Natalie was reading now, Paul could recognize some small words, and Rebekah liked throwing her wooden alphabet letters, rather than learning to identify them.

After we finished breakfast, we achieved the next hurdle—dressing everyone.

ANOTHER HOUR LATER, we were walking on the shores of the volcano island of Mulan. The children ran around in their play clothes. I couldn't fathom what they enjoyed about this lifeless place, with its black sand, black rocks, and perpetually gray sky.

Perhaps what they enjoyed most was climbing the side of the volcano.

I walked along the beach, trailing Rebekah and scanning the waves.

"Still looking for Andi?" Joshua asked.

"It's been eight years since the eruption. He said he'd reincarnate, but I never asked when."

Andi was Mulan's sea serpent, an iridescent beast who was as large as he was congenial. He had saved my life more than once, saved Joshua's life, and even saved my mother's life. I suspected he had died during the volcano eruption eight years ago. We hadn't seen him since, and I wondered if I ever would again.

Joshua put an arm around my shoulder. "He'll be back."

Rebekah sat on the black sand, digging with her small fingers and scrutinizing the smooth obsidian rocks. She played several meters from the shoreline. The waves of Mulan were no caressing laps licking the black sand. An adult could probably stand against them, but a child would be instantly swept beneath the tumultuous depths, before a riptide swept her far out to sea.

I leaned into Joshua, enjoying Rebekah's preoccupation and lack of fussing. "A moment of blissful peace."

"How many more did you say you wanted?"

"Perhaps two."

He kissed my forehead. "If you're up for it, I'll do my best to make your desires come true."

I chuckled.

Rebekah jumped up, screaming an excited battle cry, and dashed straight for an ocean wave.

I transported in front of her and scooped her into my arms mere centimeters before she plunged into the frothy surf. She wailed in protest.

As I walked back toward Joshua, I shook my head. "Honestly, I don't know how parents without magic manage to raise children." Of our three, Natalie had the most caution. The other two seemed determined to test their mortal limits.

I set Rebekah down and she ran toward the volcano to play with her older siblings.

"Neither of us would be alive today without magic," Joshua commented, pulling me close to him again.

"Perhaps we should try," I suggested. "Start with an entire day, and then a week. Then maybe a whole month."

"Are we taking bets on how long we'll last without using magic?"

"Do you think we'd even make it one day?"

"No."

With that, a wink, and a kiss, Joshua took off running to chase the children—starting a game of tag.

AFTER THE GAME OF CHASE, Joshua and the children began coloring on the black rock at the base of the volcano, using white, yellow, pink, and blue chalk we'd brought with us from home. I watched my family from a distance, listening to the ocean waves behind me.

"You know this is the dreaded island of evil? You're defacing a landmark."

I turned to Mal, who'd suddenly appeared beside me. "They're children playing."

"Making a mockery of my home." Despite his words, his expression contained more bemusement than irritation. "Natalie is probably drawing rainbows. Rainbows on the Serpent Volcano!" He made a disgusted noise. "Desecrating my temple. The next group of passing travelers won't be intimidated at all. Soon, they'll be calling it the pastel volcano. Hardly sounds threatening."

I laughed. Natalie probably was drawing a rainbow. "It's chalk. It'll wash off."

Mal opened his arms wide. "Have you noticed the lack of vegetation on this island? It rains here about once every decade."

I looked up at the volcano. I hadn't considered the rainfall. The volcano probably didn't possess enough height and breadth to capture precipitation.

"You're turning a desolate island of legendary darkness into a playground."

I grinned. "I am, aren't I?"

He rolled his eyes in feigned petulance.

I kicked at a pebble on the ground and watched it tumble over the sand. "Did you ever want children? Before you became what you are?"

His answer came swiftly. "I was twenty-three when I was poisoned and dying, and accepted my role as Malos. At that time, the armies of Bellos had marched toward Karnelik—and I'd never set foot south of the castle. I dreamt of warm coastal lands, women, and freedom at the time—not children."

Rebekah screamed in high-pitched delight, throwing a rock at Natalie's sketch on the rock wall. Natalie roared in protest.

Mal crossed his arms. "Your children do not inspire a sense of longing in me. There are many experiences I wish I could have, but managing screaming children isn't one of them. I've seen you up at all hours of the night because they were ill or cantankerous. I've seen you give them every modern luxury, and they don't even have the decency to close the front door or pick up their dirty clothes."

"Children are egocentric. But all it takes is a warm embrace or cuddling in my arms and it's all worth it."

"Cuddling?" His nose crinkled. "I'll take your word for it."

I swung my sparring stick with gusto at Baird's torso. He blocked and countered with a swing of his own. I parried. We continued to practice fighting with wooden sticks on an area of grass at the monks' sanctuary. In the distance, the low rumble of the waterfall resonated. I could smell the faint waft of cinnamon in the air from the monks' morning cider.

Off to one side, the wolf pup I'd rescued several months ago gnawed on a piece of rawhide. His coat gleamed a lustrous black, with a single speck of white on his chest and his paws painted as if the snow from which I'd snatched him still clung to the pup's fur. Baird had accepted the cub with delight and named him Fury. It seemed appropriate that a man with the Language Stone should have an animal companion with whom to converse. I tried to detect when they communicated, but it was nonverbal. Baird did the same with the hawks the Gunthi monks bred and trained.

We continued fighting, and Baird brought his baton down toward my head. I dove, rolled, and lashed out a leg—striking Baird's calf. He landed on the ground with a thud. I leaped to my feet as I swung the stick down, halting it mere centimeters from his face.

When he raised his hand in a signal of surrender, I stepped back.

"Formidable," he acknowledged. "You haven't fought this well since before you had children."

"Well, Rebekah's two now, so we're in a routine that actually involves sleep every night—although her bedtime stalling tactics grow more creative every week."

I extended a hand and helped Baird off his back.

"And to what do I owe the pleasure of a practice during your work week?"

Without making eye contact, I set down the baton and picked up a set of throwing knives. "I was given a day of suspension."

"Suspension?"

I threw a knife, which lodged in the wood stump off center of the target. "I chaperoned a group of students on an excursion when a blizzard struck."

He glanced at his wolf. "I recall you telling me. And what was the reprimandable offense?"

I threw the next knife, which also failed to find its mark. "Instead of bringing the students back immediately, because of the threat of the storm, I went to help other stranded hikers."

Baird crossed his arms.

Another knife sailed from my fingers. Closer. "Some of the

parents complained that I neglected the safety of their children and endangered them unnecessarily. My first responsibility should have been to the students."

"Where were the students while you rescued the other hikers?"

"In a cluster of trees and rocks, sitting around a fire and telling jokes."

"Hardly sounds life-threatening."

"Dean Lariat convened the board to listen to the concerns of their parents. My disciplinary punishment was to have one day's leave of absence." I pulled the knives out of the post and walked back to Baird.

"Well, they must not be terribly concerned if the sentence is so mild."

I threw another blade, but the tempo was off. The hilt struck the post and the knife flopped to the ground. I groaned. "It's a gentle slap on the wrist," I agreed. "The trouble is what the incident is representative of—I can't seem to excel at any one thing in my life. Every aspect of every endeavor is like the blizzard—I try to do the right thing, yet inevitably someone or some group ends up disappointed, or frustrated, or angry."

"You're always late," Natalie had said with disdain.

Another knife hurled through the air. This one cut smoothly and buried three centimeters off center. "Every aspect of my life competes with the other. I'm pulled away from my work or family for Queen duties—but the castle is constantly underwhelmed at my participation in continental affairs. They're frustrated they have to send runners or messenger birds, or the captain herself, to find me rather than me being present at every deliberation. The more help I offer, the more they demand. My children complain I'm not home enough —though that doesn't motivate them to behave better when I *am* home. Joshua and I hardly have any time together as a couple." I threw another knife. Bull's-eye. "I'm a wife, mother, teacher, and champion—but I'm proficient in none of those roles."

When I walked over to collect the knives, Baird followed.

"Not dedicating one hundred percent of your time and effort to an endeavor doesn't translate into a failure to excel."

I blinked at him.

"Let's take each aspect of your life and examine it: You and Joshua have careers, which you each support, and three children you share —that is success as a wife. Your children are strong and healthy— another success. No mother should spend every waking moment with her children. They need other experiences and enrichment. There's a reason people say 'it takes a village to raise a child.' Even if you dedicated your life entirely to them, they would still find something else to complain about—such is the nature of children."

He continued, "Next, your teaching. You've educated and enlightened hundreds of minds over the years—another success. If a few of them had to weather a storm then they'll be tougher for it."

I deposited the knives by the other weapons. "And my role as the Avant Champion?"

"I think you're still defining what it means to be the champion when evil has already been defeated. You're still molding that piece of clay, so it's natural for it to feel incomplete at the moment. In time, you'll form a pot ready for planting. The pieces of your life will gain balance."

He stood before me until I made eye contact. "Are you happy?" he asked.

I opened my mouth and then shut it. I had moments of happiness with my family and my career. What defined if one was happy? Was it a certain percentage of time spent in a 'happy' state of being? If I hesitated, or couldn't answer his questions, did that automatically make me unhappy?

Baird touched my shoulder. "Come. Let us meditate."

I bit my lip, hesitating. I particularly lacked skill in the art of monk meditation. I was supposed to breathe and focus on a sense of unity with the one universal deity—the Unideit—but inevitably found myself fighting not to take a nap sitting up, or letting my mind wander towards the many things I needed to get done that day.

With a barely suppressed sigh, I followed Baird to the waterfall. The sun struck the misting water, creating a breathtaking rainbow. Together, we sat by the riverside as crisp water tumbled and gurgled past us. The moist air carried the sweet scent of the wisteria growing nearby.

Baird and I closed our eyes and communed with nature. I began with deep breathing, listening to the roar of the water as it drowned out the sound of the tweeting robins and rummaging squirrels. I thought of the time I'd rafted on this very river with Joshua—cold, frothy, tumultuous water churning around us.

As we'd sped down the river, the exhilaration of surfing on top of the mighty rush of water had filled us both. Up until the waterfall. That was where we plummeted straight down into the churning water. Breaking a leg and nearly drowning was an event I'd rather not repeat.

That led me to my next thought, and I remembered when Natalie fell off a horse and broke her arm. I empathized with the pain, and I'd told her the story of the waterfall. Fortunately, having a father with a magic healing stone meant she didn't have to suffer long, and the damage to her arm wasn't permanent.

Sitting beside Baird, I noticed with frustration that my mind wandered through memories, rather than sinking into the meditation I sought.

Think of nothing.

How does one do such a thing?

I lazily blinked my eyes open. The volcanic island of Mulan materialized around me. I sat on the black sand with legs crossed.

"You're getting closer. Another ten years and you might master sixty seconds of meditation." Mal sat casually on the beach, his legs crossed as he leaned back on his elbows.

"Now you're mucking up my meditation?"

"You're mucking it up on your own. I'm just enjoying the view."

"It's your island. You can enjoy the gray and black towering volcano anytime."

"Not that view." He gave a wolfish grin.

I narrowed my eyes at him. "The view of a terrifying warrior who skewered you once upon a time?"

His grin widened. "Yes, exceedingly terrifying with your little curls about your face and your cheeks flushed."

I tucked a rogue strand of dark hair behind my ear as I glowered at him. "I *am* intimidating—ask any of my students."

"Wouldn't it be grand to have a conversation with anyone but you?"

I blew another curl out of my face. "Why should your limitations be a burden on me?"

He arched an eyebrow. "Am I a burden to you?"

"No," I admitted. Mal was entertaining, helpful, and usually annoying—but he was never a burden.

Mal cocked his head to one side and studied me. His expression softened before he looked away. After shoving himself to his feet, he leisurely walked away down the shoreline. "I'll leave you to your meditation."

I watched his predatory figure saunter away, the rolling waves lapping at his feet.

"Abigail?"

My eyes shot open.

I was still at the sanctuary—the waterfall churning behind me.

Baird was frowning down at me. "I believe you were sleeping, not meditating."

I scrubbed my hands across my face. "You try juggling three children and full-time employment! I graded papers late last night."

I sighed. I couldn't even achieve proper meditation.

Fury climbed into my lap, licking and nuzzling.

Baird put a gentle hand on my shoulder. "Go home and get some rest."

I patted Fury and his tail wagged enthusiastically. His delightfully soft fur sifting through my fingers felt more like therapy than meditation, anyway. "Hey, Fluffy. You're a good boy, aren't you? You accept me with all of my flaws, don't you?"

"His name is *Fury*," Baird corrected. "And you don't even use that ridiculous voice with your children."

I scrunched up the wolf's fur. "You like *Fluffy*, don't you? Yes, you do."

Fluffy Fury yapped with delight.

I gave Baird a giddy grin, and he shook his head with annoyance.

3

oco DeFay walked into my office, her polished black boots clicking on the floor as she circled the room.

I looked up at her over the papers I was grading. My desk was littered with books and papers—which might appear haphazard to the untrained eye, but I'd developed a vague method to counter my lack of organization.

Coco walked around the room, appearing out of place with her long, blond ponytail, glimmering silver breastplate, and clean, pressed blue tunic. Her attire was appropriate for a battlefield but out of place in an office.

"Another crisis?" I asked.

As she took a seat, Coco frowned. "I don't *only* come to solicit your help."

I grunted. With some effort, I recalled that Coco had indeed come for a social visit. Once.

But I didn't mind. I'd come to enjoy Coco's company, regardless of her motive for visiting, and I appreciated her dry personality. I wouldn't venture to call us friends, though, as we didn't socialize outside of solving disputes for the Queen.

"Your necklace is different," Coco said.

I instinctively reached up and touched the thick necklace. It was encased in carved wood now, and the silver couldn't be seen. Nor could the Warrior Stone within.

"After Windish figured out the source of my power—not hard to do when one wears a stone that glows—I took precautions to hide it better."

Coco put the heel of her boot on my desk and crossed her legs, pulling a textbook into her hands and sifting through the pages. "Haven't you had the same office for ten years?"

"Twelve." I flicked my wrist around the room. "You see what moving would involve?" I had books, beakers, papers, and minerals, all overflowing on the shelves.

I gaped at Coco's boots for a moment. She'd never taken the liberty of relaxing in my office before, so I'd never taken a good look at them. They were warrior's boots made of leather with thick soles, yet elegantly slender.

Coco abandoned the topic of my office with a frown. "Minister Tarik has been polarizing the court."

So, she *had* come about royal business.

I thought of Minister Tarik for a moment–a light brown-skinned man with a bright, insincere smile. "Isn't that what politicians do?"

"We're supposed to all work together."

"What a magnificently naive concept." I leaned back in my chair. "Is he undermining the Queen?"

"Perhaps."

I waited for her to elaborate, but Coco didn't. Often, our conversations were a series of incomplete discussions such as this.

I leaned forward, eyeing the book Coco was idly thumbing through. "Is there a particular chemical formula I can help you find?"

She snapped the book shut. "I heard about your suspension."

"Punishment for saving lives," I said grimly. "For every positive action I take, there is always a negative reciprocal reaction. Like chemistry."

"You could transition to full-time champion—no longer subject yourself to the rules and whims of academics, or ungrateful parents."

"But then I'd neglect the children of the grateful ones."

She snorted.

I shot her a warning look.

Coco dragged her boots off my desk with a bored expression on her face. "Yes—the intrinsic rewards of teaching. I remember this conversation."

Half of a conversation, like all the rest.

"There's danger in constantly exposing myself, Coco. With each little favor I do for the Queen, more people see my magic. I've noticed over the years that people are becoming less grateful of me, and more suspicious. The wonder of magic has been replaced by wariness of it."

"I'm sure you aren't feeling deprived of glory?"

I leaned forward. "I don't care about glory. I don't care if people aren't particularly grateful. What I don't want is a mob—driven by paranoia and fear—to arrive on my doorstep armed and angry."

Coco crossed her arms. "That's absurd. No one even knows where you live ... except the Queen's messenger birds."

"It's a figure of speech. And I plan on keeping my estate as secret as possible." If that *was* possible, when you had a half-dozen employees who could blab to anyone. I hoped we showed them respect and discretion, and that they'd show the same for us.

I looked back down at my students' papers, scribbling a correction to a chemical formula.

Coco watched me work for several quiet minutes. "There's a land dispute in Aithos."

I shifted my gaze to her and narrowed my eyes. "I *knew* you had an agenda."

"The people of Aithos respect you. You may be able to resolve this by little more than just showing up."

"I'm raising a family *and* trying to hold down a job. You have five dozen guards at your disposal who could easily settle the matter."

"Bloodshed could be avoided with your involvement."

I pursed my lips. "When do we go?"

She stood. "This afternoon."

"Fine."

She exited my office without a trace of gratitude.

I looked back down at my desk. If I left for Aithos this afternoon, I'd be late for family dinner. Again.

A knock sounded at my open door.

"Coco, I—"

Dean Lariat stood in the doorway.

I stood up. "Dean Lariat."

She leaned against the doorway. I'd become accustomed to seeing the Dean in this position. For a time, I even wondered if she needed the extra support—as if standing on her own required too much effort. I'd grown to understand how it conveyed that she was making an appearance without committing to a full conversation. It also enabled her to get the last word in and make a rapid exit.

"I hope you know I advocated on your behalf to the board. I negotiated them down to a single day's leave of absence."

"I appreciate that."

"I explained that you're the Avant Champion and exceptions must be made for exceptional people." She ran a hand through her short, spiked hair.

I frowned. I didn't want exceptions made for me because I was the Avant Champion. I'd have rather she advocate on my behalf because of my proficiency as a chemistry teacher or because the students found my classes invaluable.

"You do great work, Abigail. Students enjoy your classes."

"Thank you."

"And we've noticed a growth in university attendance since hiring the Avant Champion as faculty."

I swallowed, standing stiffly.

"I know you do valuable work for the Queen. My concern is your ability to do both to the fullest extent. I hear that you never miss giving a lecture, but the students can't always find you in the afternoon for tutoring."

"If they schedule ahead of time, I'm here." Students who dropped by might find a locked and unoccupied office.

Dean Lariat held up a hand. "Like I said, I'll continue to be supportive of you—given your accolades..."

I had teaching accolades, but I knew she referred to my other role.

"...but keep in mind that I can't have the university become a circus; where strangers come to see you because of magic."

"That's never happened," I said firmly.

The Dean pushed herself off the wall. "Keep your roles separate, but strong—the Avant Champion at the castle and a professor here. People always support a hero."

As she left, I sank into my chair. When had life become so complicated?

When late afternoon arrived, Coco reappeared in my office doorway, signaling that it was time to travel to Aithos. I transported us instantly to the edge of town there. Red clay buildings lined block after block as we made our way to the courthouse.

Coco wore her captain's uniform, earning stares from merchants and ranchers as we passed. I was dressed in my simple cotton tunic and pants, which I'd worn to the chemistry classroom earlier that day.

When we arrived at the courthouse, I followed Coco inside the tall, two-story building.

A man in sandals and a white toga approached. He appraised Coco's attire, indisputably a Queen's guard. "You've come about the land dispute. The farmers aren't here."

"Where did they go?" Coco asked.

"Out to Copper's farm." The man's brow furrowed. "The situation has escalated."

"How so?"

"All I know is that everyone rushed to Copper's ranch at daylight."

I extended a hand. "Take us there."

He eyed my extended hand.

Perhaps I looked disheveled after a day of teaching, and there was a small, but unsightly hole in my shirt incurred by carelessness with sulfuric acid, but I didn't look like a leper.

Coco bobbed her head. "This is Abigail Cross. If you imagine the Copper farm, she'll transport us there."

With no small measure of reservation in his expression, the man took my hand. When Coco grasped my shoulder, I transported us to the ranch. Dry, flat land with sparse trees materialized around us. In the distance, I could see the ranch house—a wood frame covered with brownish red brick walls. Horses roamed inside a fence which clearly marked the boundaries of the property.

The man in the toga swayed slightly, disorientated by the transport.

Before we could address him, though, a voice called to me.

"Abigail!" It was Allis, and his smile lit up the plains as he enveloped me in a hug.

With his straight black hair and robust belly, Allis appeared just as I remembered him from our journey, even if he was thirteen years older now. He'd accompanied me on the quest to raise—to become— the Avant Champion. Despite the arduous travel across the continent, exposure to the elements, and the stress of being part of a group strung together in a crisis, Allis' smile had never wavered. After the Battle of Marrin Beach, he'd returned to Aithos to raise a family. Now he owned a bank, and was a respected member of the community.

"I've missed you!"

I wondered if that was possible, with six children and a bank to manage.

I returned Allis' warm smile.

"Thank you for coming," he grinned.

"Captain DeFay tells me there's a land dispute?"

Several other Callabus men and women approached to listen.

Allis' expression sobered as he turned and looked over his shoulder, up towards the ranch house. "It began as a land dispute. It's more complicated now."

I suppressed the urge to tell him to *uncomplicate* it for me. I didn't have time for complicated. In an hour, I was expected to pick up Joshua from the clinic and greet the children, before preparing everyone for dinner. '*We're important, too.*' Natalie's words knifed me —daily.

As I took a deep breath, I reminded myself that I had agreed to help, which meant taking the time to understand the situation and find a solution. "Tell me what's going on?"

"Yonis Copper is behind on his loan payments."

"How far behind?"

"Unrecoverable. He's been getting further into debt every month. Not only to the bank, but to other individuals as well."

"Why? What changed?"

One of the men, with spiked hair and a short beard, shrugged. "He's never had much of a work ethic. The ranch was always skirting the edge of financial ruin. Copper seemed to lose any further motivation once he slipped into debt."

Allis continued, "Several days ago he made a scene at the bank when we discussed foreclosure."

"A scene?"

"He assaulted several clerks."

"And the complicated part?"

Allis' expression turned more troubled. "He stomped out and we presumed he went home after that event. Yesterday, when we approached and knocked on his door with the foreclosure papers, he yelled that he had a knife—and if we tried to enter he'd kill his family and then himself. That's when we sent for help from the Queen."

The bearded man added, "He said it loud enough so even his children had to have heard it."

Allis nodded. "We've been camped out here ever since, trying to sort out how to diffuse the situation."

After I recovered from cringing, the moment it was mentioned that children were involved, I asked, "So, when I separate him from his family, what happens to them?"

"Clarissa and the children can go and stay at her sister's home." Another local—a woman—joined the conversation. "Clarissa is an excellent seamstress. She can provide for the children."

I turned back to Allis. "How many people are in the house?"

"Yonis, his wife, and their two children."

"Okay. Not too complicated."

"It's not?"

"Rescue the family. Capture Copper." My gaze roamed the pastureland. "I just need ... horseshoes."

"Horseshoes?"

"Keep everyone here. I'll be back."

"But—"

I didn't hear the rest of his objection as I transported to outside the tack room, a small wooden shed set apart from the main house. When I opened the door and stepped inside, my eyes adjusted to the dim light.

Horseshoes.

I picked up two of them, hanging from a nail on the wall. After exiting the barn, I walked toward the house in plain view. As I stepped onto the porch, I introduced myself to the closed door. "Mr. Copper! My name is Abigail. Can we talk?"

"Talk." A gruff voice said.

I peered into a window, trying to see into his house. The curtains were drawn and obscuring my view except for a thin sliver. "Can I come inside to talk?" I tried to project my voice back toward the front door, so it wouldn't be too obvious I was peeking through his window.

Through the sliver in the curtains, I could see the sitting room. A woman and two children sat on the floor. Clarissa appeared distraught and sleep-deprived with disheveled hair, dark circles under her eyes, and her mouth drawn. Despite her obvious anxiety, she was trying to keep the children distracted and entertained with a deck of cards.

Now. Where is Mr. Copper?

"You can talk from out there."

I moved back in front of the door. "What if you open the door? Then we can at least *see* each other while we talk."

"I don't know you."

True—and I didn't *really* want to talk, which probably made my offer sound insincere. Joshua had treated a few patients with mood disorders over the years, and he'd explained to me how people could have systemic imbalances that heightened their emotional response to situations: Despair in place of sadness, rage in place of frustration or anger. Joshua often referred them to a woman healer he knew— not because he couldn't help them, but because the process was so time-consuming it would have limited his ability to help those with more immediate needs—like trauma and infection, the cases where his skills excelled.

Perhaps a nicer person would have wanted to talk compassionately and empathetically with Yonis. My prejudice against him had been sealed when I'd heard he'd threatened the well-being of his children. Bluff or not, I wasn't going to offer kindness to a man like that—which was one of the many reasons I was better suited as a warrior than a healer.

When Yonis cracked the door slightly, I saw part of the face of a haggard man. His blood-shot eyes darted back and forth like a wild animal. His disheveled, wrinkled shirt looked as if it had been worn for a week straight. I wondered if he smelled as bad as he looked.

Time to find out.

I pulled my knee up and then launched my foot into the door, using the full strength of my Warrior Stone. The force sent the man sprawling backward, but didn't quite topple him. The splintered wooden door now hung by one hinge.

I entered the musky house and took quick appraisal of the layout —entry room, sitting room to my right, kitchen to my left. In front of me towered Copper, a man twice my size, with his beet-red face twisted in anger and a long knife gripped tightly in one hand. He launched himself at me.

I disappeared and reappeared behind him. Yonis' momentum carried him right through the open doorway, where I'd been standing a moment earlier, and he lurched out onto his porch. He barely stopped himself from falling off the edge. The motion would have been comical, except that his wife and children were watching. My role was to restrain Yonis, not shame him in front of his family.

He stared at me, dumbfounded. In my next move, I appeared beside him and wrenched the knife out of his hand, tossing it aside. When he took a swing at me with his mallet-sized fist, I ducked—at the same time reaching up and hooking one of the horseshoes around his wrist. Using the strength of the Warrior Stone, I squeezed the iron shut, into a closed ring shape, before rolling out of the way of the kick Yonis launched next.

He unleashed a string of curse words, expressing his degree of dissatisfaction with me, and tugged angrily at the horseshoe around his wrist.

I came up from my roll, spun around, and then transported again —this time positioning myself in front of him. I hooked the second horseshoe through the one wrapped around his wrist—and then tightened it around his other hand.

As clever as it was, I instantly realized that my ill-conceived plan required me to be a lot faster—as Yonis cruelly backhanded me with his bound fist.

In the instant I realized his great hand was about to make contact with my face, I transported—but the pain that shot through me told me I hadn't been fast enough.

As I reappeared, I landed in the dirt right on my butt. The taste of blood filled my mouth, from where a tooth had cut into the inside of my lip.

Yonis released an enraged roar as he fought against his wrist restraints.

I sat on the dirt and moved my sore jaw, feeling it with my fingers. I felt relieved that it wasn't broken. If I hadn't transported exactly when I had, I'd be in agonizing pain right now.

Still, I needed to think of a safer way to restrain someone next time, especially if more of these escapades were required of me. I instantly thought of the paralytic venom of the black marsh adder. It was capable of incapacitating its victim, while it still remained conscious and breathing. The Hunju used it as a weapon, administered via carefully-aimed blow darts. I'd acquired such a device in combat, and next time I'd definitely remember to bring it.

Snarling, Yonis came barreling toward me. At the last second, before he could stomp on me, I rolled aside and stuck out one leg.

Yonis tripped, fell, and landed on his face. Blood spewed from his nose, turning the brown dirt red.

In a hurry, I transported back to the front porch and blocked Clarissa and the children from seeing Yonis bleeding in the dirt. They stood in the doorway, wide-eyed and worried, and I struggled for how to apologize. My intention was never to harm him.

Clarissa lunged at me, throwing her arms around my neck. "Thank you!"

She sobbed as she clutched me.

I hugged her back. "You're going to be okay."

The other woman approached and took Clarissa into her arms. "C'mon, hun. Let's get you packed up. We'll take you to your sister's house."

I turned back toward Yonis. He'd been hauled to his feet now, with two men escorting him away from the ranch. I wondered what would become of him. Could he be healed of his mental illness? If not, he would need to be isolated from harming others. Aithos had no prisons. Marrington had one, but it was a long way from his home.

Allis came beside me. "Thank you for that."

Coco joined us. "Your jaw is swelling."

"No problem." I turned to Allis. "I'm sorry to run, but my family is waiting on me."

"How are we going to get the horseshoes off?"

I frowned. "I have no idea."

4

———

"Mama, you're doing it all wrong."

I frowned and took down the braid in Natalie's light-brown hair. "Sorry." Apparently, there was some specific style of braided hair she'd seen during her last visit to the castle, and I was failing to adequately recreate it.

I brushed her hair again. "It's very pretty down."

"I don't want it down."

I blew my cheeks out and set to work again. I needed a manual on hairstyles. I knew a few braids, but not the latest fashions. Why wasn't there a Fashion Stone? The bearer could instantly know hairstyles, clothing styles, and how to fasten the tiny satin buttons on the green dress I had to wear tonight.

After I'd finished my sixth attempt with Natalie's hair, she scrutinized the craftsmanship.

"Close enough."

Victory achieved, I sunk into the chair.

Joshua walked by Natalie's room and paused. "Natalie, you look beautiful."

She beamed. "Thank you, Papa."

She dashed out of the room—I guessed to show off her new look to her siblings.

"Keep your dress clean!" I called after her.

Joshua leaned on the doorframe. "Well done."

"I think she believes she looks acceptable though not as glamorous as she'd have liked. Why did I agree to take her to the spring ball?"

Leaning forward, Joshua scooped up my hand and pulled me up to him. "Because you're a wonderful mother, and someday she'll show you gratitude."

I groaned. I had court politics and gossip to look forward to for the night. Joshua needed to stay home because Rebekah and Paul weren't disciplined enough for four hours of dancing and socializing in a finite space.

"Time for you to get ready." He wriggled his eyebrows.

I shook my head. "*Alone.* If you're in the dressing room with me, I'll never get ready."

He gave a slight pout, but didn't follow me down the hall.

An hour and twenty-six agonizing buttons later, I was dressed. The best I accomplished with my dark, unruly hair was an updo with dangling ringlets. I had no idea if it would be considered stylish, classic, or outdated. Regardless, I would attend the ball for Natalie's sake not for mine.

I walked through the house, looking for Natalie.

"*Stars and stones*," Joshua gasped in a husky voice. He placed his hands on my waist. "You look ravishing."

"Easy. No disrupting the dress." I rolled my shoulders. "I feel like one of Chef Mo's stuffed dumplings."

"If we're using food analogies, I'd venture you look more like a marinated shank of lamb—slow-roasted on an open fire and ready to eat."

My knees went weak under his hungry gaze. "Thank you, but I'll be mostly avoiding fires tonight."

He grinned. "Except for the ones you start."

"What does that mean?"

"You've been known to burn a few bridges." His tone stayed playful.

"I've no idea to what you're referring. I'm a perfect lady." I presented my cheek to him, as I batted my eyelashes.

He kissed the offered cheek sweetly. "Yes, you are." He moved his lips close to my ear. "And when you come home tonight, wearing that dress, I'll light a fire in *you*."

A warmth of excitement coursed through me. I turned, ready to kiss him and express the passion he stirred in me when Natalie entered.

"Ready to go?" Natalie inquired.

"Ready to go."

I took her hand, winked at Joshua, and then transported us both to the castle. I positioned us outside, under a tree and a short distance from the entrance, so we wouldn't be spotted suddenly appearing. We walked along the procession of horse-drawn carriages. Some consisted of plain wooden boxcars, while others were ornately carved from polished oak with decorative curtains.

Natalie shook her hand free of mine. "Why couldn't we arrive in a carriage?"

"We don't own a carriage." I had a cart—a rickety cart, sufficient for moving wood and hay. It wasn't an apparatus refined enough to arrive at the castle in, though.

"Couldn't we borrow one?" Natalie gazed longingly at the delicate carriages, with their cushioned interior seating.

"So we can sit in line? Walking is better." I grinned. "We get to walk to the front of the line."

"But it makes us look different."

"We *are* different. We're not politicians, or ambassadors, or bourgeoisie."

"I don't want to be different."

I frowned. Since she was my daughter, being different was inevitable. I quite liked different.

Before I could think of some enlightened analogy about flowers growing among weeds, or the four-leafed clover sprouting amidst a bed of a thousand tri-leaves, we arrived at the inner gate.

I presented our invitation, and we were permitted to pass. The courtyard glowed with bioluminescent lanterns tinted pink and yellow. Urns of green flame danced as they lit the path to the ballroom.

Natalie stared in fascinated amazement. Her wide eyes observed the decorations and the fine clothing everyone wore as they filed into the ballroom. In that instant, I knew whatever discomfort I bore this evening would be worth it as the price for seeing her child wonderment.

As we entered the ballroom, formal introductions passed between us and the court ministers, foreign dignitaries, and nobles that lined the walkway to the Queen. I heard whispers in awe as some recognized the Avant Champion. Although I seldom came to court, once here, I couldn't hide my vibrant blue eyes and dark hair.

As people met my daughter, they were immediately enamored by the small, seven-year-old girl with a polite bow and sweet smile.

Aman, the Queen's Council, swept us through the crowd to Queen Rebekah. She sat atop a crushed velvet cushion in a high-backed chair, painted gleaming gold. Servants knelt on either side of her—young girls dressed in unobtrusive gray and unnoticed by the glittering guests.

I noticed. I'd been there. I'd been a servant to Queen Rebekah for six months, until one dark night on V-Day, when I knelt in service to the Queen on the eve of Malos' attack. My life had been forever altered that night, as I'd begun my journey to become the Avant Champion.

Natalie and I gave the Queen a respectful bow.

"I am deeply pleased to see both of you," she said.

We rose.

"Thank you, mum."

The Queen's pale makeup masked the lines on her face—lines that grew deeper each year I saw her. Yet, her soft eyes lent truth to the words she spoke.

The Queen regarded my daughter. "Natalie, you grow taller and more graceful each time I see you."

Natalie's cheeks flushed. "Thank you, mum."

"How is your father?"

"He's well, my Queen. He's going to build a hospital to help people."

"So I have heard. And what do you think about a hospital?"

Natalie answered without hesitation. "Some people say my mother is a hero, but I think my father is. He helps sick people every day. A hospital would help him treat even more people. Maybe he'll treat them faster, so he'll be home more."

"I couldn't agree more," I said.

I felt a tap on my shoulder. I turned to see the Minister of Foreign Affairs offering to dance with open arms.

"Minister Tarik. How do you do?" I looked at his outstretched hands, trying to conjure words to politely decline his offer, while simultaneously keeping my face from morphing into an expression of horror.

He lifted my hands and whisked me to the dance floor.

"Abigail. We see you at far too few of these functions." His smile gleamed white and his eyes sparkled with delight. His smooth skin was the color of coffee with cream. Like the beverage, something bitter lurked beneath his pleasant aroma.

"If I come, I'm at risk of being asked to dance." Or not even asked and simply *made* to do so.

"Is that so bad?" He winked.

My gaze followed around the room as we spun. Natalie still conversed with the Queen. A few ministers watched Tarik and I dance. Another man stared. He had sun-weathered skin and appeared to be about forty. A long scar extended down one side of his face. I didn't recognize him.

Looking back at Tarik, I asked, "What foreign affairs are keeping you on your toes these days?"

"You want me to bore you with talk of tariff negotiations with Bellos?"

Anything to take my mind off the fact that I was dancing with a politician who made my skin crawl.

"I've heard they're being brutish and taxing imports too heavily."

"It's just business," he replied dismissively.

The man with the scar on his face materialized beside us. "May I cut in?"

Tarik's lip curled before a smile graced his expression. "Certainly, Ambassador." Without asking if I wanted to switch partners, he gave my hands to the ambassador. "Abigail Cross, I introduce you to Goran Foal, ambassador to Kovia."

I bowed my head in greeting, before I found myself dancing with this stranger.

Goran held my right hand in his left and rested the other on my waist. He glanced at my left hand on his shoulder. "You're married."

"I am."

His stiff posture, practiced movements, and stoic expression contained no trace of seduction—so I waited for him to explain the significance of his question.

"Yet, you dance with *that* snake." He nodded subtly towards Tarik. I noticed how the stranger's eyes scanned the room even more intently than mine. Despite his thick Kovian accent, his Crithian was still clear.

"He's not so bad." In truth, Tarik was loathsome, but I always thought my feelings against the minister were a manifestation of my own prejudice against politicians. If he was a snake, I'd envision him as more of a small, scaly ground-dweller than a venomous adder.

I continued, "I'm not here to dance with anyone. I'm just a chaperone."

He followed my gaze toward Natalie. "She's charming. But no one here is 'just a chaperone.'"

"What's your quarrel with Tarik?"

Goran grunted, as though the answer should be obvious. "He's hardly adequate at his job."

"Why do say that?"

"I had to travel all the way from Kovo to ask the Queen for assistance after our earthquake. Tarik did nothing to convey our needs in a time of crisis."

"Earthquake?" I wondered if Kovo, the capital of Kovia, had been damaged.

Goran pursed his lips. "You see how little regard is given for our country? You didn't even know about our earthquake."

"I don't spend much time at court, or within the circles who might have received such news."

"An earthquake struck our eastern shores. It's devastated thousands of lives and destroyed an entire city."

"That's terrible!" I knew Kovo wasn't on the coast, but my geography of Kovia lacked detail enough to know any of the eastern port cities.

Goran stared at me, as if only seeing me for the first time since we'd started dancing. He blinked, and his expression softened. "Yes, it is."

"Did the Queen agree to send aid?"

"She did. She's generous—but it's difficult to gain an audience with her."

"Is anyone still in danger?" My mind began churning. Perhaps I, as the Avant Champion, could help.

"No." He drew out the word as if my question were peculiar.

Goran turned my hand in his and ran a calloused thumb over my star tattoo. His eyes widened. "You are *her*. I wondered if half the room was staring at us because a disfigured man is dancing with a beautiful woman—but it's because you are the champ—"

"Chaperone, remember?" I swallowed. A fleeting stab of panic struck me.

For the first time since seeing him, Goran smiled. It transformed his appearance from rugged ruffian to handsome and approachable. "A legend, encased in a small body, wrapped in a shell of humility. How refreshing."

"And you're an intelligent warrior, poorly disguised as a politician."

"You're changing the subject again. You do that well, Champion."

"It's not humility. It's self-preservation."

"Self-preservation? Or protecting those you love?" His gentle gaze flickered towards Natalie and then back to me.

My stomach knotted.

"I think I understand. If the stories of your abilities are true, you want to help—probably even *like* to help—but you have a family to consider."

"Family comes first."

"As they should, milady."

Goran took me in one last circle before stopping and dropping his hands. "Thank you for the dance. I expect it will be the highlight of my evening. I'll maintain discretion, but if you're ever in my country, you'll find hospitality in Kovia if you mention my name." He walked away and vanished into the crowd.

"Mama, who were you dancing with?"

Looking down, I saw Natalie by my side. "That was an ambassador to Kovia, and a remarkable man." I wondered if she detected that I'd never made a similar statement about Minister Tarik. "His name is Goran Foal. He was telling me that his country recently suffered an earthquake on their eastern coast. They have a lot of rebuilding to do."

Her brow furrowed.

Had that been too much information for a seven-year-old? With a healer for a father, she wasn't shielded from discussions about the suffering of others. Perhaps images of mass devastation were too much.

Her face turned contemplative.

As I knelt beside her, I asked, "What are you thinking, sweetheart?"

Natalie blinked and seemed to gather her thoughts. "I overheard the municipal judge of Waterton. I believe her name was Bev. She spoke with another woman about a fishing boat of sailors. The boat was caught in a storm and all the fishermen were lost at sea. Bev put together a donation center, and people from the town gave food and clothing to the wives and children." Her face brightened. "We could do that for Kovia! You could transport everything we collect there."

I smiled. "That's a brilliant idea." I glanced around and, seeing Goran again, added, "Shall we go tell him?"

As I stood, Natalie began walking across the room. The way she carried herself—so unselfconsciously, and with such natural dignity—revealed a self-confidence I didn't acquire until I was much older. She looked almost queenly as the crowd parted for her.

When we reached Goran, I made the introductions. "Ambassador Foal, this is my daughter Natalie."

Natalie extended her hand, and Goran politely kissed it, with a charmed expression.

"She has a proposal to help Kovia."

As Natalie spoke, Goran knelt to listen carefully. With her in her luxurious dress, standing before a man on one knee, the scene looked like the many times I'd seen subjects bow before Queen Rebekah.

When Natalie had finished speaking, Goran straightened and adjusted his dress shirt. "I think yours is a wonderful plan."

I grinned, full of pleasure and pride. "Can you stay at the castle for a week, while we gather donations?"

He grimaced. "I've already been away two weeks, and it's another week of travel back. Can the items be shipped by land or sea when they're ready?"

I open my mouth, but Natalie was already speaking. "Mama can transport the supplies in seconds."

I shot her a warning glance, before looking around our immediate vicinity to see if anyone had overheard her.

Goran arched an eyebrow.

I gave a nervous cough as I cleared my throat. Lowering my voice, I leaned closer. "I can bring any donated objects—and you—back to Kovia. The transportation process is quick."

He cocked his head to one side. "How does that work?"

"Magic," blurted Natalie.

"Yes," I hissed at her. She knew I liked discretion.

She smiled sweetly back at me, and I narrowed my eyes in response. Turning back to Goran, I nodded once to confirm her admission. "Magic."

"That I would very much like to see."

Natalie remained dedicated to her plan. She spent the following week on the university campus recruiting students to her cause. Students set up a tent in the campus quad filled with empty crates. Day after day, the donations poured into them. When I wasn't teaching class or grading papers, I helped organize the donations, placing like objects in similar crates. People had brought clothes of all sizes, shoes, blankets, sheets, towels, pots, pans, goblets, plates, utensils, candles, bioluminescent lamps, books, and toys. The art class donated paintings and pottery. The metallurgy students donated hammers, mallets, saws, and nails. Other students donated food–salted meats, crackers, hard candies, and anything else which wouldn't perish in a few days.

By the end of the week, we'd sealed twenty full crates. As I stared at my daughter's achievement, Dean Lariat approached.

"Quite the accomplishment," the Dean commented.

"All of the credit goes to Natalie." I placed a hand on my daughter's shoulder.

She beamed.

"Well, it's wonderful. I think it reflects your commitment to the university. The whole town is buzzing about the help we're providing. The students are planning bi-annual meetings to discuss the next relief effort." She put her hands on her hips, nodding. "Well done."

As she walked away, I stood in silent disbelief. This activity was in no way intended to gain favor with the Dean. Given my recent suspension, I needed all of the help I could get, but I'd never have schemed to use my daughter in such a way. Nor did I see how a charity event was representative of commitment to the university. The idea seemed exploitive.

"Magnificent," a deep voice sounded.

I turned to see Goran standing beside me in awe.

He turned his grin toward me, before his expression faltered. "Are you okay?"

"Yes. Sorry. I'm under a lot of pressure at work at the university, and I was distracted by it."

Why am I sharing this with him?

He looked to the crate and back to me. "Is this a problem?"

"No," I said hurriedly. "No, this is perfect. This is exactly what I need. I never mind focusing on other people's problems, so I can forget my own for a spell."

Not sure why I shared that, either.

I supposed something about the jagged scar made Goran seem trustworthy.

He clasped his hands behind his back. "Well, I must admit, I've been eagerly anticipating watching how you intend to get all of this to Kovia."

"Magic," Natalie said.

I looked around the quad of the campus. The late afternoon sun bathed the trees, grass, and gray stone buildings. Since it was at the end of the week, the students had vacated the premises to spend the weekend at home. During the collection process, as we'd organized the donated items, I'd been careful to tell Natalie that she wasn't to mention how the items would get to Kovia. My plan was to take them, and the ambassador, to Kovia at dusk. The students would return in two days and, when they did, they'd assume the crates had been carted off to the east by carriage.

"I suppose now is as good a time as any," I said.

Natalie climbed onto the crates, sitting with her feet dangling off the edge.

"Ambassador Foal." I gestured toward the crates.

With a half-bemused, half-cautious expression, he climbed and sat on the wood.

"If you please, think of a location near to where these need to be delivered but far from crowds or onlookers." I laid a hand on the nearest crate and activated my star. I stretched the power around each touching crate, feeling their geometric shapes pressed against each other—and two other people touching them.

As the campus dissipated and our destination materialized, four walls formed around us. Dark wood panel walls surrounded us. Stale and musky air replaced the smell of grass and blooms from the campus.

I peeled off the wooden shell around my warrior stone necklace and set the stone glowing. Night had long descended upon this part of the world. Other crates surrounded us, as well as rusted machinery and dusty chests.

I looked at Goran. "Is this the right place?"

He hopped off the crate. "Yes. Amazing." He looked around the room. "This is a warehouse outside of the city. It's close enough to the port so we can claim the donations came by ship."

I gave him a grateful smile.

He raised his hand slightly. "It's obvious you want discretion. You don't want knowledge of your powers to draw attention to yourself. I don't want to have to explain a transcontinental trip that occurred in three seconds, either—so we'll settle on a story of traveling by ship, and I hope no one assembles the impossibility of that timeline."

Natalie climbed off the crates.

"Thank you. You'll be able to get the supplies where they need to go from here?"

"Yes."

I turned to take Natalie's hand.

"But I have two more requests."

I turned back to him.

His expression, initially amazed at the expedited form of travel, transformed into the conservative face of the ambassador I'd first met at the spring ball. "Could you take me to my home? And honor my family with the company of your family for dinner tomorrow night?"

"Yes—and no."

Natalie, whose face lit up at the mention of a social visit, turned a scowl towards me.

Goran looked troubled.

I continued, "Our dinner time is probably breakfast for you, given the distances between my home and yours. We can come during our breakfast time, which would be a dinner for you. However, my husband is working Saturday—so we couldn't come until Sunday."

Goran nodded. "Perfect. My wife would disown me if I gave her less than a day to prepare for company, anyway." He extended his hand.

I reached to accept it. "Let's get you home, ambassador."

5

Two days later, my family invaded Ambassador Goran's home.

With three children and two adults between us, he and his wife would know the full rambunctiousness of the Colt-Cross family. We brought with us a chocolate torte cake Paul and Mo had made, plus a quart of moon juice so the adults could better endure the screaming joy of children at play.

I could see the house in the daylight. The narrow, three-story building sat in a neighborhood of other homes. A broad lane stretched on either side, decorated by a spattering of cherry blossom trees.

When Goran opened the door, I realized I'd dressed more formally than the occasion required. My light-blue cotton dress, with lace and silver embroidery, contrasted against Goran's brown pants and shirt. Joshua similarly wore a decorated tunic. I'd imagined dinner to be a formal affair, at the table of an ambassador, while Goran had clearly imagined a casual dinner with new friends.

I relaxed instantly, liking Goran's approach much better.

After introductions, the children went outside to play. Joshua and Goran followed to talk while supervising the children. I remained in the kitchen and offered to help with the preparations. Lorraine, Goran's wife, waved me off as she took the cake and flask of moon juice we had brought as gifts.

She poured the spirits into a glass and handed it to me. "You're a guest, and I won't have you fixing your own appreciation meal." Her Crithian accent was thicker and less refined than Goran's but still easily comprehensible.

I sipped my moon juice and smiled. Lorraine was my height but with more robust curves than I'd ever possessed. Her bosom appeared large and generous in the cream colored dress she wore. Her long, copper-colored hair was efficiently braided back.

"You probably don't want me destroying your meal anyway."

"You don't cook?"

"I'm better in a chemistry lab than a kitchen."

She chuckled. "Goran told me you teach chemistry."

With those words, and a brief rake of her eyes from my head to my toes, I felt her appraisal. Did Lorraine wonder or worry about the strange teacher from another continent being invited to her home? Or was she happy to have guests over for a meal?

Unlike Coco DeFay's perpetual disapproving appraisal of me, I sensed Lorraine felt at ease. She didn't perceive me as a threat, and I wondered if that meant Goran hadn't told her of my powers. Or better yet, he had, and she just didn't fear them.

"Yes. I studied at the University of Marrington, and now I teach there."

"Goran said the students launched quite the relief effort."
Lorraine began to beat eggs and milk in a bowl.

"Twenty crates of supplies."

She nodded, turning to roll dough on the countertop. As Goran's
wife fixated on her tasks, she said, "Goran told me you helped bring
him home." Her voice cracked at the last word.

I swallowed and straightened.

Without looking up at me, she added, "With his ambassador position, I never know when he'll be home. Thank you." As her eyes met
mine, she blinked away tears. "He's providing for his family, but it's
still hard to be without him so often."

At a loss for words, I walked around the counter and hugged
Lorraine, not caring that flour would get on my dress from her apron.

She returned the hug. "Thank you," she repeated.

"It was no trouble at all. He seems like a nice and genuine man."

As she pulled away, Lorraine snorted. "Yes, he is. Funny though—
most people never know it because they take one look at the long scar
and rugged face and assume he's unapproachable." She placed the
dough in a cast iron pan and began pressing it into the edges. "Don't
mistake me, he's no puppy dog. He's battle-hardened and has killed
men when he saw no other way. But he's decent and fair, and he'll
always choose resolution over conflict when he can."

"A good ambassador, then."

She beamed. "Yes. Quite."

"He misses you, too, while he's away."

Lorraine gave me a quizzical look.

"When I dropped him outside your home the other night, he had
tears in his eyes and joy in his heart. For a moment, I thought he
might fall to his knees and kiss the ground in front of your house."

Her mouth quirked, as if she was trying to picture the sight.
Lorraine added the vegetable medley into the beaten eggs and grated
cheese, and mixed the concoction before placing it into the skillet.
"Goran kneels for no one and nothing."

I arched an eyebrow. "I bet he kneels for love."

Her cheeks flushed and she grinned. Still smiling, Lorraine

carried the skillet across the kitchen and slid it inside the wood-burning stove.

WHEN THE QUICHE FINISHED BAKING, we sat the children at the only table and fed them first. After they ate, the children went upstairs to play while the adults sat down for their meal.

"The quiche is delicious," I commented after my first bite. I cut into one of the fresh, sliced tomatoes accompanying the meal.

"Yes," Joshua agreed.

Lorraine sipped her moon juice. "Goran tells me you're a healer."

"That's right. I have a clinic in Marrington, and I'm working on funds for a hospital."

"Hospital?" Her face went blank.

"It would be like a large clinic, except some people who are very ill could stay there for days at a time until they recover."

"Ah. We call those infirmaries. And how did you and Abigail meet?" she asked.

Joshua smiled at the memories. "I was several years ahead of her at the university. She was my roommate's pesky younger sister, always getting into trouble."

I elbowed him playfully in the side.

"When she left to work at the castle, I didn't see her for six months. Then, one dark night, she arrived on my doorstep disheveled, distraught, in over her head *again*, and stunningly beautiful. I realize that night I loved her—and we've been at each other's side ever since then."

Lorraine wiped at her eyes. "That's lovely."

"What about you and Goran?" Joshua asked.

"I was a farmer's daughter, while Goran worked for the King's guard. He headed their anti-smuggling division."

"Smuggling?" I asked, instantly regretting the interruption to her story.

Goran swallowed the bite of quiche in his mouth. "Bellosian

smugglers have a ring on Southern Kovia. They steal salt, silks, live-stock. Local authorities couldn't manage them, so we did."

Lorraine continued. "He and his men showed up at our door one day, asking for food and lodging."

Goran absently touch the finger to the scar on his face. "We'd been defeated by a band of smugglers. They'd been ready for us."

"They spent a week with us, healing, and helping on the farm as repayment. Then Goran asked my father for my hand in marriage."

He chuckled. "Her father said: 'Why in the name of the Unideit are you asking *me*? You want to marry her? Ask her.'" Goran took Lorraine's hand into his, eyes sparkling in adoration as he gazed into hers. "She said 'yes.'"

"I think my father feared farm life would shorten my life expectancy, as it had my mother—she died in her fourth childbirth—and he believed Goran could provide better for me than a farmer ever could. And Goran has. He even quit the anti-smuggling division, so I'd worry less about whether or not he'd return home alive."

We finished the meal, talking more about the struggles, geography, and politics of Kovia. When we finally gathered the children, Joshua and I thanked our hosts and promised to return in one month's time, to transport them and host them for dinner at our house.

I spent the morning removing weeds from the garden. Small, green tomatoes hung from vines, as little buds sprouted on other vines where cucumbers would soon grow. We had peppers, lettuce, carrots, cabbage, corn, and much more planted. Marigolds were scattered between the crops to attract ladybugs, hoverflies, and mini-wasps to eat the insects that eat the plants. The flowers also repelled the worms that tended to infest the corn. Mint, planted near the cabbage and tomatoes, repelled cabbage moths and ants. Rosemary and sage also kept the cabbage moths away as well as carrot flies.

My hawk, Carrot, perched on a post, watching me tend the garden.

When I finished, I stroked the raptor's golden-orange feathers. "Are you feeling neglected?"

Carrot had only recently become comfortable with the children, and now allowed Natalie to stroke her. Paul and Rebekah were still too rowdy for her wary temperament.

"Let's go visit the wizard, shall we?"

Joshua had the children for the morning, so I had time to travel to the Black Stag Forest. After attaching my leather wristband, I let Carrot climb aboard. I transported us instantly to the edge of the forest, and we walked deep into the clearing where I usually found Orrick. Since freeing him from captivity as an oak tree, he and I had become friends, and I visited him whenever time and my obligations at home permitted.

Orrick sat on a log in the clearing, and I joined him. I enjoyed the early spring weather. When summer arrived, the incessant heat from the surrounding marsh would make the steamy forest humid and unbearable.

"I do delight in your visits, Abigail. There's such a tranquility in casual conversation with a human."

I imagined living among brownies would be taxing. The small creatures required a certain conversational finesse.

"I wish I could visit more often."

—except in the summer.

"You have obligations. I understand." Orrick looked around, adding, "Is Mal here now?"

At his question, Mal materialized.

"Yes." I transferred Carrot to a low-hanging branch. I had asked Orrick once if he knew of any magic so that he, too, could see his brother—but he'd shaken his head and mumbled something about a 'work in progress.' I didn't push the issue after that, because I'd miss these outings with Orrick and Mal if the brothers didn't still need me as a go-between.

Orrick linked his fingers. "Wonderful. What shall we discuss today?"

Mal smirked. "How about the time we were crossing the gorge on Mount Kapri and the bridge broke?"

I relayed the message to Orrick, who grimaced. He explained, "I was eighteen, and I never told Mother we nearly lost you."

"What happened?" I asked.

Orrick's gaze became distant. "We were children, confined to Karnelik all our lives. Our playground was those mountains—though they probably weren't any safer than traveling south into the territory raided by Bellosians."

I settled into his soothing tale, feeling a sense of accomplishment in bringing the brothers together to reminisce.

"I crossed the gorge first," Orrick continued. "As you're well aware, the mountains are slick with snow and ice. The bridges are no different. The wood was practically petrified from the cold and covered in a sheet of ice. As siblings often do, I dared Malakai to cross while hopping like a rabbit."

I glanced at Malakai. "Like a cute, fuzzy rabbit?"

He bristled. "I believe the request was hop like a frog."

"So, he starts hopping, and halfway across I have an ominous premonition, as if someone dropped a lump of snow down the back of my shirt. I cry out for him to stop just as the ropes maintaining the bridge snap. They were frozen, brittle, and stretched to capacity by the weight of the icy planks. The last thing I saw was Malakai grasping at rope and plank as he plummeted into the darkness." Orrick shook his head. "I thought I'd killed him. Ten seconds, which felt like a lifetime later, he's calling to me: 'Are you going to stand there, or pull me up?' I look down to see him standing on a ledge, holding what was left of the broken bridge still attached to the side of the mountain I was on."

Mal gave a *tsk*. "My own brother, attempting to murder me." He leaned against a tree trunk he'd created. "The good news was that I used Orrick's guilt against him for the next year."

I turned to Orrick. "Did Mal manipulate you after that?"

He chuckled. "Oh, yes. For the next twelve months he had me covering for him for missed sessions with the tutors, introducing him to women at court, and sneaking out to the market. I broke all sorts of codes and curfews out of guilt for nearly killing him."

I grinned. "What made you finally stop?"

"Sal," Mal said. A doleful smile suggested a mix of happy and sad memories from long ago.

"The captain of the guard. Sal Yonik. He was an enormous, burly man one didn't cross. He caught Malakai and I sneaking out after dark. I confessed our entire shenanigans."

"Sal suggested Orrick had sufficiently paid his debt to me. That was the end of it," Mal said.

"That was not the end of my brother's misbehaviors, but it was at least the end of my aiding and abetting him."

"Pay no attention to the wizard. I was always a gentleman."

The stories and bantering continued, until Baird's voice in my head reminded me that I needed to take over watching the children and bring Joshua to the Aithos river.

We are ready for fishing, Baird's voice sounded in my mind.

He and I had formed a silent communication link eight years ago, when we'd crossed our traveling stars trying to transport a sizable army. The link proved useful when crisis arose—or when Joshua and Baird wanted to organize their next fishing trip.

After I coaxed Carrot down from the tree, I bid Orrick farewell.

"Mom, why are you pacing?"

I looked at Natalie, who stared up at me from her book. Paul was slaying a chaise lounge in the center of the Inn room as if it were a giant swamp snake. Rebekah jumped vigorously on the room's bed.

"I'm waiting for your father," I explained, as I continued pacing.

Joshua had gone to speak with his parents about coordinating a group family activity; after all, we'd all taken this spring vacation together to Ntajid.

At last Joshua returned to our rented room.

I stared at him expectantly.

He rubbed the back of his neck. "They left a message at the desk that they've gone to the springs."

"Again?" For two days his parents had gone to the Ntajid springs —a source of relaxing hot water and mud pools, but not a play spot for children. "What's the point of taking a vacation with them if we aren't actually spending vacation together?" I found his parent's company an affront to all of my senses. They were loud, verbose, and generally disruptive. Nevertheless, they were my children's grandparents, and I wouldn't deny the children an important familial relationship with them, but his parents had to be willing participants.

Yesterday, while Bart and Marge went to the springs, Joshua had to spend a half-day at the clinic, and I had the pleasure of managing three boisterous children in the bustling, crowded marketplace of Ntajid all by myself. Rebekah had attempted to touch every ware on display—the ones she could reach at least—while Paul had run through the crowd with reckless abandon. Natalie, meanwhile, would stop at every jewelry booth to stare at sparkling gems. I'd tried to not lose a child in the chaos.

Joshua rolled his shoulders. "We're both a little frustrated at the lack of coordinated activities."

More than a little frustrated.

"As lovely and bustling as this city is, they don't have activities for children."

"I know, but my parents have never been to the springs, and they don't get many vacations running a restaurant."

"I'd have been happy to transport them there, if I'd known they weren't going to spend any quality time with their grandchildren."

Maybe not *happy* to do so—I might have had to restrain myself from telling them to take the train like everybody else, but eventually, I would have agreed.

Joshua gave me an apologetic shrug.

I raised my voice to the room, infusing it with cheer. "How does everyone feel about going to the beach?"

The children cheered in unison.

"We'll go to Marrin Beach. They've been cooped up in the room for half the day. Shoes on everyone."

"I'll stay," Joshua said.

I started to protest.

"This way I can speak to my parents when they get back."

Now his parents' behavior had eroded into our family time as well. I bit my tongue. Complaining further wouldn't help the situation.

I kissed Joshua on the cheek before we left. "Good luck."

"Uncle Baird!" Natalie cried in excitement. She wrapped her arms around the tall monk.

I stifled a pang of jealousy, trying to remember the last time she'd greeted me with such joy.

"Fluffy!" Rebekah called.

Fury fought to control his excitement as he crawled towards the toddler on his belly. She tumbled onto him, clasping his hair in her small fingers. She giggled as he licked her face, before he raced away to discharge his energy a safe distance from her. Fury ran toward the ocean waves, nipping at the water. Then he spun around and weaved his way between the children, barking as they chased after him.

I gave Baird a sheepish grin. "I'm glad you could join us."

"It's been too long since I visited the ocean."

To one side of us, blue waves tumbled along the shore. The water was darker, murkier, and cooler than the pristine waters of Misty Isle, but it was still a pleasant beach. On our other side stretched rolling sand dunes and wispy, marram grass—permanently bowing eastward as a result of the perpetual ocean breeze. In the distance, far ahead of us, rose cliffs along Marrin beach. Behind us were kilometers of shoreline, speckled with the wagons of people visiting the beach.

Baird had left his blue cloak in the sanctuary and wore brown slacks, rolled to his shins, paired with a white cotton tunic. He looked relaxed as he watched the children play with the wolf.

"Where is Joshua?"

"Dealing with his parents."

"Hmm."

Crisp, foamy water doused my feet as we walked. "I learned of an earthquake in Kovia from the Kovian ambassador at the Spring Festival. Do you know Goran Foal?"

"I do not. But when Zack heard of the devastation, he sent two monks to offer assistance."

"I didn't see the damage, but I delivered donated supplies from the university to Kovia. It was Natalie's idea. She orchestrated an entire relief effort."

"Fascinating."

"We took twenty crates of supplies there."

"Much needed, I'm sure."

"It seems, in the hierarchy of financially-stable countries, we rank beneath Bellos and Kovia ranks beneath us."

"Quite right—and I think that delineation has widened over the years. It's contributing to unrest."

I scooped up a white seashell and ran my thumb along the ridges. "Mal and I often talk about man's repossession of his own evil. I don't understand what's changed. Since I'm the most recent Avant Champion, I feel responsible somehow. I'd fix it if I knew how."

"Perhaps the source will reveal itself in time."

Would I be able to make such calm, casual statements once I'd lived for over a hundred years? Perhaps, by that time, I would have finally learned to juggle the many facets of life; and problems that now seemed monumental would be minor.

Baird breathed deeply of the salty air. "Tell me this: Does the sense that you have contributed to the unleashing of evil drive you to intervene when the Queen and Coco ask for assistance?"

"Yes, but there are other factors."

"Such as?"

"Such as knowing I can resolve situations faster and with less risk to the safety of others."

"Since times are changing, as you pointed out, perhaps people will need to learn how to remain civilized in the face of incivility —*without* the fear that magic will be used to control them."

Were my interventions as the Avant Champion acts of controlling people through magic? "You're suggesting that by intervening, I'll create a society that only behaves so long as they fear me?"

"It's a possibility."

I watched the children play in the frothy waves. Fury had strayed toward the dunes, chasing crabs and seagulls.

"Wonderful. Yet another way I can screw up the world."

He grinned. "How is your meditation coming?"

6

"Did you enjoy the springs?" I asked Marge.

We ate at a large dining table, big enough for the three children and all four adults.

Bart had been given the task of feeding Rebekah. Thus far, more food had landed on his face than in Rebekah's mouth. I made an effort not to laugh out loud.

"Oh, wonderful, dear," Marge said to me. "I feel ten years younger. I wish we could come every year, but the restaurant can't be closed so much." Her eyes sparkled above a set of round, rosy cheeks.

Bart dragged a cloth across his face, wiping away the food. "Oh, I don't know, maybe our favorite daughter in law could ferry us on occasion."

Only daughter in-law.

I started to open my mouth in protest, when Joshua lifted a bite of food to my mouth. "Abbey, try this steak, it's wonderful."

I glared at him, reluctantly chewing the bite of meat.

Bart's eyes twinkled. "While we were soaking in the mud pit, I had a brilliant idea. Imagine, Abigail, you could have your own business transporting people to vacation destinations. You could charge them half the cost of train or carriage travel and still make a fortune. People would pay to go places they've never been before."

"Dad," Joshua interjected, "Abbey has a full-time job at the university."

As I had since they'd known me.

At last, I swallowed the mouthful of steak. I opted to change the subject. "Since Meredith is close to Kovia, do you get any news from that country?"

Marge bobbed her head enthusiastically. "Yes, we have travelers who visit from Kovia."

"I met a man named Goran, a diplomat from Kovia, who said an earthquake struck."

"Oh, yes. Probably two months ago, would you say, Bart? It was the east coast though. Far from us. They said a lot of people were displaced. Did you know anyone affected?"

"No." I sipped my tea. The warm lemon flavor lingered on my palate. "I just wondered why news of it seemed so slow to travel across the continent."

She frowned. "Well, of the ten continents, they aren't even in the top half of the wealthiest."

I gaped at her. What did that have to do with anything?

Natalie sat straighter. "We organized a relief effort. All the university students donated supplies. Mama transported them to Kovia— and we met ambassador Goran, and had breakfast with him and his family."

"Oh, how pleasant."

"Imagine the advertisement," Bart continued, his mind still dwelling on the concept of my under-utilized transport abilities. "'Holidays by Abbey.' Oh, you could truly spice it up with 'Champion Holidays.'"

I shot Joshua a look as I abandoned any further effort at sensible conversation.

"My beautiful wife." Joshua ran a finger along my cheek, before tucking a stray strand of hair behind my ear.

We each lay on our side in bed, looking at each other by the flickering light of the bedside candles. In the other room, behind a closed door, the children slept peacefully. They'd worn themselves out playing at Marrin Beach and filling their stomachs over dinner with their grandparents.

"You're saying that because we just made love."

He grinned. Satisfaction emanated from his expression. "That type of physical activity, after a disagreement, is always pleasant."

"Makes me wish we could extend our holiday." I knew such a wish to be impossible. Even the few days Joshua had spared meant more patients would be awaiting his return. Before he could remind me of that, I added, "But I know you need to get back."

Joshua rolled onto his back and positioned his hands behind his head. "It's difficult being the only magical healer. People, from infants to elderly, travel from across the continent. For every person I heal, magically or naturally, three more arrive. I love helping people, and it may surprise you to know that I gain more satisfaction when I achieve it naturally, rather than by magic. But the cycle can be exhausting."

I listened quietly. Long ago, I'd abandoned my demands that Joshua find an alternative to using his stone. Constant use drained him, but I finally accepted his passion, realizing his call to healing. The best way to help him—help *us*—was to support him.

I ran a finger along his bare chest. "I'm happy to be your source of distraction and recuperation."

"I'll never say 'no' to that." He reached over and pulled me towards him.

I suppressed a laugh as I straddled him.

He pulled me down closer for a tender kiss. "I may heal my patients, but you heal me." He brushed a thumb across my lips. "Your love gives me strength. Each night with you is a gift—whether we're exhausted after a day with the children or making love."

I stared at him, amazed that after thirteen years of marriage he could still make such a heartfelt statement.

"Though preferably making love," he added with a boyish grin.

I didn't have words for how much I loved him, so I kissed him again and made his wish come true.

Summer arrived, with the trees brimming in green leaves and the blossoms of spring gone. The temperature hadn't turned hot yet, so the children spent long days outside. I watched them, and realized I needed to buy more warm weather clothes for Natalie and Paul, who'd both grown since last summer.

After our usual morning routine of getting dressed and welcoming the household help into our home, I walked with Joshua to the end of our driveway before transporting him to his clinic. From inside the walls, I heard the murmuring of people already waiting outside the front door.

"Sounds like you'll be busy."

"Evidence that I need a hospital." He wrapped his arms around me and gave a squeeze.

As I returned his embrace, my gaze roamed the room. Joshua had expanded the clinic over the years, but judging by the line at his door, more space was still needed—and more healers.

"I'll pick you up this evening."

I transported to my university office to prepare for my morning lecture.

An hour later, I stood in my classroom and began my lecture. I wrote a chemical equation on the chalkboard:

$$3I_2 + NH_3 \longrightarrow NI_3 + 3HI$$

I turned to the demonstration table and held up a glass beaker. "This is one gram of ground iodine crystals. I'm pouring it over concentrated aqueous ammonia. While we let that sit and dry, here's what it looks like when you pour that solution over filter paper."

The filter paper was secured to another beaker by twine. Dark brown crystals clung to the paper. This pre-prepared demonstration had already been given time to dry. "The dark clusters are the nitrogen triiodide. This compound, in its dry form, is very unstable."

I pulled out a feather and a meter stick from my demonstration table. After securing the feather to the end of the meter stick, I took two steps back from the table and situated a pair of glass goggles over my eyes. The students, seated in the theatre-style room, were a safe distance from the table.

Gingerly, I dipped the feather into the filter paper with the dry nitrogen triiodide. A loud boom erupted, and a cloud of purple fumes plumed over the table. Gasps of surprise were followed by cheers. As the gas dissipated, I wrote on the board.

$$2NI_3(s) \longrightarrow N_2(g) + 3I_3(g)$$

After I dismissed the late morning class, Dean Lariat approached me in the classroom. Her short, gray hair looked disheveled, and her lips were stretched thin.

"Class attendance was abysmal today," I commented. "I had my big explosion. Chemical reaction of nitrogen triiodide. Usually they all come." I began putting the beakers and supplies in a crate to take back to my office

"For twelve years you've been trying to destroy this classroom."

I followed her gaze to the charred and scarred demonstration table, the victim of my many experiments.

The last of the students trailed out the door.

She glanced around the room as though a spy might be lurking. "You'd know why students were sparse if you lived in town."

I placed the iodine crystals in my box. "Enlighten me."

"A lot of people have fallen ill. We're closing school for the rest of the week."

"Closing school?" I'd never heard of such an occurrence.

"People are beginning to panic. Some are leaving the city."

"What news from the Queen?"

Dean Lariat shook her head. "She's issued a public notice to stay home and not panic, which naturally means everyone is doing the exact opposite."

I thought of Joshua, recalling the throng of people outside the clinic door that morning. If "a lot of people have fallen ill" meant an outbreak was occurring, his clinic could be overrun by patients. If people were in a state of panic, as Dean Lariat had suggested, Joshua might need help.

"I need to get to Joshua."

She straightened. "Yes, that makes sense. Don't worry about the mess."

As I gave her a grateful nod, Mal's apparition appeared by the door. "Don't go to the clinic, Abigail. It isn't safe."

"What?"

Dean Lariat took a confused step back. "I said don't worry about the mess."

I looked back at her. She hadn't heard Mal, since only I could see and hear him. Like almost everyone else in my life, she didn't even know of his existence.

I gave her a forced smile. "Thank you. I'm going." I scurried out of the classroom and wound my way through the halls to my office. Enroute, the lack of students and professors mulling about the hall created an ominous silence. I shut my office door.

"Mal, explain yourself." I'd experienced enough of his warnings over the years to know to heed them.

He reappeared, the same solemn expression on his face. "A sickness spreads."

"What sickness? Spreads where?"

"A plague." His voice was grim.

"Is Joshua in danger?"

"No. The Queen's guards relocated him to the castle when the clinic flooded with patients. If you go to the clinic, you'll be exposed."

"But Joshua is unharmed?"

"He is unharmed." Mal lifted his arms and projected a scene for me. He was somehow capable of re-creating images of past events so that I could watch them unfold as if I had been there.

I instantly recognized Joshua's clinic. Instead of the peaceful, tidy interior I left him in that morning, I saw wall-to-wall patients resting on cots or on the floor. Some had blankets others gripped flasks of water. Some huddled close, together as families, with looks of devastation marring their faces. Some of the patients were flush with fever, while others looked pale and sickly. One woman—ashen, with bloodshot eyes and a bleeding nose—cradled a small, pale corpse.

As I swallowed, I averted my eyes to the ground. The images Mal showed me had no sound or smell, though I imaged if they did, it would be of blood and human waste.

When I looked back, I saw Joshua rushing between patients to administer elixirs and tonics. He looked ragged but focused. He wasn't using his healing stone. I wondered if that was because he recognized the masses would strip him of his strength if he did, or because he didn't have an understanding of the illness and therefore couldn't heal it.

Joshua could heal many ailments, but only through careful study over the years. His stone worked by rapidly helping the body heal through mechanisms he'd come to understand.

As I watched, castle guards entered the crowded clinic. Their pristine blue garments, with silver-embroidered horse and metal vambraces, contrasted with the dirt, and blood, and human secretions that filled the clinic. They were young men and women, eager to serve the Queen, but not hardened soldiers. Since Mal's scepter absorbed evil, no human wars had happened in over seven thousand years. Aside from minor skirmishes, the guards had little experience with true battle.

Their determined gaze found Joshua. One of the young guardsmen spoke to him, and Joshua looked at the man with incredulity. He signaled around at the patients in the clinic. The guard's face became stern. He gave Joshua some type of command.

One weak and feeble woman pushed herself to her feet. She spoke through a swollen tongue and ulcerated mouth. I couldn't read her lips, but she was clearly angry. Others joined in protest.

The energy in the room shifted from silent suffering to heated hostility. The guards' eyes flickered around the room, and their hands reached for the hilts of their swords.

My mouth went dry, my heart hammering in my chest. I reminded myself that these were prior events and I could take no action to change them. Whatever happened next, Mal had already assured me Joshua was presently safe.

Patients started shoving to their feet—the ones with enough strength to do so.

Swords were drawn from their sheaths.

Joshua raised his hands as he addressed the crowd. I could tell he had tried to provide words of reassurance, but the people didn't appear placated.

As the guards escorted Joshua out of the clinic, they had to force their way through—physically pushing the mob of people aside. Agitation erupted into anger as the patients continued to protest. The guards grew more protective of Joshua as the hostility in the room escalated.

As the guards shoved their way through the mob, Joshua was ushered into a waiting carriage. Someone on the street—a yellow-toothed man dressed in worn clothing, who looked like he might have walked fifty kilometers to get to the clinic that day—grabbed Joshua's wrist.

The man spoke, his face a mixture of fury and pleading.

"I'm sorry." Joshua's lips formed the words even though they weren't audible to me. He tried to gently pull free, but the man held tight.

One of the guards punched the man in the face. As he stumbled back, the carriage door slammed shut. The crowd exploded with rage, hollering and banging on the carriage. The horses were signaled and took off with a jolt, knocking those crowding the carriage to the cobblestones.

I turned and looked at Mal. "*Merciful Monks*," I gasped. I felt relieved they'd evacuated Joshua—he didn't have the resources to treat so many—but their evacuation tactics left something to be desired. I didn't see the other healers who normally worked with him, either. Were they ill?

I complained, "If he was needed urgently at the castle, they could have sent some of their own healers to take his place. They abandoned all of those people. Patients often travel hundreds of kilometers to see Joshua."

Mal didn't reply.

I realized his silent imaging of the past still played past events. I turned back to watch the angry mob. They began attacking each other now. Arguments erupted, both internal and external to the clinic. Pushing and shoving escalated to fighting. When one of Joshua's burners was knocked over, flames spread up nearby curtains. Bottles of chemicals became superheated and began popping, spewing chards of hot glass.

"No! His clinic!"

I watched in horror as people began evacuating. Some stole items as they fled. Others left invalids on the floor. No one attempted to put out the fire.

The image faded and vanished.

I stared at the wall of my office. "The clinic?"

"Ashes."

I thought of all of Joshua's books and ledgers and healing remedies. He'd be devastated. He might not even know yet.

I started to ask Mal why he hadn't told me sooner, but restrained myself. Whenever I asked him this question, he always explained that he could only see parts of current or future events, and the timing was variable.

"Why didn't you tell me sooner?"

My restraint is often short lived.

"You would have gone to help," Mal answered.

"Absolutely," I snapped.

"Then you would have been exposed to the illness."

Mal had been protecting me, again, even when I might have failed to protect myself.

"Where is Joshua now? I'll go to him."

"You're missing the bigger picture, Abigail."

"What's that?"

"This is a plague—rapidly spreading, highly contagious, and deadly. You are, as of yet, unexposed. If you go to the castle, you will be exposed."

If I was exposed, then I couldn't go to the children without exposing them. Could this illness reach our rural estate? "I need to move the children to safety."

"Yes."

"Misty Isles is unaffected?"

"Yes."

"Okay. You're right." I paced my office. "You did the right thing."

He crossed his arms and arched an eyebrow as if to say: *Did you expect anything less than perfection?*

"Alright. No need to further inflate your ego. From what you've shown me, the disaster has only begun." I walked out of my office and down the hall.

Mal's lean apparition walked casually beside me. "Where are you going?"

"To talk to Sunny. I need a history lesson."

He nodded in understanding.

"But you have to vanish. I lose all credibility when people see me looking in your direction and talking to no one."

"As you wish." His form dissolved before he finished the sentence.

7

———

I found Sunny, the university history professor, in her office with her nose buried in an excessively thick book on the history of sea travel.

I knocked on her open door.

Sunny looked up at me over her reading spectacles. "Oh, Abigail, is it our lunch date? Did I lose track of time?" She started to stand.

"No, no." I waved her back into her seat as I entered. "You've heard about the infection spreading?"

She nodded, pulling off her glasses. "Many students are out and classes are being cancelled."

I sat down in the chair opposite her desk. "What do you know about the—" I hesitated. I never asked Mal the specific name of the plague.

"*Omega* plague," Mal whispered to me.

"—Omega plague."

She straightened. "What? Why do you say that? No one has called it that?"

I was startled by her alarm. "I spoke with someone earlier—"

"Someone tall and dashing," Mal purred.

"—someone annoying, but who is often right about such things. He hypothesized that this could be the Omega plague. If that's true, what are the ramifications?"

"Not a hypothesis," Mal corrected.

I sighed.

Sunny pursed her lips, stood, and walked over to close her door. "Stop saying that out loud."

"Omega plague?"

"Yes," she hissed. Her curly brown hair bounced as she shook her head at me. When the door shut, she sat back in her chair. "The Omega plague decimated the continent of Kovia eight hundred years ago. We don't throw around the name carelessly."

I frowned. "It's not as though reciting the name of a disease incurs its wrath."

"No. But you could insight panic."

I thought about Joshua's cremated clinic.

Too late to avoid panic.

"Can you tell me about it? How did it spread? What are the symptoms? How was it stopped?"

"You should take my history of medicine course next semester."

If there is a next semester.

Sunny continued, "I don't know if anyone who studied it lived to write about it. Historians think it was viral, but unlike the Jau virus, a vaccine was never discovered. Exposure or inoculation to symptom manifestation is three days. From the appearance of symptoms to the occurrence of death is usually five days."

Bile tickled the back of my throat.

"Symptoms start with a rash and escalate to bleeding organs—bloody stool and urine, coughing up blood, oozing blood from eyes and nose."

I thought about the people lining the walls of Joshua's clinic. Their mouths were crusted with blood.

"Don't look so worried, Abigail. The plague hasn't reared its ugly head in eight hundred years. It's eradicated. That's why it's in my history books and not in your husband's medicine books."

I bit my lip. I couldn't share the source of my information with her. She wouldn't believe me. "How was it finally stopped?"

She walked to her bookshelf and pulled a book. "Everybody died. There are no precise records of how many, but hundreds of thousands in all likelihood." She spoke the words in the frank tone of a history professor—coldly reciting facts about distant events without any thought on their bearing on the present.

Sunny opened the book she'd selected and slipped her glasses back on her nose. "I always use this poem during class because the imagery is so vibrant." After looking over the page, she turned the book for me to read.

> *See the devastation of the disease,*
> *Smoldering in the breeze.*
>
> *Death destroys hope with decay,*
> *Indiscriminately, every life is prey.*
>
> *All obscured by the ashes,*
> *Overshadowed dismay crashes.*
>
> *Death's tentacles ensnare all,*
> *Merciless, cataclysmic, curtain call.*
>
> *Stone of Blood, Stone of Health,*
> *Save the lives considered wealth.*

Beneath the poem was a notation:

The Omega plague has not cursed this land for over two-thousand years. It is the obligation of the living to document devastating events as they unfolded so generations to come may know the suffering and the heroism. The plague's origins were traced to Kovia, where its first victims succumbed.

Further transcription illegible.

FS Klux
Circa 6280

"So, it occurred eight-hundred years ago *and* two-thousand years before that." I stood and paced her office. I wondered if eight-hundred years ago, history professors were declaring it eradicated.

Sunny sat back down in her desk chair. "Someone saw the devastation and wrote it down, or at least passed it along verbally until somebody else wrote it down. The history is rich in these few lines. They burned all of the bodies, so you can imagine a gray sky of smoke and ashes day after day."

"And the stones?"

"Mythical legend. Some historians say magic was used to finally end the plague."

"You don't think so?"

She stared at me. "You're exceedingly level-headed, Abigail, but I see your imagination running rampant at my words."

"I'm worried."

"I can see that."

"I'm going to evacuate my family until I have answers about what's going on. I can relocate you as well."

"I'm an academic, not an alarmist." She shut her book.

I stopped pacing. "And I have magical talents, so I believe the possibility of magical intervention merits a bit more consideration." She knew I was the Avant Champion, and although Sunny had never seen my Traveler's Star or Warrior Stone in action, she had heard of their capabilities.

Sunny blinked. "Do your talents include seeing the future?"

"No."

"Mine do," Mal said.

"Not helpful," I murmured.

"Beg pardon?"

"Nothing. Thank you for the history lesson."

"Perhaps take a holiday. When you return, you'll see you worried about nothing."

"I hope you're right," I said, as I pulled the door open and left.

I ARRIVED home via my usual surreptitious route—inconspicuously transporting to the end of the long roadway to my house, and then walking down it. I felt the urge to run. I picked up my pace. Soon my feet were flying beneath me.

When I reached the house, I panted for air. After three children, I hadn't taken the time to rebuild my endurance—and I was feeling it.

I still sparred with Baird, but less frequently than I used to. I'd lapsed into the comfortable stability of my family life, mindful that it might be disrupted but not diligently preparing for the next catastrophe.

I stood outside, catching my breath. My impression of this new dilemma was that it would require more cunning than strength. This wasn't a fight against evil, or a bloody civil war; it was a plague—the worst plague in the history of the world.

This was a healer's domain, not mine. Joshua's war. So why did I feel the same angst as I did before battle?

I opened the door and stepped inside my house.

"Mama!" Rebekah squealed. She left her blocks on the floor and ran into my arms.

I squeezed her tight to me. No matter our disagreements at mealtime, naptime, and bedtime, she was always delighted to see me. Her greetings were in contrast to Natalie's—from whom I usually received little more than an obligatory "hello."

Too soon in our hug, Rebekah squirmed out of my grasp. I set her down, and she turned her attention back to her blocks.

Gert stood and smoothed the bun of her brown hair. "Lady Cross. You're home early."

"Yes." I turned toward her. "There are quite a few people ill in Marrington and Oxville. I'm taking the children to my mother's. The staff can have days off until we return. I recommend everyone take similar precautions."

Her brow furrowed as she nervously fingered the hem of her dress. "Similar precautions, m'lady?"

"Yes. Somewhere remote. With family."

"Your estate is quite remote m'lady."

"And it may be sufficiently so, but I'll be taking the children to my mother's nonetheless. Please let all the staff know they will receive holiday pay on the days they would have worked. I'll send word when we're back at the estate."

"Yes, m'lady. I believe Cook Mo has already prepared several meals for the week."

"Excellent. We'll take some with us, and all the staff can divide the remaining rations among themselves."

"Yes, m'lady."

"Can you watch Rebekah while you spread the word? Just until we're packed?"

"Yes, m'lady."

"Where can I find Natalie?"

"Riding lessons."

"Thank you."

I left the house and walked toward the barn. The six-stall wooden building still looked pristine, as it was only two years old. To the left stretched a mixture of open pasture and woodlands for the horses to roam. To the right was a corral for riding and training.

I spotted Natalie atop my horse, Phobus, cantering around the perimeter of the corral. Phobus' chestnut hair glistened in the sunlight.

Natalie's long brown hair flowed behind her. She maintained perfect posture in the saddle. I wondered if I'd ever looked so graceful riding as she did. Natalie made riding look like art; a dance.

I walked to the perimeter of the fence and Phobus caught sight of me, cutting across the center of the arena towards me.

Natalie let the reins fall. "Hello."

"You're riding beautifully." I stroked the short hair between Phobus' eyes as he lowered his head to me.

"You're home early."

"Yes. We're going to Nana's."

"So suddenly?"

"So suddenly."

She looked around the barn, house, and garden. "Where's Papa?"

"He's still in Marrington. There are a lot of sick people. He's helping take care of them."

She pouted. "He's not coming with us?"

"He's not," I confessed, apologetically. "I'm taking you to Misty Isle. Then, I'll go help your father."

"Why can't we all go help?"

I considered how "helpful" the children would be, running through the castle halls, knocking over fine Bellosian vases, banging on Taco silver, and causing mayhem.

"You can't go because there'll be sick people everywhere. I don't want any of you getting ill."

"You and Papa are going."

"Yes, and I'm not risking anyone else in this family."

"That's not fair."

"It's called being rational. Now, before you continue to wear down my patience, go back to the barn and tell Will to ready the carriage."

She scowled, but had the good sense not to argue with my stern expression. "Yes, Mama."

She retrieved the reins and whirled Phobus around. She loped one last time around the arena before heading to the barn.

My gaze roamed around the estate.

Paul. Where would Paul be?

The kitchen.

I walked around the house to the kitchen. The small building was linked by a covered walkway to the main house. This separation was designed to reduce the chance of a kitchen fire spreading to the house. Fortunately, we'd never had such an incident; probably because I seldom cooked.

I opened the door and stepped inside the kitchen. Warmth and a variety of mouth-watering aromas filled the air. To my left, something simmered on the stove. Opposite me, the pantry stood—where canned food and drying meat were kept along with an insulated bin with an ice-filled bottom for keeping glass jars of milk and blocks of cheese fresh. I kept it cool with ice transported directly from the mountains. To my right sat a table for chopping and mixing, above which hung bushels of drying herbs.

I was always amazed at how much food was required to keep the household and helpers fed each week. I couldn't imagine doing everything myself around the house either. With three children needing food, clothing, and an education, I would have had to quit the university position if I hadn't had help.

The only other option would have been to live in Misty Isle where my mother, stepfather, and half-brother lived. Although the island possessed breathtaking beauty, I wanted more space for my family than a minuscule hut.

Cook Mo emerged from the pantry, carrying milk and eggs. Paul was in tow.

Paul spent hours with the bulky, dark-skinned cook, learning about herbs and recipes. I liked that my children received both text-book and real-worlds educations. My parents had taught my brother and I similarly, and I think that was why I chose electives involving excursions and explorations when I attended the university.

"Lady Cross," Mo greeted me with cheer.

I smiled. "What's Paul cooking us for supper?"

Mo set down his ingredients on the table. "He's making chicken and sausage stew for dinner. We heard the news 'bout you heading for your mother's, so I thought we'd assemble pancake batter to take with you on the trip."

"Very thoughtful. Thank you."

"Mama, why are we going to Nana's?"

I leaned down toward him, placing my hands on my knees. "We need to leave home for a little while. We'll be back." I knew it wasn't the location that troubled him but the abruptness of leaving.

Mo began breaking eggs into a wooden bowl. "Gert says you're alarmed 'bout a sickness."

"Yes. Alarmed enough I'm taking the children to my mothers." I laid a hand on his thick forearm briefly. "And anyone else who wants to go."

He stared at me for a moment, before giving Paul instructions on measuring out the flour.

"That's generous of you, m'lady."

I had met Mo at Joshua's clinic. He'd traveled from Ntajid to Marrington utterly penniless and alone, looking for work. He'd asked Joshua about working at the clinic, but Mo knew nothing of healing remedies. On further inquiry about what skills he did possess, he admitted to being proficient in the kitchen.

We hired him on at a time when Natalie was a toddler and Paul was on the cusp of eating regular food. The new house and external kitchen were still under construction. Mo cooked for us, sleeping in what would eventually be our completed barn. Now, he had his own small house on our property and made wages comparable to a teacher's salary.

"If I introduce you to my mother's village and you cook for them, they may never let you leave."

Mo flashed his brilliant white smile. "I believe I'd like to meet them, but I'll stay here this trip. I'll tend to the chickens and horses while the house staff is gone."

"Thank you."

I turned to Paul, who was mixing batter in a bowl. "Can you be at the carriage in an hour? I'll go pack."

Mo looked at Paul. "What do you think, Cook Colt? Will we be wrapped up here in an hour?"

"Yupperdos."

"There you 'ave it m'lady. An official yupperdo."

I chuckled and left the two of them elbow deep in flour.

After exiting the kitchen, I entered the main house through the dining room. I walked through the living room, past the fireplace, and on towards the bedrooms.

Baird? I called to my friend.

Yes, Abigail. His replies were always prompt—though I worried about invading his privacy. Our link formed a mental communication with words only, and I couldn't see or sense where he was or what he was doing when I began a conversation.

Are the monks aware of an illness in Marrington?

Watertown, Ntajid, Marrington. We have word of many ill in several places.

Mal tells me this is the Omega plague.

Baird fell silent.

I wondered if he doubted Mal, and was thinking how to refute my companion's claim—or if he knew enough about the Omega plague to be speechless.

That's a frightening claim, Baird replied.

He hasn't been wrong in eight years.

"I haven't been wrong in over seven-*thousand* years." Mal appeared in front of me, leaning on the doorway to my bedroom.

I scowled at him. It was unfair he could eavesdrop on my silent conversations with Baird.

I turned my attention back to the monk. *I'm taking the children to my mother's, then I'm going to the castle where Joshua has been summoned.*

Do you need my help?

Probably, but not yet. I'll be in touch.

I could have asked him to begin investigating the outbreak, but I knew that my mere mention of it, and the seriousness of our conversation, would already propel him to do so.

· · ·

AN HOUR PASSED, then two, before the entire mound of luggage was finally packed and loaded and the children were herded on board the carriage.

I couldn't seem to keep them all corralled at once. Paul recalled another book he wanted to grab. As he went back to the house, Rebekah used the distraction to run toward the barn. Natalie remained on the wagon with arms crossed, glaring at me.

At last, I had them all in one place. We rode the wagon to the end of our lane. When out of site from the house, I transported us instantly to Misty Isle, wagon and all.

A salty breeze enveloped us. I hadn't been raised on the beach, but I'd been frequently visiting my mom here for thirteen years. The island felt like a second home. I gazed around at the small, thatch-roofed houses. A few pedestrians wandering about waved at our arrival.

Paul and Natalie leapt off the carriage, rushing to find Nana Nadine. Rebekah screamed to join them as I held her. She couldn't safely jump off the wagon like the other two.

I snapped the reins and the horse, Brawny, ambled forward, toward my mother's cottage. I pulled him to a halt in front of my mother's door. The children had left it open. After I lowered Rebekah to the ground, she rushed inside the house as well.

I dropped the reins and hopped down from the wagon. Brawny was a well-trained gelding. He'd stand complacently as long as the reins rested on the ground.

Frowning, I looked at the packed wagon. Prior to children, travel had been as simple as appearing somewhere at will. Now, every excursion demanded planning, and packing, and snacks, and endless changes of clothing.

My mother appeared in the doorway with Rebekah wrapped around her neck. Despite my mother's age, betrayed by long, brown and grey hair, she carried the toddler with ease and adoration.

"Surprise," I said meekly.

8

My mom smiled at me. "This is an unexpected visit." She looked around. "Where's Joshua?"

"I'll give you all of the details when the children are distracted."

"Ah, well." She gently pinched Rebekah's cheek. "What do you say about a walk on the beach?"

"Beach! Beach!"

"Beach?" Paul said from inside the house.

I called to him. "Yes. Can you let Natalie know?"

"I don't want to go," Natalie called from somewhere inside the house.

"I didn't ask if you did. Spit, spot, on the dot."

Paul snickered, as Natalie gave a complaintive groan.

Trad, my half-brother, appeared in the doorway.

"Trad!" I gave him a warm hug and had to stand on my tiptoes to kiss him on the cheek. When had the once lanky teen grown into a young man? He stood taller than me now. He had fine stubble on his chin and shaggy brown hair framing an oval face.

"Good to see you, Abbey." He returned the embrace.

When everyone came outside, we followed the trail through to the beach. I recalled eight years ago when all of this vegetation had been flattened like a pan-pan from a devastating harbor wave. Mulan had erupted and seismic forces had created an enormous wave. The wave sped to Misty Isle and leveled foliage and buildings. Fortunately, Mal provided me advanced notice; Baird and I were able to evacuate the island. Within a few months, the villagers rebuilt their homes. Years later, there was no trace of the devastation.

Paul, Natalie, and Rebekah ran ahead with their dutiful uncle keeping pace.

I walked beside my mother. "Mom, I need to leave the children here."

"Absolutely. What's going on?"

I explained the plague on Crithos. "Joshua is helping at the castle. I want to see what I can offer. Perhaps I can take people to the Healing Springs or bring water from the springs to them."

"How long do you suppose you'll be gone?"

"I'm not sure. None of us have been exposed. If I *am* exposed, I'll want to wait a few days to ensure I'm not contagious. If I had to venture a guess, I'd say a week—but it could easily be longer. I brought enough food and clothing for the children for five days."

"We'll manage."

When we finally reached the beach, it was easy to follow the footprints to the children. I looked down at my moccasins as they left prints in the dry sand, side-by-side with the small footprints of my children. Beyond the sand, shimmering emerald water stretched to the horizon, darkening in the distance to a deep sapphire. Gentle waves lapped the taupe sand.

"The beach is so beautiful. It's breathtaking no matter how many times I see it."

I thought of Mal, who loved the beach.

He instantly appeared beside me, walking yet making no impressions in the sand. "Did someone say beach?"

I arched an eyebrow at him.

"I shouldn't be denied the pleasure of beautiful scenery."

"Indeed."

"What was that?" my mom asked.

I shook my head. "Nothing. I'm anxious to get to the castle and check on Joshua."

"And leave this serenity behind?" Mal asked.

I ignored him.

My mom called to the children to come say goodbye. Trad tried to coax them over, but they evaded him and continued playing.

"Ungrateful urchins," Mal commented.

I shot him a warning look.

"It's okay, Mom. They're having fun. I'll be back as soon as I can." I suppressed my disappointment that they weren't rushing to hug me goodbye. After I embraced my mom, I walked away from the beach, reluctantly leaving my family behind.

"In their defense," I told Mal, "I always leave and I always return. They don't understand the danger of the current situation. They don't know they should give me a proper farewell."

"Ungrateful and spoiled." He smiled. "And they'll miss you."

I arrived back at my mother's house as Bellok, my stepfather, unloaded the last of the trunks.

"Oy! That's a heavy one."

"Paul likes his books."

I followed him as he lugged the trunk inside and deposited it on the floor.

"Thank you for that. I've filled Mom in on the details. I hope to be back in a week."

"No problem—as long as you know that's an abundance of days your mother will have to spoil them."

"Well, if you need to enforce a little discipline, remind them you're royalty."

He chuckled. "None of that, Abigail."

Bellok had been a prince of Bellos, though a distant fifth in line for the throne. He was traveling on a diplomatic mission to Crithos over twenty years ago when a storm had taken him off course and shipwrecked him on Mulan. Andi, the sea serpent, brought him to Misty Isle. Bellok's life since then had been that of a simple farmer and father. His hardworking and honest personality meant no one doubted his claim to royalty, but we all enjoyed teasing him about it. I'd asked him once if he ever wanted to return home. This *was* his home, he'd replied. He had all of the riches he needed on this island.

We walked back to Brawny and the wagon.

"Do you want to keep the horse here?"

Bellok considered the question. "Yes, leave him. We'll put him to good use."

"I thought you might. I put a pad of hay and bag of feed under the carriage seat."

"Be safe, Abigail."

"Always." I gave him a farewell hug and vanished.

I RETURNED HOME and found the quiet stillness of the house disconcerting. In my bedroom, I pulled a rectangular chest from under the bed and brushed at the dust on its surface. As I opened it, the smell of cedar filled my nostrils.

My champion attire lay inside, unused for eight years. I slipped on the black leggings, boots, tunic, and silver breastplate. I'd thoroughly cleaned and shined everything before storing it, yet all the pieces bore the scars of battle. I ran my fingers along the smooth, red cape. It was the only unworn piece of clothing. During the Hunju civil war, eight years ago, I'd shredded my original cape to fashion red armbands out of the fabric; which we used to identify friend from foe on the battlefield. Although I'd replaced that piece of the outfit, I hadn't had occasion to wear it yet.

After dressing, I fastened the new cape to the shoulders of my breastplate and reached for my sword—a Ballik blade, forged in the icy mountains of Karnelik. I had sharpened it before stowing it; but the blade still bore small scratches and gouges from use. Terrible use. I had shed blood during the Hunju civil war. The end result was new leadership and less discrimination, but the cost of the lives lost in the conflict seemed like such a high price to pay.

Finally dressed, I took a deep breath. I was prepared to offer my services to Queen and country. By Mal's imagery, I knew Crithos faced a crisis, and it would get worse before it got better. I had to help fight a plague, which meant battle armor wasn't likely to be the most suitable outfit. However, it was the attire that would earn me instant recognition as the Avant Champion at the castle and thereby facilitate a fast-track audience with the Queen and her ministers.

From outside the house, I heard the battle cry of a bird of prey followed by the terrified screech of another bird. My pet hawk, Carrot, was evidently protecting the perimeter. Why she thought other birds were a threat remained a mystery. Still, she was a loyal companion, and I sensed she watched over the children when they played outside. Although I hadn't seen any dangers near our house, bears and wolves were known to wander too close to civilization and take farm animals and small children. It felt good to believe Carrot was looking out for them.

Less than thirty minutes had passed since seeing my children, and I was already missing them. These would be a stressful few days —but at least I knew Natalie, Paul, and Rebekah were safe.

I TRANSPORTED and appeared at the inner castle gate. The hefty wooden doors were shut. I gazed around the outer courtyard, observing the well-trodden ground stretching between the outer walls and the inner walls. Normally, shopkeepers had open storefronts set up there, and street vendors lined the wall selling fresh produce, baked goods, flowers, clothing, accessories, and more. Now, desolation had replaced the usually thriving marketplace.

An eerie chill ran along my spine.

I knocked on the large doors. "Open the gate!"

A guard from the watchtower called down, "Gates are sealed by order of the Queen!"

"Tell her the Avant Champion requests entry."

"I've orders that no one enter. Be off with you."

So much for a polite entry.

Instead, I transported to the inner courtyard. Once there, I walked past the larger than life-sized alabaster statues of the six previous Avant Champions and towards the doors that lead to the meeting rooms of the castle. The courtyard smelled pleasantly of blossoming pink sweet peas as I strode through it.

"You there! Halt!" A guard dressed in armor marched toward me, his royal blue tunic embroidered with the insignia of a silver horse.

I didn't stop walking toward the doors.

He ran around in front of me, drew his sword, and pointed it toward my chest.

I stopped and regarded him. "You'd better know how to use that thing if you're foolish enough to threaten me with it."

His throat bobbed, but I could tell the guard didn't know me by my reputation. He was young, eighteen maybe, with trim blond hair. He'd have been just a boy when Crithians fought the forces of Malos.

The most recent time I had arrived at the castle wearing the armor of the Avant Champion had been eight years ago, and even then only the inner court had known of our scheme to help the Hunju with their civil war. It explained why he didn't recognize me or offer the deference the Avant Champion usually received.

My plan to limit my notoriety by avoiding courtly functions might have worked to my detriment today.

In the seconds he stood before me with uncertainty, five more of his fellow guards rushed to the young man's aid. They surrounded me, their swords drawn.

"I am—"

"Surrender your sword. You've trespassed on castle grounds."

I glared at a different, older man—the one with the audacity to interrupt me.

"I don't surrender." Taking a step back, I drew my sword.

The older guards, knowing who I was, braced themselves, but they didn't retreat. The young ones looked confused, witnessing what they presumed was a regular woman boldly prepared to fight six guards.

The first of the guards lunged. I parried and struck his sword with enough force to rattle his arms. Another swung from behind me. I blocked, spun closer to him, and kicked my boot heel into his knee. He fell to the ground with a grunt.

Two more moved toward me, swinging. I blocked each of them, grateful Baird's training included fighting multiple adversaries. The challenge of my current situation was to disarm these guards, and teach them a little humility, without causing serious injury.

Perhaps I needed to make a habit of carrying a stick instead of a sword, like Baird did.

I transported—vanishing and reappearing instantly behind one of my attackers. Confused, the two other guards stumbled through their next swings. With the flat of my blade, I smacked one of them on his rump. He let out a howl of surprise and pain as he turned to take a wild swing at me. I caught the wrist of his sword arm with my left hand, flipped my sword around in the grip of my right, and then *popped* him square in the forehead with the blunt end of the hilt.

The guard stumbled backward, and I wrenched his sword from his grip as he tripped over a decorative pot of flowers.

Four guards remained on their feet—four swords against my now two blades.

"Enough!" A woman's voice boomed.

The guards straightened and sheathed their swords.

I looked up at Coco DeFay, standing in the doorway to the inner castle.

"Captain DeFay," I greeted her cheerily, waving my captured sword in hand.

Coco strode toward us, her blond ponytail swishing like the tail of an irritated horse.

"I appreciate the welcoming party, but tea would have sufficed." Not ready to sheath my own sword or relinquish the one I'd deftly confiscated, I held them both casually pointed towards the ground.

Coco cracked a slight smile—before correcting her expression and glaring at her men. "Do none of you recognize the Avant Champion?"

The eldest guard stepped forward. "Yes, Captain. But she trespassed and didn't explain herself."

I scowled at him. I'd been interrupted *before* I'd had the chance to explain myself.

"You're dismissed," Coco snapped. "Back to the wall."

I tossed the one humiliated guard his sword back as the six of them dispersed.

"It's good to see you, Coco." I sheathed my sword.

"Good to see you, too, Abigail. Are you here to help?"

"However I can, against a plague."

I gauged Coco's reaction. Her expression suggested more suspicion than surprise.

"What do you know of the illness spreading?"

We walked inside the castle and down a towering corridor.

"I know it fits with the symptoms of the Omega plague." I paused for effect, but her continued calm demeanor suggested Coco didn't know just how cataclysmic such an infection had historically been.

I looked around. "Where is everyone?"

"Last night, when it was clear people were falling ill, we cleared out the outer market and shut down the gate," Coco explained. "This morning we started screening citizens for red splotches on their skin before they'd be allowed inside—but by the afternoon it became evident the sickness had already breached the inner castle."

We took one of the stairways and started the winding climb upward.

"Now we're keeping the throngs of people from overtaking the castle."

"Who's ill?"

"Probably half of those inside the castle, including Queen Rebekah and much of the court."

"The Queen?" My stomach lurched.

"Yes. She manifested the rash about an hour ago."

We finally reached the top tower.

I followed Coco's gaze over the stone edging and to the land beneath us. Below, hundreds of tents had been erected, spread across the grounds outside the castle. Since I'd transported directly within the castle walls, I hadn't even seen those left suffering outside the walls.

"Those are the sick, and the few who've volunteered to help them."

I thought of the poem Sunny had read to me.

See the devastation of the disease,
Smoldering in the breeze.

Death destroys hope with decay,
Indiscriminately, every life is prey.

I swallowed. "The disease kills within five days of the rash."

"That's what Joshua said."

I turned to her. "Did Joshua say it was the Omega plague?"

She shook her head. "He didn't have a name for it, but the people who had come to his clinic all gave the same report. They lost their loved ones two days shy of a week."

"*Crithos,*" I swore. "Can Joshua cure it?"

"It seems he can slow the course but not reverse it."

"He can't do that indefinitely." I thought of how the stones worked, taking some element of the user's life force. "Please, take me to him."

She nodded grimly. "I'll take you to the deliberation room."

I followed Coco as we made our way to the deliberation room.

When we quietly entered the large room, quarreling voices could be heard from the far end.

I looked around the large room, with its high arches towering above us. The last time I'd been in here it had bustled with activity and the seats were filled with citizens from all across the country, each waiting to discuss issues with the court. Now, only a handful of people milled around the front of the room, and they seemed to be conversing while attempting to keep their distance from each other.

Joshua stood nearest the Queen. Tarik, Minister of Foreign Affairs, paced the room. Holden, Minister of Strategic Defense, sat looking exhausted in a chair, his grey robes wrinkled and his beard yellowed. There were a dozen other people, a mixture of ministers and council representatives; some of whom I recognized, and others who I didn't. They were all too engrossed in discussion to notice our appearance.

Mal materialized to my right and watched silently.

"I need time to work on a cure," Joshua was saying.

"You said yourself: You don't even know where to start." Tarik continued to pace, his hands clasped behind his back. "You said something about needing to find the first patient infected."

"Yes. If we can find the source of the disease, and the first people exposed, those who survived might have developed a defense mechanism in their bloodstream that I can mimic."

"How long would that take?" Holden asked.

"Finding a survivor and replicating the serum could take weeks," Joshua admitted.

"We don't *have* weeks," Tarik protested.

"The city will be a graveyard by that time," Holden added.

Another man nodded. I suspected, by his light blue robes, that he was one of the castle healers.

Joshua lowered his head and added, "There are no guarantees I can synthesize a cure, but many healers have cured other diseases this way."

Cure.

I whispered quietly, *"Stone of Blood, Stone of Health, save the lives considered wealth.*" Sunny had mentioned references to a magical cure in the history books.

Coco cocked her head to one side.

I looked at Mal. "Could there be a magical cure?"

"Orrick would know."

I nodded.

"Who are you taking to?" Coco asked.

Ignoring her, I walked toward the front of the room. All eyes turned to me in surprise.

"My Queen." I bowed.

"Abigail!" Joshua said. "You're not supposed to be here!"

I frowned at him briefly. He might have at least shown some relief to see me.

"I sent you a messenger bird."

"I've been a little busy," I retorted. Then, I recalled Carrot accosting a bird and wondered if that poor thing had been the messenger.

I turned back toward the Queen. "There may be a magical cure."

"We're listening, Abigail," the Queen said.

I rose from my bow. "The pattern of infection suggests this is the Omega plague."

Joshua's face blanched.

I continued talking over the murmurs of disbelief. "I'd like to consult further with Wizard Oak—Orrick Dallik—in the Black Marsh forest. An ancient poem claims a blood stone and healing stone can be used to stop the disease."

Queen Rebekah wasted no time in her reply. "Consult with him. Return to us tomorrow to report what supplies are needed."

Tarik flashed a dazzling white, politician's smile before speaking, "Perhaps Captain DeFay can accompany you. Two sets of ears are always better for instructions this important." Tarik's request suggested I wasn't to be trusted with Orrick's instructions.

He had no grounds to distrust me—and I suspected his distrust reflected his own untrustworthy character.

I smiled sweetly in return. "I have no objections to Coco's company."

"If this is the Omega plague, we need to warn others," Holden suggested.

The Queen nodded once. "We can deploy messenger birds, but we can't send runners—or we risk spreading the disease."

She turned to me. "We will see you back here before dawn."

I gave a slight bow. As I turned to leave, Joshua walked beside me. I noticed he didn't touch me.

"The children are at my mother's."

"Good thinking. Did Mal suggest the Blood Stone?"

I inadvertently glanced at Mal who had continued to linger by the entrance. "No. I spoke with Sunny. She read me a poem. Mal suggested Orrick may know more."

I hooked an arm through Coco's, while still speaking to Joshua. I wished we could touch and hug. "I love you. I'll be back at day break."

"I love you, too."

I activated my star tattoo and vanished with Coco.

9

Coco and I appeared at the edge of the Black Marsh forest.

In the distance, the sun dipped below the horizon, casting long shadows toward the east. Coco and I hiked through dense foliage and over a log that laid across the path of a small stream. I knew the path to Orrick well, even though it wouldn't appear to be a path to the untrained eye. The forest smelled like fresh rain mixed with freesia.

"Who's Mal?" Coco asked.

"A friend of mine."

"You can communicate with him like you can with Baird?"

"Similarly, yes."

Her gaze roamed the forest. "Eight years is too soon to be back at this place."

"Really? I've returned several times a year or so to visit."

"You didn't wake up in a brownie pit."

"No—I woke up with my arms and legs bound, as Grey Wolf and Night Owl discussed the best way to sacrifice me so they could free Orrick from that tree."

"Oh. You never mentioned that."

"We've never spent time talking about the quest to help the Hunju."

We never spent an abundance of time talking about anything. Coco was devout in her dedication to the Queen, and she couldn't comprehend how I wasn't. We constantly disagreed on how my skills should be used and with what frequency. Admittedly, Coco had eased her judgment of me over the years but not to the extent anyone would consider us friendly. Today, her disposition was pleasant enough, but I suspected it was because I'd arrived of my own volition to offer help to the castle.

As we walked, the forest grew darker—a combination of the dense trees and setting sun.

"We should have talked about it more," Coco said, pushing a branch aside. "Other than the battle of Marrin Beach, the marsh was my one great adventure. Everyone asks how exciting it must have been to go on a quest with the Avant Champion."

I snorted. "Not as grandiose as they might imagine."

"Oh, I don't know. Enormous, man-eating snakes, an enchanted forest, an ancient wizard restored, a civil war among giants."

I wondered if she'd ever forgiven me for her capture during the quest. I hadn't predicted Windish's betrayal. As a result, Coco and Joshua had been hostages for a night.

"And brownies," I added.

She shuddered. "They're creepy."

I laughed. "They're an acquired taste. You have to get to know them."

"Not likely."

Ahead of us, yellow light lit a section of the forest.

I felt the trip wire seconds late. I had already triggered the trap.

"Duck!" I yelled.

Coco and I flattened our bodies onto the ground. Above us, two large sacs of sleeping dust collided. We rolled to the side to avoid falling red particles.

A conch sounded from the direction of the brownie village where the light emanated.

"Our welcoming party," I grumbled. As I stood, I brushed leaves and dirt from my clothing.

I could hear tiny, panicked voices and urgent rustling from the leaves in the trees above. Coco and I walked into the lit opening, surrounded by the towering arbors. Above us, fireflies flew in circular patterns, bathing the forest in luminous yellow light. Dozens of small houses rested in every tree. All of the doors were firmly shut.

"It's Abigail," I announced, hoping to get the words out before the brownie warriors, hiding in the trees, hurled spears or more sleeping powder at us.

Usually intruders came to cut down their trees, so the brownies had long ago learned defensive measures. Their clever antics had made people believe the forest was haunted; and that was as much as a deterrent as their traps.

A brownie emerged on a branch above us, standing tall and carrying a walking stick the size of a twig. He wore a gray hat woven to look like the head of a wolf, complete with black pebbles for eyes and tiny, yellow canine teeth—real teeth that I suspected had once belonged to a squirrel.

Even with the hat, Grey Wolf stood only about a third of a meter high.

Others emerged from the trees and shadows, whispering. "Red goddess."

Coco put her hands on her hips and cocked her head to one side.

I stifled a groan. I had wanted to eliminate the foolish title, but the brownies clung to it.

"Password."

I crossed my arms. "Grey Wolf, you know who I am—and you remember Captain Coco DeFay, I'm sure." She'd been *Lieutenant* DeFay when they'd first met her ... and put her in the pit. But I knew they'd remember the beautiful, tall blond woman regardless of her new title.

Grey Wolf stood straight and stoic. "Password."

I bit my tongue to suppress my annoyance. "I swear by mystical moons, wizard runes, and silver spoons that I come in peace."

"Silver spoons?" Coco asked in a whisper.

A few brownies snickered.

"I'll explain later."

"Welcome, Abigail the Bold," Grey Wolf announced.

An agile brownie dressed in black feathers swung from a rope, landing on my shoulder.

"Raven! Good to see you." I smiled.

"It's good you've come," she said gravely. "The wizard is ill."

A LUMP FORMED in my throat. Mal's brother had looked well when I'd seen him recently. Had the virus spread this far south already? I had no way to heal Orrick. Something about the strong properties of the forest prevented me from using my traveling star within its boundaries, which meant I had no way to easily transport him to Joshua, either.

"Follow me." Grey Wolf sat astride a plump, rust-colored squirrel that began scurrying across the limbs of trees above us.

We followed, stumbling over roots with nothing but the dim light of a few fireflies to guide us. I already knew the way to Wizard Oak's home, but Grey Wolf's led us, increasing the sensation of urgency.

Wizard Oak had a small, single-bedroomed abode wedged between two, large oak trees. When we reached it, the door hung open. I walked inside, my heart thudding with fear at what I might find.

Coco followed with wide-eyed, open-mouthed nervousness behind me. I wondered if her concern were for Orrick's health or how his condition may interfere with our mission here to gain knowledge.

Orrick lay in bed flanked, by furrow-browed brownies. Night Owl, dressed in slate, with his decorative owl hat askew, sat on a table beside the wizard's bed. Orrick appeared pale but resting comfortably. No rashes marred his skin, and no blood oozed from orifices. This was not the Omega plague. Was it something curable?

I knelt beside him and took the old man's hand, brushing a gray strand of hair from his face. "Orrick?"

Pale, blue eyes flickered open and focused on me. He smiled. "Oh, Abigail. I was hoping you'd visit soon." His voice sounded raspy and dry.

My heart sank. "Of course."

Raven hopped off my shoulder. "Out! Everyone out!" She ushered the brownies out of his home.

Grey Wolf turned his squirrel, gave me an acknowledging nod, and left. Night Owl walked somberly behind him.

Coco sat in a chair off to one corner, watching observantly.

When all who remained in his home were me, Raven, and Coco, Orrick squeezed my hand. The grip possessed strength, even though he appeared weak.

I shook my head, hating to see how feeble Orrick seemed. How had he declined so quickly since I'd last visited? I needed to fetch Joshua to heal him. As soon as I thought the words, I remembered I *couldn't* fetch Joshua. He was busy keeping those infected at the castle alive. They wouldn't let me just waltz in and take him—not without a fight.

Even worse, Joshua was likely to have contracted the virus himself by now, which was why he hadn't touched me at the castle. If I brought Joshua here, the entire forest could be exposed. I could transport Orrick to the healing springs, but I would first need to carry him out of the forest.

Orrick glanced around the room one more time, with a mischievous twinkle in his eye. Then he sat straight up in bed.

He cleared his throat. "Oh, *merciful monks*. They haven't left my bedside in days. There's no privacy in a forest of brownies!" He gave me a wink. "So glad you came, Abigail."

Startled, I rocked back on my heels.

Orrick continued speaking as he scrubbed his hand across his face. The color instantly returned to his cheeks. "I'm suffocated day and night by the entire tribe!"

I turned to Raven, whose wry grin told me she'd kept Orrick's secret.

"They mean well," he explained, "but there's no peace in a brownie village. They constantly want my council or my blessing. I'm consulted for every childbirth, every funeral, and every full moon. At least when I was a tree, I could turn into myself and hide. I've taken to feigning illness just to get a moment of respite!"

Orrick flicked a hand in the air in my direction. "Judge me all you want, young warrior. When you get to be my age, little lies aren't the worst of your worries."

I let my body relax, my prior angst leaving me. "I can help you leave. Perhaps you need a drier climate to heal what ails you? We can set up a home for you somewhere else. But I can't do that yet. There's a crisis in Marrington."

"Is Malakai here?" As he asked the words, Mal appeared.

I nodded.

"I have a gift I want to give you, Abigail, but I need his help. Lay your left hand in mind. And Malakai is to do the same."

I searched Orrick's expression for signs of more trickery but found none. Tentatively, I laid my hand on Orrick's. With a leery look at his brother, Mal placed his hand through mine and into Orrick's. Wizard Oak closed his eyes.

Suddenly, I began hallucinating. Streams of light floated through us, connecting Mal and I. We appeared to be outdoors, bathed in sunlight. I could feel the heat, smell the bloom of magnolias, and see flecks of gold dancing on the breeze around us. It was all so real.

So too, suddenly, was the connection between Mal and I. Warmth, where our hands met turned to searing fire. I gasped, withdrawing my hand and recoiling away.

The bright light dimmed when our connection broke. I found myself back in reality—back in Orrick's home.

In eight years, Mal and I had never touched. I'd tried to bump elbows playfully once, and I'd gone right through him. Every object I ever hurled at Mal, whether in anger or frustration, had sailed cleanly through him.

I always assumed we simply couldn't touch. Had Orrick created some type of bridge? If so, I wanted no part of being burned.

I looked around, but Mal had vanished.

"Are you well?" Coco asked me. She sat in the only human-sized chair in the room.

"I'm okay."

"Who is Malakai? He's the Mal you talked to in the castle?"

"Long story. I'll explain later." *Maybe.*

"What is this crisis you mentioned?" Orrick asked.

I looked down at my throbbing palm. A tattoo of two blue moons—one large, one small—was etched on it; as if it had been there for years. No burns marred my skin, and yet moments earlier my palm had felt scorched.

Staring at the new tattoo, I told Wizard Oak, "There's a plague inflicting Marrington."

He stared out the window, his blue eyes turning gray. "The Omega plague. Hmm. Yes. It's not only Marrington. It spread from Kovia then worked its way through all of the major cities east to west. Unchecked, it will eliminate eighty percent of the world's population." He blinked and shifted his weight. "Raven, take the Captain and fetch my books. We'll find an answer in there."

The small brownie departed with Coco in tow.

Now that she was gone, I looked at the tattoo on my palm and asked, "The moons?"

"I've given you the gift of moon magic and moonlight."

Which explained nothing. "Meaning?"

"All in good time. I'll show you the meaning of the moons on our next encounter."

I narrowed my eyes at Orrick, wondering if this was his way of ensuring I returned to rescue him from the brownies. I respected him too much to doubt his gift, but also knew him too well not to suspect mischief was involved.

"Why did you need Mal to make it work?"

"All in good time," Orrick assured me.

Raven returned with Coco, carrying a stack of a half-dozen books. She lowered them onto a table in his room.

"I've been writing everything I can remember of the magic books of my days," Orrick explained.

I stood and leaned closer. "Magic books?" My voice was barely a whisper.

What did I know of magic? My skills were acquired from the stone I wore. Mal had spoken of his mother's magic and Orrick's magic—magic not beholden to magic stones. Long forgotten, ancient magic.

"Magic books," I repeated, feeling a rising excitement, a wave of hope.

"Raven, more light please." I drew my hand across one of the brown leather covers.

Fireflies swarmed into the room and hovered above us, casting their glow over the pile of books.

"You've written *six* books?"

Orrick shrugged. "I've been out of captivity for eight years. I've been attempting to document all of the magic I can recall from my mother's books—as well as any I've witnessed used during the last seven thousand years."

I touched the spine one of the smooth, leather covers. "Which book shall we open? We need anything about cures, the Omega plague, or the Blood Stone. We need to find the answer tonight."

"Try the red one," he suggested.

AN HOUR LATER, I found a passage within the book resembling the pieces mentioned in Sunny's poem. I passed the open, red leather book up to Orrick—who'd reclaimed his chair from Coco. "Will this work?"

Recipe for Mass Healing

The formula has been applied in the past with success to
multiple infectious outbreaks.

Ingredients:
Healing stone and activator
Blood stone
Blood of the host creature
Bowl

Depending up on the type of disease, the carrier vector
may be animal, insect, parasite, or man himself. The
blood should be fresh and in sufficient quantity in
proportion to the number of people to be healed. For
instance, a room full of people may only need a drop
of blood—whereas a large population will need the
entire stone doused in blood.
Around the bowl, arrange the Healing Stone and its
activator. Place the Blood Stone in the bowl. Add drops
of blood from the carrier animal. The activators of the
stones will then work the magic to heal the masses.

Orrick looked up, blinked, and looked back at the book he held. "Yes. This one will do. But the addition of a Wind Stone will carry the healing farther."

I let out a breath of air I'd been holding. "Is it enough to heal a continent?"

"The addition of a Wind Stone will carry the healing as far as the wind takes it."

Coco, who'd been flipping through a blue, leather-bound book in deep fascination, looked over his shoulder at the red book. "Carrier vector? What carrier vector?"

Orrick closed the book. "A bat."

"A bat?"

He stared out the window of his home, deep into the dark forest, as if it held the answers of the universe. "The Kovian salt mines. You'll find the bats you need there."

"Bats in Kovia?" Raven asked.

Orrick turned and looked at me. "You'll need to travel to the salt mines on southeast Kovia. The mines have the bats that carry the disease. You'll need the blood of a bat for the cure."

Coco tapped a book on the wood floor, simultaneously tapping a finger to her chin. "Joshua has the healing stone, but where do we find the Wind Stone and Blood Stone?"

"I have a book Mama Duski gave me." I realized no one in the room but I knew the former gypsy leader. "She bequeathed me The Book of Stones on her passing. The book contains the last known location of all Che stones. I can't testify to how accurate it is, but the stones are sacred to the Dubik gypsies, so I'm sure they made every effort to track them down."

"Then we have a plan?" Coco asked. "Book, then stones, then bat?"

As I looked back over the stack of books, I nodded. "We should skim these tonight before we head back to the castle to ensure we aren't missing anything."

Raven began walking toward the door. "I'll grab some snacks."

"Abigail, wake up."

I started suddenly, clutching an object in my lap. I looked up to see Coco standing over me and then down at the red leather book in my arms.

I blinked at the sunlight streaming through the window of the small cabin we'd slept in last night.

Four hours was a scant amount of sleep, but it was all we could afford. My stomach rumbled. The brownies had brought us nuts and fruit for snacks as we worked our way through the magic texts last night, but those were hardly sufficient for a human-sized appetite. As I stood unsteadily, I shifted the book in one crux of my arm and exited the house. I was grateful the brownies had agreed to allow us to rest in their camp until morning.

"Let's go."

Raven swung down from a tree, landing on my shoulder. She carried a sack over her shoulder, and she gripped my ear with her free hand.

I glanced at her without turning my head. "Where do you think you're going?"

"With you."

"I don't have time to list the many reasons that's a bad idea."

"Then don't. Accept my company."

I continued walking to the forest edge. "Do you have permission to leave?"

"I don't need permission."

"You could be killed by the plague."

"No, I won't. We're going to make the cure."

"You could be trampled by a horse."

"I'm agile."

"You could be eaten by wild dogs."

"I can communicate with animals, remember?"

"There isn't any black fingernail polish where we're going."

She grinned. "Good thing I brought my own."

When we reached the edge of the woods, I said, "Last chance to change your mind."

"I've lived my entire life in that speck of forest. I want to see the world."

I placed a hand on Coco's shoulder and transported us to my home. Raven clutched tightly to my collar as she sat on my shoulder. The first few times transporting could be disorienting, and I'd neglected to warn her of that.

"I'll be right back. I need to grab the Book of Stones."

I left Coco outside, and walked into the house. A moment later, I snatched the book from a shelf in my study.

"Your house and land are so big," Raven commented, still perched on my shoulder.

From her perspective, as a brownie, my estate spanned larger than the entire brownie village.

"What's the book for again?"

"It's a list of all of the stones and their last known location."

"Handy."

I ran a hand over the worn, blue leather cover. "The former leader of the Dubik gypsies gave this to me."

Mama Duski had been instrumental in helping me find the Warrior Stone. Without it, I wouldn't have defeated Malos. She died eight years ago, and the book arrived at my doorstep shortly afterward. Why had I kept it? It belonged in a library.

When I returned to Coco, she was stroking Carrot who was perched on a fence post. I watched, absorbing the picturesque moment of Coco enjoying the camaraderie of another creature.

"Carrot is probably worried because my family is gone. I can't exactly communicate that we haven't abandoned her."

Raven made some odd cooing noises as she looked at Carrot. In response, the bird shook out her feathers.

Raven explained, "She understands now. She also said you'd better take her on any upcoming quests—and if you protest, she wanted to remind you that she saved you from the swamp snake."

I blinked at Carrot. "Duly noted."

Coco gave the hawk's feathers one last caress, before stepping back to me.

I placed a hand on Coco's shoulder, and instantly transported us directly to the deliberation room.

10

The large chamber materialized around Coco and I, appearing exactly as we'd left it.

"Abbey!" Joshua's excited voice was music to my ears.

"It's about time," Minister Tarik snapped.

I ignored him, walking to place the books on one of the tables. My gaze roamed across the room—taking in the Queen, who sat on her large wooden chair, and the various ministers flanking her. Aman, the Queen's Council, wasn't present. I wondered if he'd fallen ill too.

Raven hopped off my shoulder to stand beside the book. Judging from several of the minister's wide-eyed expressions, they'd never seen a brownie before. Her gothic appearance added an element of apprehension to their judgement of her.

I opened the book to the page describing the cure. "Cave bats on Kovia are the carriers of the Omega disease. We need blood from the bats, combined with the Healing Stone and Blood Stone, to make a cure."

"How does it work?" the Queen asked. Purplish half-moons had formed beneath her eyes, accentuating her pale skin.

"Once all of the components are combined, a healer activates them. We'll also need the Wind Stone. It can carry the effects of other stones over distances. Adding the Wind Stone would spread the effects of the Healing Stone." And do what to Joshua? Healing half the continent sounded like a dangerous tax on him.

"This sounds like magical speculation."

I turned a hard gaze toward Tarik. "Certainly, Minister Tarik—but your solution is?"

He glowered at me.

The Queen spoke. "This needs to be resolved quickly to preserve the most lives. We can send one team to collect each of the needed stones and another to collect the Kovian bats."

I opened the Book of Stones. "The last known location of the Wind Stone is ... Ntajid. Looks like south of the city." I continued to skim the pages. "The last known location of the Blood Stone is Karnelik." The book listed more details of the specific locations. The one in Karnelik lay deep in caves northeast of the town, just before the point at which the rolling hills turned to stony mountains.

"You should be the one to capture a bat," the Queen told me. "It's the furthest away, and you can transport back the fastest."

"Yes, mum." My eyes still roamed the book.

"I'll go with Abigail." Coco stood beside me.

I gave her a grateful smile.

"We'll need two other teams." Tarik straightened. "Captain DeFay, do you have lieutenants still well enough and suited for the task?"

"Yes. Lieutenant Guy is from Karnelik and Lieutenant Jok is from Ntajid. They can each assemble a team."

I ruffled the edges of the Book of Stones. "I'll take Baird and Joshua and—"

"Not the healer." Tarik held up an authoritative hand, which I wanted to use to smash his nose.

"The cure *needs* the healer," I protested.

"You can bring the ingredients here. We'll have the other stones brought *here*."

"It would be faster—"

"If you stopped arguing," he interrupted.

I looked at Queen Rebekah. "My Queen," I pleaded. She wouldn't ask me to take this trip and leave my husband behind.

"I'm sorry, Abigail. We need him to continue his work here while you collect the stones. If you don't succeed, he's our best hope to help us with alternative plans."

I straightened, turning a cold, hard look on all of them. Uncaring, unfriendly faces stared back at me. I sensed they'd already discussed the possibility that I'd want Joshua to accompany me. They'd already unified their response. The truth was, there'd be no alternative plan if I failed. They were keeping Joshua as a hostage—to make sure I came back to the castle.

I turned to Coco. "You have two hours to prepare. I'll meet you at the stables."

I closed the book with an echoing boom. Raven climbed back on my shoulder, and I turned to leave.

"Abbey." Joshua's voice cracked.

I couldn't look at him. If I did, I might run to him, embrace him and disappear with him. Doing so would brand us both as traitors. Even if we cured everyone, we'd never get his clinic rebuilt. He'd most definitely be denied the hospital he'd been fighting to build.

"I love you, Joshua. I'll be back for you."

I left.

I TRANSPORTED to the barn and let Raven from my shoulder onto one of the stall doors.

The horses snickered in greeting.

"Do all of your quests start so dismally?"

I sniffed. "Yeah. They quite often do. I imagine that's why they call them crises."

I walked to the back room and dropped the magic book into one of the saddlebags hanging there.

Baird? I called silently to my friend.

Abigail, what news?

Can you come to my barn?

By the time I walked out of the tack room, carrying a blanket and saddle, Baird had already arrived.

Raven was startled by his sudden appearance. "Oh! He's got magic like you."

"Baird, Raven. Raven, Baird."

He gave her a warm smile. "It's a pleasure to meet you."

Grabbing the beak, she tipped her bird head hat at him.

I opened a stall and walked into the stable. Phobus stood still as I brushed dirt from his back. I tossed the blanket and saddle atop him.

"You're angry." Baird stood, watching me work.

"They're holding Joshua hostage."

"They who?"

"The Queen and council."

"Why?" His voice held pure astonishment.

I swallowed the lump in my throat. I had no time for tears. "To keep the Queen alive. To make sure I'm motivated to find the cure."

"Is that what they said?"

"Not those exact words." I cinched the saddle. I walked to the tack room, grabbed the saddlebags and bridle, and walked back to Phobus.

"Can you find a cure?"

Maybe.

Hopefully.

"Yes." After I secured the saddlebag, I placed the bit in the horse's mouth. "We need a Blood Stone, a Wind Stone, Joshua's Healing Stone, and the blood of a bat. Our job is the bat."

"Blood of a bat?"

"A bat from the Kovian salt mines. They're the harbingers of the plague—we *think*, as long as we trust that Orrick channeled his wizarding abilities accurately. Also, we'll need a map of Kovia." I stroked Phobus. His ears perked up and he lifted his tail. He suspected an adventure.

"Interesting."

When I walked out of the stall and looked at my friend, I lost my composure. I stepped into Baird's arms and tears streamed from my eyes.

He patted me gently and with unconcealed surprise. "We'll get Joshua back. It sounds like you have a plan. I'll go prepare and get a map. I've a trainee I'll bring, too. The four of us will make a great team."

"Coco is coming."

"Five of us then."

I nodded, my face still buried in his blue robes. In our thirteen years of friendship, I'd never cried on Baird's shoulder. Finally, I stepped back and tried to pull myself together. When I glanced at Raven, she respectfully looked away from the emotional scene. Her first big adventure had started with the Avant Champion bawling her eyes out.

I wiped at my eyes. "I'm sorry, Baird. I've had only a few hours of sleep."

He pulled me back in for a hug. "Don't apologize. Friends are intended to be used for comfort."

"And adventures?"

"Especially adventures."

"Can you be packed and ready in a few hours? The monk library has a map of Kovia?"

He nodded as he released me. "One hour. I'll bring a map. Have you extra horses? If not, I can borrow some from Aithos."

"I've two more," I assured him. "Joshua's horse, Unis—he's older and he'll be slower than the rest—and Butterfly. She's a young mare. She'll need an experienced rider."

"I'll be back in under an hour." He disappeared.

I busied myself brushing and saddling the other horses. I packed snacks of oats and apples. Raven was bonding with Phobus, sitting on his mane, stroking his hair and talking to him.

During all of my preparations, I was cognizant of Mal's absence. I would have valued his council, but his disappearance had been sudden, causing me to wonder if he was upset with me or with his brother. We had shared a searing touch of our hands, and I hadn't seen him since.

As I looked at the moons tattooed on my palm again, I shook my head. Another mysterious "gift." No one stopped to ask me if I *wanted* them. However, I wasn't going to argue with a wizard capable of seeing the future—especially not if he thought to grant me a gift that might prove useful. My angst originated from not having had enough time to learn more about the tattoo's purpose from Orrick.

Scrounging around in the kitchen, I gathered dried meat, bread, and cheese from Mo. I snacked on a few pieces, since breakfast had consisted of only few slices of bacon, and lunch had been nonexistent.

Next, I went to my bedroom where I packed a blanket, tent, clothes, soap, and a water flask. Lastly, I reached for the weapons stored in my trunk. I picked up a blow dart and the case with darts, plus a glass vial of snake venom. I also took a few small sacks of brownie sleeping powder. When I'd finished, I filled the flask with water and carried everything to the barn.

Baird and his young trainee were already waiting for me. I stared at the dark-haired, rosy-cheeked lad.

"Hans Stallman." I felt satisfaction at having remembered his name.

He wore the blue cloak of the Gunthi Monks, but his eyes were still dark green.

"Thank you for joining us," I added.

He gave me a bright smile, which illuminated his face and eliminated all traces of his usual insecure awkwardness. I'd known Hans as a university student, but as he'd been an English major, we had seldom crossed paths. His father was one of the English professors—one more reason why I remembered who the young man was.

"And are *you* joining us as well?" After setting down my supplies, I walked over to Baird's wolf, bent down, and scratched behind his ears. "Hello, Fluffy. *Such* a good wolf. Yes, you *are.*"

Fluffy Fury melted into my affectionate hands, showing me exactly where to rub and scratch with his body language.

"That's amazing. He never lets anyone except Baird touch him." Hans took a friendly step toward the wolf. The animal stiffened and eyed Hans cautiously, causing the poor young man to halt.

Baird crossed his arms. "Only Abigail pets him like a domesticated dog."

I grinned as the wolf gave me a slobbery kiss with his tongue. "That's because I saved you, right, Fluffy?"

"His name is *Fury*," Baird corrected me with barely contained exasperation. "And I need to introduce him to all of the horses."

"Raven, do you want to meet *Fury*?" I asked.

"I'd rather meet Fluffy."

We chuckled.

She slid down Phobus's outstretched leg the way a child rides a slide, walking over to me and climbing onto my shoulder as I knelt on the ground. Fury sniffed Raven's extended hand. She dropped to the ground, and he lowered his head.

With a final pat to Fury's head, I left him and Raven to become acquainted.

I stood and turned to Hans. "You have much experience with horses?"

"A little, professor."

I led him to Unis, standing by a fence post outside the barn. "Call me Abigail, Hans. We're not in class anymore. You graduated—what —three years ago?"

"Four milady. Four, *Abigail*." He fidgeted nervously with his hands, looking from my face, to my breastplate, to my sword. I wondered if my battle armor made him skittish. Hans had been accustomed to seeing me in either dresses or trousers at the university.

"Always mount from this side," I warned him. "The horse's left. Unis is a good horse, he'll follow the other's lead, but horses in general don't like sudden movements. Keep everything slow and smooth."

I stood by the gelding's neck as Hans approached. I pushed at a clump of dirt on Unis' chest. Since he'd been put out to pasture for most of the week, his white coat had patches of brown dirt spotting it. Not that it mattered. We were embarking on a quest, not a parade, so his appearance was acceptable enough for the task at hand. Haste trumped beauty at present.

Hans stepped into the stirrup and hoisted himself shakily into the saddle, his face flushing.

I put a hand on Han's calf and made eye contact with him. "*And* they can tell when you're nervous, so take a deep breath. You're going to be fine."

With a nod, Hans swallowed and tried to force himself into a more relaxed position in the saddle. As the son of an English professor and city dweller, Hans wouldn't have needed to learn horsemanship as a lad.

I left Hans to hyperventilate and walked back past Baird to escort Butterfly out of the barn. I shot Baird a look.

The corner of his mouth quirked. *You were young once, too, Abigail. And inexperienced.*

I grunted and handed him Butterfly's reigns. Baird loaded a sack of supplies into her saddlebags.

Finally, I walked Phobus out of the barn and mounted him. "Coco is meeting us at the royal stables."

Baird nodded.

I whistled. Carrot dutifully glided from a tree, through the air, and landed on my outstretched forearm.

"You have a hawk!" Hans exclaimed, eyes wide in astonishment.

"Hold on," I warned Raven, who'd climbed back onto Phobus' mane.

She grabbed a fistful of the horse's sleek hair as I transported us all to Marrington castle.

WE ARRIVED at the royal stables—me and Raven on Phobus, Baird riding Butterfly, and Hans still nervously situating himself on Unis. The stables possessed an eery silence, like the rest of the vacated outer castle. The stables consisted of three long rows of horse stalls. The animals inside snickered at our arrival.

Baird dismounted and secured Butterfly's reins to a post. He disappeared, and reappeared moments later with Fury. Looking around the stables, Baird asked: "I wonder if these horses have been fed and watered. This place is deserted." He began pumping a faucet to fill a bucket with water. Hans followed suit, dispensing hay and feed to the horses.

As I dismounted, I transferred Carrot to the saddle. She perched herself there, and I stroked her feathers as she clucked. "You saw the family packing, didn't you? You didn't think I'd leave you behind?"

"Can you talk to animals like Baird?" Hans asked.

"No. Nothing coherent. I'm sure my communication is mostly one-sided." After I found a barrel of feed, I began to distribute grain to the other horses.

Many years ago, I'd given Baird the Language Stone, enabling him to understand and speak other languages, including, as we soon discovered, animals.

As we worked, I explained the gruesome progression of the plague to Hans, Baird, and Raven. Hans's complexion turned greenish, and he looked like he might lose his breakfast. Raven, on the other hand, merely picked at her black fingernails.

"Tell us about the cure," Baird said.

"The Queen has sent guards to secure the Blood Stone and Wind Stone. Our quest is to collect bats from the Kovian salt mines. We have your map, Baird—though a guide would be better."

Hans dropped a pad of hay to a grateful horse. "I've been to Kovia. There's a train that runs from Moontown to the salt mines. It makes several stops, but it's faster than horseback—and more comfortable."

I gave Hans an appreciative nod.

Some of the color had returned to his face. "My father gave a guest lecture at Parvia University on the southern peninsula."

"Then, we have a guide," I announced triumphantly, though I suspected Baird already orchestrated such. "The only place I've been is outside Kovo. What's the closest you've been to the mines?"

Before Hans could answer, Baird spoke. "I know what you're thinking, Abigail, but we don't know into what conditions we might be transporting. Also, the only way to keep our bearings on the map would be to travel without the star."

I frowned, but couldn't disagree. "The train it is, then. If the Kovian trains are like the ones in Crithos, they'll have livestock quarters so we can still take the horses for the off-rail portions of our trip."

Coco arrived at the stables carrying a saddle pack, water canteen, and tent roll. She gave a quick glance at our group and greeted Baird curtly. Baird introduced her to Hans.

As Coco left to fetch her horse, I turned an inquisitive gaze toward Baird. He mounted and patiently dealt with Butterfly's shifting weight without acknowledging my look.

My understanding was that Baird and Coco had courted for a short time after the Hunju civil war but found they weren't compatible. I assumed it had to do with her ambition to be Captain of the Guard—thus confining her to the castle. Her behavior suggested it was at least partially his fault.

Baird scowled at me.

There's a story you haven't told me, I privately communicated, since Hans stood close enough to hear spoken words.

And you've no business knowing it, he retorted.

I narrowed my eyes at him suspiciously, but he didn't reply.

Coco emerged with a black gelding, sporting a black leather saddle. The horse boasted two hands in height over Phobus, and his hide shimmered a gleaming obsidian.

"He's a beauty," I said.

"He's from the Queen's royal stock. His name is Prince."

I scratched behind one ear, which earned me a jealous snicker from my own horse.

Coco stopped in her tracks, seeing the wolf for the first time. She gaped at Fury, who'd been patiently waiting away from the stables. I had seldom seen true fear on Coco's face, but the brief expression was unmistakable—before it transformed into irritation.

"He's my companion. His name is Fury." Baird explained.

"You never had a wolf."

"Abigail gave him to me. He's still young."

Coco gave me the briefest, frosty glower before jerking her head back to Baird. "You don't have a leash for it?"

"A leash?" Hans scoffed playfully as he mounted Unis, oblivious to the tension between Coco and Baird. "Put a saddle on him. He's big enough to ride!"

Coco speared a diminutive glance at Hans, but he'd already turned Unis away and missed her icy glare.

Coco mounted Prince in one smooth motion, her ponytail swishing to one side. I found myself inspecting the bare skin on her arms and neck. No rash.

"Are the other teams off?" I asked.

"Lieutenant Jok and his crew are off to Ntajid, but Lieutenant Guy fell ill. They're finding a new team leader for Karnelik."

I started to mount Phobus when I hesitated.

"To Kovia?" Coco asked.

I shook my head. "I can get the Blood Stone. Orrick knows the land." So did Mal, but of this group, only Baird knew of my personal guardian angel—er—prince of darkness. Regardless, Mal was intangible, so he couldn't help me transport to any caves in Karnelik. I still needed Orrick.

"That will delay getting the bats. *That* is our assignment." Coco adjusted her seat in her saddle.

I looked up at her. "I can do it faster. Ride east, and when I'm done, I'll let Baird know, and he can come get me."

I lifted my reins to Baird. "Will you take Phobus and Carrot?"

Neither of my companions would appreciate me taking them into a dark cave.

He nodded. "You should take Fury, though."

"How will Baird let you know where we are?" Hans asked.

I would let Baird explain that one.

I turned to Raven. "You with me?"

She gave a crooked grin as she leaped from Phobus' neck onto my shoulder, and then skittered down my arm to land on Fury's neck. Her splendid agility was a sight to behold. The wolf didn't seem to mind a small rider.

"Where should we begin?" Baird asked Coco and Hans.

I grabbed my water from my saddle pack and threw the strap over my shoulder.

"Not a town or city," Coco replied. "We don't want to appear suddenly in a populated area and provoke fear, nor do we want to land amongst the ill and acquire the sickness ourselves."

"I've only been to cities on Kovia. They'll all be populated," Hans warned.

Baird scratched his chin. "We can start outside Meredith then, east of Lake Wahla. Then ride to Moonshadow canal and take the ferry across to Moontown on Kovia. We can board the Kovian railway there."

As they prepared to transport, I cautioned Coco, "I know your Prince is royalty, but he's never transported abruptly. He may spook."

She blinked irritably, but I noticed her grip tightened on the reins.

They formed a line side-by-side—Hans, then Baird, then Coco— each touching their adjacent rider. Then they vanished.

I opened a palm to the wolf. Fury, well-trained in the art of travel, lifted a paw for me to touch. We instantly transported.

11

____

Fury, Raven, and I materialized at the edge of the Black Marsh forest and walked our way back to the brownie camp, carefully avoiding the trip wires. Fury stayed dutifully at my heel, watching his surroundings warily.

Winding my way through the woods, I greeted several of the brownies I'd met over the years—Rabbit, Brown Bear, Hawk Eyes, Rooster, and Ferret. I nodded to Grey Wolf when we encountered him and saw his eyes widen at the sight of Fury. In all there were thirty little pairs of eyes staring at us, all surprised to see us so soon.

"I didn't expect to be back here again already," Raven grumbled.

"We won't stay long."

We reached Orrick's home. Before I could lift a hand to knock on the door, the wizard swung it open.

Startled, I stammered, "Wizard Oak."

"Abigail." He tipped his head. "Welcome back."

He wore gray robes and carried a woven sack, which appeared to be full. "You've come to take me on an adventure." His eyes shone bright and his smile was broad. "I've packed snacks and water. I couldn't see where we were going—somewhere dark—but I'm ready."

I gaped at him. "You had a premonition I was coming for you?"

"Wonderful, isn't it? It struck me a half hour after you left this morning."

The timing might have been better if he'd seen it before I left, but he was fortuitously packed and already motivated to go.

"Um," Raven began in a hushed tone, "what about your illness?" She looked around skeptically at the watchful brownies on trees.

The old wizard leaned closer to her and lowered his voice. "I'll tell them I'm better."

He motioned with a hand for us to move. "Lead the way, Champion."

I whirled and began walking back through the brownie camp—with a wolf, a brownie, and a wizard in tow. "Can I carry something for you?"

"I'll manage," he replied.

Grey Wolf caught up to us as we passed back through brownie town. He brought the squirrel he rode to a halt on a tree branch. "What is this?" he barked.

"I need to borrow the wizard. It's important," I said.

Grey Wolf looked back and forth between me and Orrick.

"I'm better," Orrick said, still maintaining his broad smile.

"But—"

"I don't have time to explain," I interrupted. "I'll bring him back."

Grey Wolf narrowed his eyes at me. Since several hundred generations of brownies had looked after the oak, my confiscation of

Orrick would cause alarm. The leader of the brownies opened his mouth.

"I *will* bring him back," I repeated. "Raven will make sure of it."

She nodded.

"You'd better," Grey Wolf warned, keeping his eyes locked with mine.

Orrick and I resumed walking, the sound of gasps and astonished murmurs retreating behind us. Soon, we progressed beyond the village.

"What's the quest?" Orrick asked.

Raven glanced at him. "You're so eager to go on a quest that you didn't even wait to learn the details before packing?"

"Yes."

I chuckled, thinking of his complaint yesterday about the brownies' oppressive presence. "We need to fetch the Blood Stone. The last known location was the caves in Karnelik."

"In the mountains?"

"At the base of the mountains but nearer the city. I thought you might know something of the caves, since you were raised in Karnelik."

"Caves under the city?" His brow furrowed. "Those aren't caves. Those are tunnels. The tunnels of the catacombs of my parents' castle."

"Tunnels? Surely no part of your castle could have survived thousands of years." The Karnelik I knew was a town of homes and stores, most of which belonged to metal forgers. There was no trace of a seven-thousand-year-old castle—at least not above ground.

Orrick swatted at a bug. "Those tunnels were made of stone and Ballik ore. Nothing is stronger. If someone documented caves in that area, they likely connect to the catacombs."

Splendid. I'd be foraging among corpses for the Blood Stone.

I stepped over a log. "What do you know about the Blood Stone?"

"Purification. It's especially good for poisons, but works on any disease circulating the blood stream."

"So, the Healing Stone is better for trauma and the Blood Stone is better for poisons and blood-borne diseases?"

"Correct. Did you know Malakai had been poisoned? Perhaps if we'd had control of the Blood Stone at the time, events would have unfolded differently."

"Malakai wouldn't have become Malos."

"What do you think, brother?" Orrick asked to the air. "I was skeptical of Mother's plan and refused. Would you have done it even if you weren't poisoned?"

Mal appeared and walked backwards a few meters in front of us. He wore a contemplative expression.

"Who is he talking to?" Raven asked, glancing at Orrick skeptically. "He did that in his home, too. He asked you if Malakai was with us. You nodded, but no one else was there."

"I can see the ghost of Orrick's brother, Malakai."

"Huh. What does he look like?"

Mal replied, "Tall, dark, and seductively handsome."

"A pudgy midget with green skin," I lied.

"Really?" Raven asked.

"No. He's human—tall but a few centimeters shorter than Orrick. He has dark eyes and dark hair. Looks about thirty years of age."

"Does he haunt you?"

I grinned at Mal. "Yes. Yes, he does."

Orrick spoke again. "If you knew it would save Anastasia, would you have made the transformation without being on your deathbed first?"

"Who's Anastasia?" Raven and I asked in unison.

"Hmm." The sound emitted as a low rumble from Orrick.

I wondered if Wizard Oak was surprised I didn't know or now regretted mentioning an obviously personal detail.

Mal continued walking as he spoke, "She was the love of my life —when I *had* life. And she chose to go to war for Karnelik, rather than stay with me. She was the epitome of bravery, and grace, and self-sacrifice. My transformation to Malos, and absorption of evil, enabled her to live."

I swallowed, but it didn't ease the ache in my heart I felt for him. "But then she had to live without you."

"She found happiness." He sounded at peace with the concept.

Mal had obviously had many millennia to accept what had happened to him: The choices he'd made—or was forced to make.

I tried to assess how I would feel if I died and Joshua found another love.

Yes, I'd want that for him. I would wish him happiness, even if I couldn't provide it myself.

"What's he saying?" Raven asked.

"He loved Anastasia. He had to leave her when he became Malos."

"Malos is who you defeated as the Avant Champion?"

"Yes."

"And now he's a ghost who haunts you?"

"Yes."

"Seems unfair to save so many lives and be rewarded with your enemy's ghost, forever haunting you."

"It does, doesn't it?" I mused.

Mal narrowed his eyes at me. "You're being ungrateful."

When we reached the edge of the forest, Orrick gazed across the marsh stretching before us. His eyes blinked in the brightness of a bland, bluish gray sky.

"Wonderful," he said, in sheer astonishment.

"Hmm. You say that because you've never had to hike through it."

He looked down at me.

I elaborated, "Kilometer after kilometer of mud, and muck, and insects—and if that isn't enough fun, add in giant snakes."

He stroked his beard. "Oh, yes. The Black Marsh adder. It's good they're not extinct after all these years of being hunted by Hunju."

I blinked at him. "You only say that because you've never been bitten by one." I rubbed a hand along my thigh, vividly remembering the horrible pain of such a wound.

"Anyway," I hooked an arm through his, "we don't have to cross it now. I need you to concentrate on where you think the cave or castle entrance might be on the northeastern-most corner at the base of the mountains. Hold an image of the location in your mind, and I'll transport us there."

He closed his eyes and nodded. "Done."

Fury gave me his paw. "The travel can be disorienting and nauseating the first few times."

Orrick patted my arm, keeping his eyes closed.

I continued, "We don't want to be inside the castle or cave, because the architecture may be different than you remember owing to wear and tear and ceiling collapses. I don't want to know what happens if we land within a kiloton of rock."

"I'm ready."

I transported us, and tall pine trees materialized around us. The air turned crisp and dry. Beneath us was ... nothing but air. Ten meters below flashed the dirt and rock.

"What the—?"

Raven screamed as she clutched Fury.

I corrected our position to a few centimeters above the ground, but we were already falling. We landed on our feet, but Orrick and I crumpled to our knees from the force of the fall. Fury remained nimble and upright.

I helped Orrick to his feet. "What was that? Were you a *flying* wizard when you lived here?"

He looked around, as though expecting to see something he would recognize. "This must represent several thousand years of the ground settling."

I scanned our location. Among the trees and rocks and foliage, no obvious cave entrance presented itself. I turned south, away from the mountains. "We need to find an entrance, assuming there still is one."

"Over here!" Mal called.

"Oh, your brother is making himself useful after all," I told Orrick as I helped him step from one rock to another. I led everyone toward the sound of Mal's voice.

"Did he find it already?" Orrick asked.

"That, or he's found another orphan cub for me to shelter."

"What do you mean?"

"He introduced me to Fury one stormy, blizzard day."

We reached Mal, who was pointing toward a downward climb that led to a path between two large boulders. The path was obscured by ferns, and I knew I'd never have found it without Mal.

Step by step, I eased down the embankment, watching Orrick and being prepared to help him if he slipped. His footage stayed secure.

When we reached the bottom, we followed the path into a gaping cave. Soon, the darkness enveloped us. I activated my Che stone with my will, but the darkness was so encompassing—and my stone nearly completely covered by the wood casing around it—that we only gained a little visibility, immediately in front of us. I pried off the wooden cover, but the light still extended only a meter.

"Do you have a spell of light?" I asked Orrick.

"Use your moon magic."

"How do I do that?"

"Let the moon magic glow within you and around you. Will it, the same way you will the magic of the Che stone."

I concentrated on thinking of light—pure white light—as I imagined the beauty of Mother Moon. The cave lit. I blinked to adjust my eyes as a soft white glow emitted from within me and lit our way. Every exposed surface of my skin was illuminated.

"Spectacular." Raven's voice held genuine awe for once, rather than her usual sarcasm.

Mal stood with his arms by his side and his mouth slightly open.

"What are you staring at?"

He blinked. "You're *glowing*."

He took a step back and slipped his hands into his pockets. A grin spread across his face. "Shall we call you Baby Moon?"

"I was thinking more Moon Goddess," I retorted, striking a pose with my hands extended dramatically over my head.

From her seat on the back of Fury, Raven kicked a tiny foot into my calf.

"Ow."

Mal leaned closer, and his voice turned sultry. "To make that determination I'd have to see you in less clothing. Do you glow *everywhere*, I wonder?"

I lowered my hands and cleared my throat.

"Everything okay?" Orrick asked.

"Fine." I began walking deeper into the cave. "Your brother was being ... well, *himself*."

Behind me, Mal chuckled.

As we walked deeper into the caves, we were forced to stoop and then crawl over a pile of rocks. The cave soon transformed from walls of natural rock into an organized structure of hand-laid stone.

"Underground castle it is," I said.

"This was once our home." Mal's voice filled with raw emotion.

I turned to Orrick. "Are you okay?"

"Yes. I'm honored to have the privilege to see these walls again, and I'm humbled by the memory of friends and family long since passed."

The walkway led to a large room. I watched Fury. He was a ball of tightly-coiled observation, his ears perked and nostrils flaring, but at no point did he seem to sense a threat.

Orrick stopped. He mumbled something followed by a shout. "Illuminate!"

A ring of glowing golden light circled the ceiling, revealing a large, oval chamber where we stood. Tall stone pillars surrounded us interspersed with square and rectangular shapes representing windows—long since filled with dirt and rock.

"This was the announcement and banquet hall," Orrick said.

"This is where they announced the death of the king," Mal added.

He referred to his father.

Raven shifted her weight on my shoulder. "I've never seen a room so big."

"We're not at the level of the catacombs though." Orrick turned in a slow circle. We need to go down a level."

"Northeast stairs." Both men spoke simultaneously.

Mal led the way and I followed. As we left the illuminated room, my moon magic gave us light once again. We wound down stone steps, as the air grew staler and more dank. Thick wooden doors, which appeared to be petrified, sealed off several rooms.

We followed the tunnel to the right and reached a juncture. Straight ahead, the hallway appeared caved in. To our left a door of stone towered to the ceiling. On our right, the hallway continued.

As I turned right, Orrick turned left. I stopped and turned back to him.

He placed a hand on the long-petrified door, as if caressing it. "Mother's in there."

Mal walked through the wall.

Moments later, he returned and gave a quick nod.

"You're right," I told Orrick. "Mal confirmed it."

I turned to Mal. "Did you see any signs of the Blood Stone?"

"I did not, but I can't see well in the dark. I'll go back and perform a more thorough search."

As Mal left again, Orrick still stood motionless, facing the door.

I placed a hand on his arm. The last time he'd seen his mother, he'd fought with her, refusing to become the vessel for evil as she'd wanted. She'd cursed him to the oak tree, trapping him there for generations.

I felt for Orrick, and I wanted to give him time to spend by his mother's tomb—but time was working against us.

"I'll bring you back," I promised. "I can force the door open, but I worry about causing a cave in." Could I force a door open which had been sealed for seven thousand years? Even my strength had limits.

Orrick turned to me. "You could try, but mother has warded this place. Her magic and skillful craftsmanship are the reason this much of the castle survived."

He patted my arm. "Come. I'll visit her another day. Today, we save lives."

Thirty meters further down the corridor revealed another pile of rocks, blocking the only path left to us.

How could we ever find a stone in this place? "Another dead end."

"Maybe not." Raven pointed at a rat, as it scurried up the rocks and through a hole in them, disappearing from the intrusive glow of my moon magic.

She leaned forward. "Get closer. I'll climb through."

When I stood near enough to the rocks, Raven jumped onto one and crawled up into the hole she'd spotted.

"Watch out for the rat," I warned.

"I can communicate with small animals, remember?"

Orrick and I waited.

Mal returned. "As far as I can tell, no stone is in her tomb—unless it's hidden in her coffin. The other path is solid rock and dirt for ten meters."

"Raven is inspecting this path."

A moment later, she called, "It's too dark. Abbey, stick an arm through the hole so I can see."

I started to advance my fist, but hesitated. "You'll tell that rat not to bite me?"

"Yeah, yeah."

"You're afraid of a rat?" Mal asked.

I grimaced as I turned to look at Mal. "It was a big rat," I said defensively. I slowly pushed my arm into the hole and tried not to imagine chunky teeth gnawing on my flesh.

Mal leaned forward and inspected the hole my arm now filled. "Couldn't have been *that* big."

"How about you be helpful and look around with Raven, instead of standing there harassing me?"

Mal grinned, before walking into and through the solid rocks.

Orrick shook his head. "I don't have to hear both sides of the conversation to understand all of it. Do you two always carry on like this?"

"Mostly."

"Found it!" Raven called.

"Can you carry it back through? Or drop it in my hand?"

"Sure—when pigs fly. You try picking up a boulder half your size —*without* your magic stone."

"Okay. Is the room big enough for me?"

"Yes."

"Touch my hand and imagine us standing in the middle of the room."

A small hand touched mine. I blinked and brought us into the chamber. The small room was lined with sarcophaguses. They were either unmarked or the etchings had worn off long ago. Everything was coated in a dense layer of dust and dirt, and black moss clung to the mortar between the stone bricks, stretching its fuzzy tentacles ever upward.

In the center of the small room stood an empty stone pillar. I wondered if whatever it had once held had been stolen long ago.

On a small, carved recess of worn stone, sat the Blood Stone—a deep, dark red that was almost black. The stone was bigger than any Che stone I'd ever seen. I looked around the room again. Why here? Had whomever hidden it here intended to fetch it again later? Had he or she been prevented from doing so due to the collapse of the ceiling?

I grasped the large, cool stone. "Let's go."

Raven crawled up my arm to my shoulder.

"Wait," Mal said.

I turned to Mal, who was staring at the stone pillar in the center of the room.

"I remember seeing this. I remember Mother would turn the dial on top to open it."

"It opens?" I saw a layer of dust, but nothing resembling a dial.

"Yes. Place your hands on it and turn it counter-clockwise."

I started to protest—to explain that we didn't have time for seven-thousand-year-old hidden compartments, but his earnest voice stopped me. When had Mal ever asked me for anything for himself, in earnest? Not once.

I set the Blood Stone down, grasped the top of the stone pillar, and tried to turn it. It wouldn't budge. I attempted again, this time using the Warrior Stone. Something metallic sounded from within. It creaked, and then finally gave way. A piece of stone moved aside to reveal a hidden compartment.

"Great. Another opportunity to stick my hand into a dark hole."

I glanced at Mal, who was waiting impatiently. Sighing, I reached down, deep inside the pillar. In the darkness, my fingers grasped something cool and smooth. When I pulled it out, I found myself holding a cylindrical object made of glass. Etched into the glass were blue markings. The glow from my moon magic shone partially through the semi transparent white glass. The complex structure seemed to be made of seven pieces, all fixed around a central shaft.

Mal peered closer at the object.

"What is it?" I asked.

"I'm not entirely certain. I remember seeing it in Mother's library."

"Do you know these markings?"

"Yes. Ancient Karnelik. It looks like some type of puzzle box."

The room began to shake and rumble, causing my heart to leap into my throat. Fine dust and loose dirt shimmied from the walls. Had forcing the pillar open caused disruption of the stability of this ancient room?

With Raven on my shoulder, I snatched the Blood Stone and transported us to the other side of the fallen rocks. There, I reached for Orrick. The rumbling reverberated around us, as if we stood in the belly of a hungry beast.

I glanced up.

"Look out!" Mal called.

As I lunged for Orrick, Raven leaped to Fury's back. A boulder fell from above, missing Orrick's torso. He cried out in pain. At first, I thought his outburst was from me landing on top of him. Then, I saw the stone block had landed squarely on his ankle.

I coughed out dust and my eyes watered. Fury and Raven

appeared uninjured. After touching a hand to Fury. I whisked us all to the edge of the Healing Springs.

I blinked against the bright sun, as our surroundings turned from a dark and dusty cave to a hot spring with wooden patios beneath a blazing sun.

"Let me help you dip your foot in the water." After setting down the stone and the glass artifact, I carefully took off Orrick's shoe.

Together, we moved him closer and eased his foot into the effervescent water.

Fury sniffed at the water.

"What is this place?" Raven asked.

"The Ntajid springs. This particular one has healing power. That's why it has a high fence around it."

"Abbey?" Jo approached, his large, muscular brown body so much bigger than when I first met him as a ten-year-old boy working at the springs.

"Jo! Pleasant seeing you here."

He shook a finger at me. "I *work* here. You keep showing up unannounced. I need to charge you for your visits!"

I waved a hand at him. "Sure. Send me a bill."

Jo's claim was unjust, since I hadn't randomly showed up at the springs since the Hunju Civil war. Well—except for that one time my chemistry experiment got away from me. Oh, and then there'd been the sprained ankle a year ago. Yes, I suppose now I thought about it, I had continually showed up here—rather than having Joshua use his healing stone to fix what ailed. Guilty.

Orrick withdrew his foot and inspected the healed tissue. "Wonderful." He smiled broadly.

I gave him his shoe back and gathered my new belongs.

Jo began walking closer. "Abbey—"

"Sorry, no time." With a hand on Orrick and another hand stretched to Fury, I transported us all back to the edge of the Black Stag Forrest. I didn't have time for lectures on trespassing at the springs.

"Orrick, I—"

"Yes, yes. Tick, tock. Go save the world. I can find my way back." He slipped on his dirt-splattered shoe, and we both stood.

I stretched on my tiptoes and kissed his cheek.

"Wonderful." He continued grinning. "Did Mal see that?"

Mal appeared and crossed his arms. "Tell him I didn't."

I chuckled. "Thank you for your help, Orrick. I promise I'll return."

He placed a gentle, wrinkled hand to my cheek. "I know, dear. I know."

I TRANSPORTED us to the castle, back into the deliberation room, with Fury by my side. Gasps sounded as guards backed away from the wolf. Fury, accustomed to people's apprehension of him, remained calm.

I tossed the stone to the nearest guard. "That's the Blood Stone."

I looked around the room. Joshua gave me a soft smile.

"I'm joining Coco now for the bat. Has the other team left for Ntajid?"

"They have," Tarik confirmed.

I hoped they'd be back before us.

Baird?

Yes, Abigail.

I've retrieved the stone, and I'm ready to join the group.

We are outside the port of Moon River. The place seems deserted.

Pick me up outside the deliberation room.

With a nod to the gaping group of onlookers, I exited the room, Fury by my side. By the time we'd reached the hallway, Baird had already arrived.

I offered him my hand, careful to extend it in a way that our stars wouldn't touch. I had no desire to swim through Baird's sea of memories the way I had the day our stars first touched. We had planned the mass transport of an entire army and joined hands to do so. Something about the contact of our star tattoos sent us both into a flurry of each other's memories, and gave us this permanent communication link. With that in mind, I also didn't want to know what would happen if my moon tattoo touched his star.

Our hands touching, it was time for Fury to extend a paw to Baird.

He transported us instantly, far away to the waiting group.

Coco sat on Prince and Hans on Unis. Above, I heard the familiar raspy greeting call of Carrot from a tree-top in the distance. I didn't signal her to fly down to me. Instead, I tucked the mysterious glass cylinder I'd recovered into my saddlebag.

"Did you succeed?" Hans asked.

"We now have two of the four required components—the Healing Stone and Blood Stone," Raven triumphantly declared.

I grinned and admitted, "I couldn't have done it without her."

As I mounted Phobus, I looked over my shoulder. To the west, toward where the sun stretched, was perched the lovely town of Meredith. My in-laws lived there. I worried the plague had struck there. After we succeeded in securing the components of the cure, I would need to check on Joshua's parents. I squelched the dismal thought that if the disease had struck there prior to Marrington, deaths in the town would be mounting by now.

I held up my arm, and Carrot swooped down to land on it.

Together, we all rode through the port market at a cautious pace, passing storage warehouses and empty storefronts. An eerie quiet disconcerted me. As the sun set, this would be the time for people to be busily concluding transactions and finishing unloading commercial boats.

The clicking of horseshoes against wooden planks sounded as we reached the docks. A few small, empty boats swayed faintly in the water, tethered to the docks.

Coco halted Prince. "There's nothing here large enough for four horses."

"The ferries should be here," Hans said. "This is all wrong."

I walked Phobus along the long, wooden dock. The channel water rippled deep blue with wisps of sunlight glinting in reflection on the gentle waves.

I spotted an object in the distance, jutting partially out of the water. As I brought Phobus to a halt, I gaped at the site of a ferry sunk in the channel. The submerged boat lay on its side with the port hull touching the bottom of the channel and the starboard side barely protruding from the surface of the water.

"*Merciful Monks.*" I looked at Baird. "Do you think people were on that boat when it sank?"

Baird nudged his heels in, patiently positioning Butterfly next to Phobus. His expression looked troubled. "The passengers wouldn't have had far to swim to escape—but they clearly aren't in the marketplace."

"If the ferry is sunk, how do we cross?" Coco asked, bringing her horse on the other side of mine.

Baird replied, "We'll have to use the star. We won't know what we're transporting into at Moontown, or how we'll be received."

"There's no time for anything else." I extended a hand.

Moontown materialized around us, and we were suddenly enveloped by a dense, slate-colored sleet. I blinked to clear my vision, but our surroundings remained gray. I strained through the haze to see. This was no commerce town—at least not anymore.

Ash coated every building, walkway and tree. The town smelled like death and decay. Burnt cedar wood scent mingled with the smell of burnt flesh. I turned my gaze south, to where the source of the scent seemed to originate.

Hans and Coco put sleeves to their mouths, as if that might block the odor.

The buildings of Moontown were twisted, charred ruins. For a moment, I thought perhaps I was staring at the remnants from Malos' forces of destruction, but that wasn't possible. I would've asked Mal what happened, but I didn't need to add Hans to the list of people seeing me talk to myself.

We all gaped at our surroundings, as we nervously advanced through the ash-covered city streets. The horses' hooves left impressions on the soft, slate powder layering the ground.

"Hans," Baird said softly, "show us the way to the train station."

We followed Hans and Unis south through the dilapidated city. I was certain I saw the outlines of long bones and skulls amongst the rubble. Amidst all the charred wood, blackened stone, and fine ash, I didn't see any fires still actively smoldering. Whatever calamity had fallen upon this town, we'd arrived days late to witness it.

Our horses, keen to our alertness, kept their nostrils flared and ears perked. Fury trotted alongside us, his head low and nose sniffing the ground, and his ears pricked and alert.

After twenty minutes on horseback, we arrived at the train station. Since night was descending, we made torches using sticks dipped in a jar of bioluminescent algae Baird had brought. Blue-green light emitted from them, lighting our way.

The abundance of train tracks converging from the north, east, and south was evidence of this port city's robust trade and commerce —yet, there was no movement at the train station. The train itself lay on its side, askew from the tracks. It appeared to have collided with a railcar and overturned.

"Well, the train is no longer an option," Coco noted.

"Looks as though we'll be on horseback." Baird slid off Butterfly and looked into the cargo hold of the overturned train. "We'll travel again in the morning. From what we've seen, night travel may be dangerous. We can sleep here and alternate night watch."

I took first watch.

Having had three children, I'd learned that sleep was a precious commodity—but one I could capture enough of in short, concentrated doses to still function the following day.

Falling asleep would be challenging between the danger we faced and the urgency of our trip. Taking first watch would help with that. Sleeping on the hard floor of a train cart wasn't very appealing right now, but would grow more and more attractive the more tired I grew.

As I kept watch, I pulled the mysterious glass cylinder from the Karnelik castle catacombs out of my bag to inspect it. The translucence of the material made it seem fragile, yet the bulky weight suggested a robustness to the glass. Why would Isabel Dallik, the mother of Mal and Orrick, need such a puzzle box?

When I twisted one of the seven pieces, a set of symbols aligned. Everything around me shifted.

I blinked, and suddenly found myself standing beside a woman my own age with long, brown hair and a shimmering blue gown. She was staring out over a balcony, and made no startled motion to indicate she'd even seen me.

The woman looked out over the stone balcony, down to a courtyard where two boys swung wooden swords in play combat with each other.

I recognized them instantly. Young Malakai had a mop of wavy dark brown hair. He was slim and agile, and probably about ten years old. Orrick looked thicker and more svelte, with straight blond hair. The clank of wood striking wood echoed through the courtyard.

"My boys," Isabel Dallik began, her lips not moving, "play confined to these castle walls not knowing the war that rages to the west." She seemed to be narrating what appeared to be stored memories. "How long can we defend Crithos? The war has spread from continent to continent with Bellos conquering them one by one. So long have these battles been raging that generation after generation have known no peace."

Isabel gripped the stone edge of the balcony. "Will this same be true for my boys? I feel it. I see it. My powers grow the more I study magic. I'm fortunate Karnelik has such a wealth of magic books. I hadn't known that when my marriage to the king had been arranged. I'd worried this castle would be my prison. In truth, I've more freedom here than I did on the plains of Aithos, where my magic skills were disdained. My parents hadn't told the king of Karnelik about my unique skills when I was betrothed. Fear of persecution kept me silent, until I learned I could trust my husband.

"Now, within these fortified walls, with a wealth of resources, I can practice and perfect my skills. I might make more progress with an experienced mentor, but I'm making progress nonetheless. All other wizards are deployed as spies, or in battles against Bellos." Isabel's satin-brown eyes watched her sons play and fight below her. "My hope is to find a use for this magic that will benefit my children and my country. I want to make the world a better place."

"Abigail?"

I blinked, and suddenly Baird stood before me, back in the train yard.

"How long was I gone?"

He gave me a quizzical look. "You weren't gone at all. You were staring at that device in your hands."

"For how long?"

He shrugged. "A few seconds, but you didn't answer me at first. You looked like you were in a trance. Or meditating." He spoke the last word hesitantly as though knowing that couldn't possibly be the case. What've you got there?"

I rotated the object, careful not to move any pieces. "I think they're the stored memories of Isabel Dallik. It's a visual journal with her narration. I found it in ruins outside Karnelik."

"Malakai's mother? The first champion?"

I nodded.

"That's quite a prized piece then. There are no written records that have survived seven-thousand years."

He seemed to be practically salivating at the idea of long-lost history suddenly becoming accessible. I guessed he would want to see it and document what it contained.

"Now that I know what it is, I believe it belongs to Orrick."

Baird's expression deflated slightly. "You're quite right. I'm sure the wizard would treasure his mother's memories."

I placed the cylinder back in my satchel.

"I'll stay up with you. Shall we gather wood?" he asked.

Together, Baird and I broke apart a few of the empty wooden crates we found in the train yard and made a fire from them. He began with flint and wood shavings. When flames flickered to life, we added larger strips of wood. I wasn't sure which would pose a larger threat—sleeping in darkness and risking an animal attack or sleeping with fire and risking a human attack.

When a shard of wood cut into my skin, I was reminded of our vulnerability on the quest. This scratch was minor, but we had no healer with us. If any one of us sustained injuries in a fight, regardless of who the aggressor was, Baird or I would have to transport to the healing springs, which would take ourselves out of a fight in which we might be needed.

My arms were laden with firewood, the old barrel staves I'd collected. I used my star to transport them to the fire Baird had started.

He glanced up at me inquisitively. It would have taken me mere steps to toss them into the fire without the use of my star.

As I dropped the wood strips on the flames, I adjusted the staves, explaining, "I was surprised when I discovered I couldn't transport into or out of the Black Stag Forrest on our last quest. With all of this new land we're going to traverse, I thought I ought to test the ability from time to time."

Soon, the fire was roaring. I sat down before it, next to Baird. Fury curled up beside me and lay his head in my lap. His soft fur felt sleek and fine in my fingertips. Carrot had flown away, probably in search of rodents or small game.

"I believe Fury likes you more than me." Baird's tone was jovial rather than jealous.

I grinned. "I'm snuggly."

He chuckled. "What am I?"

I hesitated. "Stiff."

"Stiff?" He began to pet his wolf.

Wonderful friend that he was, Baird was all calm composure. Yet, if the eyes were the window to one's soul, his bore all. Even when he kept his body language indecipherable, Baird's eyes betrayed his every emotion—humor, compassion, worry, frustration, and resolve.

When I didn't elaborate, he gestured toward my hand. "You have a new design."

I opened my palm so he could see the moons. "Orrick gave me the moons," I said wistfully. "He said he was giving me moon magic."

"What does that mean?"

"That's exactly what I asked him. He said he'd explain later. So far, I can glow in the dark."

"Useful."

I poked the wood in the fire. The flames danced before my eyes. Shifting on the makeshift stool I'd assembled, I reached into my saddlebag and withdrew the Hunju darts. One by one, I dipped the tips in the snake venom.

"Those are new, too," Baird commented.

"I've had them for a while. Never had an occasion to use them. The serum is concentrated Black Marsh adder venom which paralyzes its victim."

"Yes, I recall."

I'd shown up at the monk sanctuary once, paralyzed, with the caged leader of the Hunju. It was back when our supposed rescue mission had turned into an escalation of the existing civil war.

"The serum will remain potent on the tip for up to a week."

"Don't inadvertently poke your finger, then."

Indeed, careful handling was paramount. The pouch that held them consisted of thick ox hide so the tips wouldn't protrude through the leather and cause a mishap.

"I'm glad to have you on this quest." I wrapped the darts back in the ox hide and stowed them in my pack. "Still, it feels incomplete without Joshua."

Baird patted my shoulder. "All of your quests have had a mix of old friends and new ones. This one will be no different."

I disagreed, though I kept silent. Under the circumstances, I didn't share Baird's optimism. This time, Joshua was being held as collateral. This time, I had my children to consider—and, as evidenced by the destruction surrounding us, more lives were at stake.

13

I walked a hallway lit by bioluminescent lamps.

The corridor stretched onward before me, seemingly infinite. On either side, doorways extended the length of the corridor, covered by sheer iridescent curtains that hid their contents.

I waited. Most of my unusual dreams could be blamed on Malakai. When I didn't see or hear him, I asked, "Mal?"

No response came. I looked at the palm of my hand, surprised to see the tattoo of the moons pulsating with a vibrant azure glow.

That's new.

I could hear murmuring from people within the rooms. Brushing aside one of the soft, thin curtains, I peered inside the room. Amidst grunts and groans of pleasure, I discovered Minister Tarik bedding a woman.

I drew back, swallowing down my revulsion. *That* had no place in my dreams.

The next room opened to flowing stream under a midday sun. Joshua was fishing with Baird, their lines pulled taught by the tug of water. As they casually conversed about Joshua's clinic, I noticed Joshua looked solid and whole, while Baird had a translucent shimmer.

I pulled aside another curtain, and saw a woman floating on the gentle ocean current. Her eyes were closed, as a smile danced on her lips. Her long brown and gray hair fanned out in the water.

I smiled, "Mom."

She put her feet down, stood, and turned to me. "Abbey! What a pleasant surprise."

I stepped into the room, walking atop the gently rippling ocean water. "You can see me?"

"Better now that you're closer. You looked a little fuzzy at first, but dreams often are."

"I haven't dreamt about you since the time you disappeared."

Nadine gave me a quizzical look. "I thought I was dreaming about *you.*"

"Huh." I looked down at the moons on my palm again, as I thought about the corridor of rooms. Was this the moon magic?

"I think I can enter other people's dreams."

"So, you're really here?"

"As much as I can be, in a dream."

My mother rose up, so she stood on top of the ocean water like me. Around us, water met sky in the horizon, but no land was in sight. Faintly, I could still see the outline of the doorway.

"How goes the quest?"

"The plague is bad. Catastrophic actually. Entire towns on Kovia have been wiped out. I feel better knowing the children are safe with you." My gut clenched as I expressed my concerns aloud. "If our quest fails, or the magic doesn't work, Crithos won't be the same. The devastation will be absolute."

She reached toward me and touched my hand. The embrace felt warm, solid, and secure. When Mal walked in my dreams, he was as intangible as he was during my wakefulness. This was a different magic.

"The children are fed and happy. Your focus should be on what you need to do to save Crithos."

My chest quivered. "I don't know if it will be enough."

"Do your best, as you always do." Her soft brown eyes conveyed encouragement and pity.

"Joshua will contract the plague soon—if he hasn't already. He's elbow-deep in those infected with it." My heart squeezed in my chest as I spoke the words. "We're racing against a clock to save his life, too."

"Then, it's fortunate the country has the Avant Champion on its side."

"Thanks, Mom." I squeezed her hand.

We stood together silently, watching the ocean. In her dream, the water rested calmly, more like a pond—but too vast to be anything other than the ocean. As she placed a hand against my cheek, I closed my eyes to enjoy the comfort of her touch.

"Get some rest, Abbey."

I woke with a start. The sun crested the horizon, casting long, distorted shadows. We were surrounded by a sea of gray—light ash and dark shadows—representing the remnants of Moontown.

Hans, Coco, Raven, and Baird were already packing their belongings.

I sat up and patted my hair to smooth the wild waves. Between night watch and the difficulty I'd had falling asleep, I guessed I'd managed about four hours of rest. After I shoved myself to my feet, I began to roll my blanket. Four hours would have to suffice. For every minute of our journey, someone died from the Omega plague.

"The horses and Fury are fed and watered," Hans said, handing me a stick of beef jerky.

I accepted it with a thank you.

We packed, mounted, and left the ghost town behind us. Carrot took her place on my arm, and Raven was content to continue riding Fury.

Since the train was no longer an option, we'd be on horseback all the way to the salt mines. We followed the road Hans suggested, leading east. Baird consulted the map and confirmed we were on the right track. When the ashen town faded behind us, the flat landscape stretched from farmland, to prairie, to woods.

We kept a steady pace, alternating between galloping and walking. The galloping was reserved for stretches of level road.

At late afternoon, I dismounted to run beside Phobus as he trotted. I let Carrot perch on the empty saddle.

"What are you doing?" Coco asked, looking down at me from atop Prince. Her golden hair was pulled back in a severe-looking ponytail.

"I've been in that saddle for hours. I need to move my legs, and Phobus could use a break from the weight of a rider."

"I've never seen anyone run—except the Queen's runners."

"I used to be in better shape. Less winded. I haven't run consistently since having children." I chased after the children constantly, but that was more about building emotional endurance than physical.

Hans hopped off Unis. Keeping hold of the horse's reins, he joined me in a jog. He grinned. "How long do we do this for?"

"The Queen's runners can do a hundred kilometers. The most I've ever managed is about ten." I breathed heavily between sentences. "Again, that was before having children."

"What happens after children?" he asked.

"What do you mean?"

"What do you intend to do with your longevity? Will you be a chemistry teacher forever? Will you take up more quests?"

I didn't spend an abundance of time considering what my life would be when my children had grown. Since my life expectancy would be considerably longer than Joshua's—provided these Queen's quests didn't do me in—growing old together by a warm fire wasn't in our future. With the way Joshua used his healing stone so freely to help others, that time together might be even less than I'd anticipated.

"Perhaps more travel," I said, with forced cheer.

Hans was attempting casual conversation, and I wanted to avoid making him aware of the thoughts that burdened me when I thought about a future without Joshua.

He beamed. "I'd love to see Bellos. The Emerald Caves. The city of Victoria. The Bakshi mountains."

"Sounds lovely."

If Hans kept his course to become a Gunthi Monk, he'd have a long life of adventure ahead of him. What I didn't understand was why he'd choose such a life in the first place. As the son of an English professor, his life flourished among the middle class. Why sacrifice that for a life among the monks? Rotating between isolation and service to mankind? I understood Baird's motivation—he'd lost the woman he loved many years ago.

I decided to probe. "The lifetime commitment as a monk seems a steep price to pay for traveling the world."

A shadow flickered over Hans' expression, before his rosy-cheeked, boyish grin returned. "I'm fascinated with magic and the legends of what it once was—stone bearers in every village, sorcerers, and wizards. They were gods among men."

"Some of them were demons."

"True."

I'd heard vivid descriptions from Mal about what the world had been like thousands of years ago—trapped in a cycle of war and devastation. We'd had many philosophical discussions about whether mankind deserved the power of magic. History suggested that, with magic, we cycled in a state of perpetual war. When some of our evil was removed from the equation, magic became less important. Seven thousand years of peace had passed without the existence of magic-bearing wizards or war.

"You can learn history in the monk library without becoming a monk," I said.

"I have more than a lifetime of learning ahead of me."

"Oh? You reached that conclusion at a young age."

He scowled a moment, and I wasn't sure if he felt offended at me calling him young or at me casting doubt on his motivation. My inquisition wasn't meant to be unfriendly.

I tried to recover. "It's noble of you to want to become a monk. I'm sure you'll find fulfillment and learn more history than you can possibly imagine."

His eyes sparkled in amusement, making me think my flattery worked *too* well.

"You have your own noble actions." His breathing was heavier now with the exertion of the run.

"They are few and far between. I made my choice. I chose a family and teaching career over permanent service to Queen and country."

"But you never turn away from a crisis."

"True. Yet the power to influence a situation with force and magic —and of knowing if that's the right course of action—are not one and the same."

Hans chuckled. "You sound like Baird."

I grinned. "I do, don't I? I'm at least fifty years younger, so you're better off taking advice from him." I was in my late thirties, looking like young thirties. Baird, in contrast, looked like he was in his late forties, but I suspected he was actually over one-hundred years old. He never divulged his true age. Since he had continuous access to the Aqua Santos, I imagined I'd look older than him someday.

"Baird is—," Hans began.

"Look," interrupted Baird from ahead of us. "There's a village ahead."

I slowed to a walk.

With living people, or corpses? I wondered dismally.

As we approached, the village emerged—wooden, block-shaped houses and stores circled with a series of stone walls.

I climbed onto Phobus' back and Carrot took flight. Raven chose to ride on my shoulder for a better view.

Baird consulted a map from his saddle pack. "Perhaps this is Billington. It should be the town before the geysers."

"Geysers?" I asked.

Hans replied, "That's a stretch of protected land containing hot springs and geysers. It will be the shortest way to the salt mines."

"Protected land? Why does it need protection?" I lamented how ill-prepared we were for a quest on foreign land. What dangers lurked on our cross-country excursion? Then again, on our last quest we'd had preparation, and I'd still nearly been eaten by a swamp snake almost as large as a sea serpent.

Hans shrugged. "Legend says people need protection from the geysers, not the other way around."

"Why is that?" Above me, Carrot circled once, before landing back on my arm.

"Some superstition about the misting water's ability to drive people insane."

I stared at Baird. "As a practical academic, I mocked superstitious beliefs—until I learned of the world of magic."

Baird gave me a patronizing smile as he rolled the map and stowed it in his saddlebag. "I'm sure we'll keep our wits about us. A trip around the springs would be a travel delay."

Phobus snorted, and his ears rotated from front to back. He sensed something—even though nothing stirred as we walked past the first stone wall.

Fury released a low, grumbling growl. He stopped abruptly, turned, and stalked around the edge of one of the walls. I suspected Baird conveyed nonverbal instructions to Fury through the use of his Language Stone. My suspicion was confirmed by the light glow emitted from his ring. To the casual observer, it might appear as if the sun were reflecting off the embedded stone, but I recognized the white flicker as stone magic.

I dropped my arm to let Carrot take flight again. On my arm, she was a target. In the sky, she was a weapon.

As we entered the town, rows of shops rose around us. They were built with wooden walls painted in shades of white and tan, with square windows and flat rooftops. Most of the buildings stretched two stories high, with a balcony above the store on the ground floor. The owner's living quarters were presumably on the second floor.

The town could have been described as picturesque were it not for the silence that raised the hairs on the back of my neck.

A man stepped out onto the cobblestones. He was dressed in a suit a size too large for his frame, with a button-red vest and flaring white sleeves. With his disheveled brown hair and pitchfork, he had the appearance of a wealthy farmer or, more likely, a farmer wearing stolen clothes.

We brought our horses to a halt.

The pitchfork-wielder spoke in Kovian—a language I knew little of. I'd heard it in different major marketplaces in Meredith, Marrington, and Waterton. An odd bulge under his lip gave his mouth a lopsided appearance.

Baird translated for us: "Welcome to Billington. What brings your party to our humble town?"

The next time Baird spoke, he addressed Pinsky, explaining our origins—and that we didn't speak the language. "We come from Crithos, under our Queen's order, in pursuit of a cure for the plague on our lands. My name is Baird Fox. With us are Hans, Abigail, and Coco."

The farmer spat black tarry phlegm onto the ground. His dark, beady eyes assessed our group, as he squinted up at us. Around us, dozens of people were emerging from the stores and rooftops. Some were dressed in oddly fine clothing of satins and silks, while others wore laborers' clothes more suitable for a farm or mine.

The men and women hovered around us, as though waiting for instructions.

The hair at the nape of my neck tingled.

Phobus kept his ears back, a sign of distrust toward the gawkers.

"My name's Preacher Pinsky. It sounds as though you have quite the expedition ahead of you." He rotated the pitchfork slowly, keeping it pointed upward. As he spoke, Baird continued to translate. Even though I couldn't understand his exact words, Preacher Pinsky's speech was slow and deliberate. "How can we be of assistance to such an important group of travelers? We are but humble farmers and miners."

"We're simply passing through," Baird assured him.

"We have food, water, and supplies. Lee, over there?" He pointed to a woman staring at us nearby. "Why, she is a delightful cook. Makes a mean pasta dish. We could all have an amicable dinner together. We've never had the honor of dining with a Queen's fine servants."

Lee wore a crinkled red dress and her hair was wild and wind-blown. The hungry way she stared at us had me wondering if we were invited *to* dinner or *for* dinner.

I'm thinking they don't have both oars in the water, I told Baird.

He didn't answer me, but continued to address Pinsky. "That is a generous offer, but our mission is time sensitive. We can spare no daylight on diversions."

"You've already trespassed. The least you can do is accept our hospitality." Pinksy drew out each syllable of the word. His eyes flashed with hostility, despite his crooked smile.

Tension blanketed the air—thick enough to stick a fork in it. Or a *pitch*fork.

"Then we'll go around your town, and we apologize for our intrusion." Baird had Butterfly take several accommodating steps backward.

"Problem is," Pinsky began, as the other villager's expressions turned to greedy anticipation, "you're not ill. There are two types of people surviving this curse on our land—those chosen by Borlov to start a new, pure civilization; and those who possess magic and caused this chain of events in the first place."

"Magic didn't—" Hans began, but Baird silenced him with raised hand.

Borlov? My mind raced. He'd been an ancient god of man, back when we believed in many deities. I thought the Unideit had replaced false gods several thousand years ago. Were the old religions resurfacing?

"I assure you we only want to pass. We won't trespass again."

Pinsky gave us a pitying grin, revealing yellow-stained teeth. "Now, that's not how this works. You've the option of joining our accommodating group—," he looked around at his followers, "—and serving Borlov. Or you can be *cleansed* by us."

14

I wondered briefly if offering these lunatics money would placate them, but I suspected they stole whatever they wanted —including their garb—so a bribe was unlikely to work

The sooner we leave, the less likely we'll be to injure these religious zealots, I told Baird.

"We serve the Unideit, not false gods," Hans declared, his voice laced with fear and false bravado.

Although Baird didn't translate his words, the defiance in them rang clear.

Had Hans ever been in a fight? What he didn't understand was that these farmers, with their pitchforks and bravado, didn't stand a chance against Baird, Coco, and myself. We needed to negotiate out of this for *their* sake, not ours.

The horses sensed the escalating danger and shifted their weight restlessly from side to side.

Preacher Pinsky's expression filled with anger, before he gave us a full, feral smile. "Then, by the power bestowed on me by the great Borlov, I declare you heathens. Your lives are forfeited to us."

His followers cheered.

"You will show respect to the Avant Champion!" Hans bellowed.

Mother Moon, I swore silently.

Does he know the difference between escalating violence and curbing it? I asked Baird.

I remember a young woman who used to pick fights when negotiation might have been a better option.

Since he'd made his point, I didn't reply.

Pinsky pointed his pitchfork at me. "Seize the witch first."

Thanks to Hans, I'd been singled out.

Pinsky's ruffians descended upon us, battle cries filling the air.

As I pulled my blowdart case from my saddlebag, I told Baird, *I don't have enough paralyzing venom for this many attackers.*

We'll spare the lives we can. Unfortunately, we can't spare them all.

As hastily as I could, I loaded the dart and blew.

One, then another, then another. A few seconds after being struck by my darts, each target faltered and fell to the ground—paralyzed. The effects would last an hour or so, while the individual could still breath—and still feel pain.

While I blew darts, Coco drew her sword and dismounted Prince. She fought with grace and practiced precision. The two men and woman attacking her were clumsy, but rabid enough to be dangerous. Baird and Hans fought on foot with their batons.

Raven climbed out of hiding and onto my saddle. As she clung to my tunic with one small hand, she began handing me small bags with the other—filled with the sleeping dust brownies used on intruders.

I flung them at the onslaught of zealots, until the supply was depleted. Beneath me, Phobus spun and kicked his hind legs, knocking an attacker backward and onto his back. Carrot, meanwhile, dove down from the sky and dug her sharp talons into the backs and scalps of an onslaught of attackers.

"You take Phobus. I'll fight on the ground."

Raven nodded and scampered to the front of the saddle, where she straddled the saddle horn and took the reins. In her small hands, it looked as though she clasped giant straps of leather. As long as she kept the reins off the ground, I knew Phobus would protect both himself and her. I saw her moving her lips as she held the reins—as though speaking with my horse.

Pulling my sword, I leaped down, landing on top of an attacker who wielded blunt iron pincers used for metalworking. I struck him in the head with the hilt of my sword, powered by the strength of my stone. He stumbled back.

Baird moved with ease, vanishing and reappearing in the throng of attackers as he struck their knees, debilitating them. The dizzying spin of his blue cape and blur of his magical movements disoriented the crowd.

Hans fought with both red-faced anger and fear, tackling a tall, thin man with a receding hairline who brandished a poker stick.

After sheathing my sword, I picked up the blunt, metal pincers and swung them like a club, trying to inflict temporarily crippling injuries but nothing fatal or permanent.

"Abigail!"

At Baird's warning, I disappeared and reappeared several feet from where I'd just been standing. A pitchfork sailed through the air where I'd been and into a woman in a pink dress who'd been attacking me.

I followed the trajectory to see that Preacher Pinsky had thrown it at me. In a cowardly move, he'd tried to impale me in the back. Instead, he had skewered one of his own villagers.

Coco also had an attacker at her back—a burly man wielding an axe. As he lofted it high above his head, ready to swing, Fury launched himself from between two buildings. The large, black wolf sunk his teeth into the man's throat. Gurgling and an eruption of blood followed. There'd be no more calling him Fluffy after witnessing *that*.

I transported and appeared in front of Pinsky. I used the pincers to clasp his neck. With the strength of my Warrior Stone, I held him up and away from me, as he writhed and twisted with his feet dangling beneath him.

Pinsky tried to swing and kick at me, but he couldn't reach. Wrapping his hands around the iron, he tried to tug the pincers from around his neck but to no avail. I held them tight enough to prevent escape, but so he could still breathe. Barely.

"Order your people to stop their attack," I commanded.

Baird translated.

Pinsky spat in response, but without being able to move his neck, the dense brown phlegm dribbled down his chin instead of launching at me.

Around me, Coco, Baird, and Hans had closed in to defend my flanks. They'd disarmed the last of the zealots, and the remaining villagers began to scurry away from us. I surveyed the scene—three dead, six paralyzed by my darts, three sleeping from the brownie dust, and six more wounded and unable to flee.

Considering we'd been just four against forty, I thought we'd well to minimize damage.

Pinsky writhed again. "Borlov will strike you down! You are the magic users responsible for this calamity! You will be punished!"

As I held him, I felt my sword pulled from my sheath.

"Hans, no!" Baird cried.

Hans thrust my sword into Pinsky's chest. Crimson red stained his shirt. As Hans withdrew his sword, blood poured out of Pinsky's wound and down his clothes. The preacher went limp in my grasp.

Lowering him to the ground, I turned to Hans in horrid astonishment. "He was unarmed!"

Hans' face was still red from the exertion of fighting and sweat matted his hair. Fierce eyes burned with green flame. "He called you a witch, and he tried to dishonorably kill you from behind."

"I—" I stammered, still shocked and trying to control my dismay at the situation.

Leave it be, Abigail. I will speak with him privately, Baird said.

Dumbfounded, I turned to Coco, "Are you okay?"

She raised her eyebrows as her mouth quirked. "Farmers with pitchforks? This is another first for me, Abigail." Naturally, the only time she wasn't grumpy was when she got to fight.

Raven approached on Phobus.

"Well done, warriors." I gave the two of them a bow.

Phobus mimicked my movements, and Raven laughed.

"Show off," I murmured to my horse.

I patted Fury's head as he padded up beside me. Carrot flew down, and landed on Phobus. I stroked her breast feathers. "You did good, too, girl."

Hans knelt over Pinsky's body. After working his hands along the dead man's belt, he removed a sheathed dagger. I was about to tell him we didn't steal from the dead when he turned to me and presented it as a gift. "His apology in death, since he was incapable of doing so in life."

The gesture was unnecessary, dramatic, and some form of misguided chivalry, but I didn't want to shame Hans in front of his mentor and Coco. I took the dagger. As I stared at it, I noticed the gold-colored handle and inlaid ruby. Pinsky may have been last to possess this finely-wrought blade, but he couldn't have been the rightful owner.

"I vote we pass through this creepy town *quickly,*" Raven said.

"I concur." Coco wiped blood from her sword, sheathed it, and whistled for Prince.

AFTER WE CLEANED OUR WEAPONS, we mounted our horses and progressed through the town. I'd used all of my paralytic venom and all of Raven's sleeping dust. If we encountered another skirmish, I wouldn't be able to avoid inflicting serious injury.

We moved through the town cautiously, wary of another attack or retribution for the death of their leader. Carrot took her perch back on my arm. Shops and restaurants sat eerily abandoned. Unlike the last city, this one remained unmarred by fire—but where had all of the people vanished to?

"Did you hear that?" Hans asked.

We halted and listened. Banging and cries of help were barely audible. We turned in the direction of the noise. Behind a butcher shop stood a large wooden shed. A plank bridged the doors and kept them from being opened from the inside. Whoever was locked behind the doors had been intentionally imprisoned there.

Baird and Hans dismounted and worked to remove the plank. Baird glanced back at me, receiving my nod before they lifted it away from the doors.

We didn't know if we would unleash friend or foe by opening these doors, so we needed to be ready to fight.

Fury, too, stood poised to attack.

Baird and Hans set the plank aside and pulled open the storage doors. From the depths of the dark recesses emerged a half-dozen people, blinking at the light as they staggered out of captivity. They appeared stunned and timid in their tattered clothing and haggard uncleanliness. Exposed skin surfaces—arms, legs, and faces—didn't appear to have any signs of a rash.

Two of the six people sprinted away from us immediately, as if fleeing for their lives. I supposed four well-armed horseback riders, fresh from a fight, would be an intimidating sight for anybody to behold.

"You're free," I called after them, "but be careful. Preacher Pinsky's men are still out there even though he's dead."

Baird spoke as his language stone glowed. He translated my words into one of the Kovian dialects; but I'm not sure if those fleeing heard or listened to them.

The events of the last few minutes started to sink in. The combination of devastating disease, mass death, ignorance, and religious fanaticism had brought the people of this village together with the idea they could lord over and kill others. I worried what other surprises we might find on our journey.

Not all of those we'd freed fled. A tall, bronzed man turned toward me. "You killed Pinsky?" His accent was the melodic flow of a wealthy Bellosian. I could identify it from the transient court members I'd had met at the Queen's castle.

"We did."

Technically, a young, foolish boy killed his first human in a fit of irrationality—but I decided to omit that part.

"Thank you! We've been prisoners for several days. Have you any food or water?"

"The town still has an abundance, but you'll need to be careful to avoid capture again."

"If it's no burden to you, I'd feel safer if I traveled with you out of town."

I looked at Coco and Baird, who gave wordless ascent with their eyes.

"Very well," I began, my voice loud enough for the remaining onlookers to hear, "everyone take thirty minutes to gather supplies. We're heading east if anyone wants to join us to travel in that direction. The pace will be swift. Anyone who doesn't want to come is free to go their own way; but I hope you will remember what it's like to be prey, and treat your fellow man better than you've been treated."

There I went, sounding like Baird again.

As the captives scattered, the four of us gathered together on our horses.

Baird said, "If we acquire travelers, we need to take precautions that they don't see an abundant use of magic unless absolutely necessary."

"I agree. We don't know who we can trust, or who else has superstitious beliefs."

When a half-hour had passed, all of the captives we'd freed had scattered. Only the man who'd originally asked to join us returned.

He carried a sack, presumably of food and supplies, and had

changed out of his tattered clothes into a red, shimmering tunic with gold embroidery. His dark brown hair was neatly combed. I wanted to remind him we were traveling on horseback, not dining with dignitaries.

He introduced himself formally. "I am Boyo Vinchenko, Ambassador to Bellos and King Artemis Stout."

"I am Baird Fox. This is Abigail Cross, Hans Stallman, and Coco DeFay. Captain DeFay heads Queen Rebekah's guard on Crithos. We are traveling east to find a cure for the plague."

"Thank you for the rescue. I will accompany you as far as the edge of the Waterlands, if that is not a burden."

"Can you ride?" I asked.

He nodded. His gaze flickered from me to my hawk to the wolf beside my horse.

"Take my horse." I swung a leg over and dropped off Phobus with Carrot still perched on my arm. "We need to move quickly, though, and make up for lost time."

I gave the stranger Phobus' reins, ignoring the surprised looks from Coco and Hans. We didn't know if Boyo was trustworthy— though his mannerisms and proper speech suggested his claim of being part of the King's court were true. Yet, I felt secure. My horse and I shared a special bond, and I knew Phobus would never allow himself to be stolen and ridden away from me.

I turned to Coco as she sat atop Prince.

"Climb aboard," she offered a hand and freed a stirrup for me to use.

First, I turned to Hans. "Take Carrot." I gave him one of my leather vambraces and transferred the bird to his arm.

Although he looked stiff and uncertain, Hans smiled in awe at the hawk as she settled on his arm. He admired her shimmering orange and brown feathers.

After I hoisted myself up onto Prince, I situated myself behind Coco's saddle.

We started moving— winding down the road away from the butcher's shop. After a spell, we encountered what I presumed to be the work of Preacher Pinsky. Bodies were strewn up on trees with thick rope. Their mutilated corpses testified to terrible suffering and painful death. Those who hung there had clearly been tortured—beaten, blinded, and eviscerated. They'd not been given so much as a grain of peace or dignity.

Flies circled the corpses, and gaping holes in their torn flesh were evidence that wild animals had scavenged these bodies. The stench of decay and defecation hovered near them.

"*Merciful Monks.*" My eyes watered. What had mankind become? Who were we if we were capable of such horrors in times of crisis?

Boyo's face looked pale as he stared at a fate he had barely avoided himself.

"I'll not regret killing Pinsky a day of my life after seeing this," Hans said, through clenched teeth.

"We need to bury them," Baird said.

"We can't spare the time," Coco said. "We'll come back and do it when the quest is finished."

"A prayer then for now." Baird remained on his horse as he recited the Callabus prayer for the dead. His voice was deep and melodic.

> *"My time to rest,*
> *My place to nest.*
>
> *Take my soul home,*
> *End my weary roam.*
>
> *Light a torch for me,*
> *My body from sand to sea.*
>
> *From the sea to the moons,*
> *By the stars rests my tomb."*

We lingered only a moment in silence, before riding away from this scene of death.

15

Our group quietly rode down a dirt lane, heading east and leaving Billington far behind us. I was grateful to be moving away from the zealots and their victims.

A well-groomed road spanned ahead with alternating stretches of woods, grasslands and farmland on either side.

"You trust him?" Coco asked, turning her head and keeping her voice low.

I knew she referred to our new guest—Boyo Vinchenko. "I don't have a reason not to. You don't?"

"I don't trust anyone on first introduction."

I looked at Boyo as he rode, then down towards Fury as he trotted along beside Unis. Fury seemed neutral toward Boyo—neither friendly nor wary. He behaved the same toward Coco, and she was friend, not foe.

"Well, one thing's for sure. He won't challenge the four of us and a wolf. We can rotate our watch tonight. We want to be alert for attackers anyway. Our night vigil can include watching our guest."

"Let's do that."

As the sun began to set, we made camp. We selected a site well out of view of the road we traveled. I started the fire as Baird prepared a meal. Coco and Hans constructed the tents.

Using flint, I showered sparks onto soft, dry grass. When it began to smoke, I added twigs and then larger branches from the woods nearby.

Baird situated a pot over the fire. He added water, dried beans, and dried beef to the pot before letting it simmer. I stole a glance at the stew and frowned. I missed Mo's cooking already.

While the food was cooking, Hans and I fed the horses. Fury and Carrot left in search of their own dinner.

When the food was ready, we sat around the fire eating bowls of soup. We formed a circle with Coco to my right and Raven to my left.

"How long have you been in Kovia?" I asked.

Boyo took a long sip from his flask. I suspected he filled it with moon juice rather than water. After suffering in captivity, I imagined he needed a drink.

"Two months. I've been traveling from city to city, meeting delegates of the court. My next stop was Kovo, the capital, when the plague struck. They shut down travel into the city. There are rumors it's a city of corpses now. I decided to escape to Sylvia. It's a port city where I hoped to secure passage back to Bellos. In the process, my carriage was stolen and my manservant killed. I travelled on foot when Pinsky captured me two days ago. Elliptical zealot. He planned to kill me—planned to kill all of us! They burned a captive a day."

We sat in silence for moment, contemplating the horror of awaiting one's own execution. Out of all of us perched around the fire, Coco had come closest to such an experience. She'd been taken hostage and brutalized by the Dantajists—a bloodthirsty band of giants on Southern Crithos. At the time, she hadn't known if she'd survive captivity.

I glanced at Coco. Her face looked paler than normal, even with the orange glow of the fire to light it.

"I met the ambassador of Kovia." I thought back to the spring ball and hoped my friend with the long scar still lived.

Boyo gave me an appraising look, as though my association with the ambassador elevated his impression of me. "Goran Foal. He's an honorable man, if a bit gruff. He was part of the Kovian guard before an injury rendered him lame. During his recovery, he learned Bellosian, Crithian, and Sellosian dialects. His linguistic abilities make him good for international work, but his diplomatic skills need polishing."

My question uncovered information on Goran I didn't know; but more importantly, it lent validity to Boyo's assertion that he was an ambassador to Bellos. How else would he know so much about another country's ambassador?

"Do you actually think you can find a cure?" Boyo asked, looking around the group.

"We intend to try," Baird replied.

I explained, "The Omega plague originated from exposure to bats —carriers of the disease. The same way we know rats carry the Jau virus. Securing a carrier is one of the components to formulating a cure."

"Please take no offense to this, but it seems a bit late for a cure. Eighty percent of the population is already dead."

Coco set her empty soup bowl aside and reached for her cup of water. "Too late for Kovia, yes. But Crithos can be saved."

"Do you know if it's reached Bellos?" I asked Boyo.

He shook his head solemnly.

I added. "Do you know why you were unaffected?"

"Through no reason of valor." He pursed his lips as he looked into the fire. "I immediately left every place I traveled to that was infected. I heard the rumors that nothing could be done to save the plague's victims, so I did nothing except keep moving to keep myself alive."

"We're going to find a cure," Hans said. "If you want the opportunity to help, you can join us."

I wouldn't have made the same offer. We didn't have an extra horse or the spare food for an additional team member. Yet, when I looked at Hans, he seemed to be analyzing Boyo, assessing his character. If Boyo declined, then perhaps he feigned guilt rather than felt genuine remorse at not offering to help the sick and suffering.

Hans continued, "Another day or two's ride east, and we'll be at the mines."

"Two days?" Boyo shook his head. "It's at least five days to the mines from here by horseback."

Hans frowned.

Baird produced the map from his bag and unrolled it. "Our map has been to scale thus far. Here we are—and here are the mines." He pointed to each location.

"Yes," Boyer concurred, "but you cannot go directly through the Waterlands."

"Is it impossible on horseback?" Coco asked.

Boyo blinked at her. "It cannot be traversed by any modality. The Waterlands are filled with springs and geysers. The land is cursed—everyone on Kovia will tell you that."

"Cursed waterworks?" Raven asked skeptically.

Boyo glanced at Raven, as though unsure how to behave toward such a small, yet intelligent creature.

"I've read about the claims," Baird said. "The Waterlands assault one's sanity. Something about seeing the future?"

"It's worse than that. Most lose their minds or become infatuated with solving the mysteries of the images they see." Boyo took another drink from his flask.

Baird's expression turned grave. "Seeing glimpses of a fluid future can be unnerving for some. The very nature of seeing an event might alter one's actions, and affect the outcome."

"It is forbidden to trespass on the Waterlands," Boyo stated.

Coco leaned forward with her legs crossed. "It is forbidden? Or cursed?"

"Both."

Coco crossed her arms, and for a moment, she and Raven held the same skeptical pose.

"Everyone says it's cursed because the people who emerge—well, they're not the same. It drives people mad. Trespassing has been against the law for hundreds of years. Only the king is allowed to ordain men to enter."

I arched an eyebrow. "So, the king is monopolizing the ability to see the future?"

Boyo shook his head in frustration. "You make it sound conspiratorial. The king is only trying to protect people."

"We can't afford the time to travel around it," Baird said. "Tell us everything you've heard about the geysers."

"Rumors claim that when you look into a geyser, you see the future."

"Any future? Or one specific to you?"

"I've never asked."

"So, conceivably, we need only *not* to look into a geyser?"

Boyo's expression grew more irritated. "Certainly—but if it were so simple, the land would not be cursed."

"Does it have any effect on animals?" Baird asked.

"I don't know."

I tilted my head towards Baird. "What are you thinking?"

"We could blindfold three of us and have one take the lead. Horses and blinded riders can follow the lead horse."

Boyo stood and stretched. "I see I cannot dissuade you. I wish you safe passage. I'll travel with you tomorrow to the edge of the Waterlands, and then I'll venture south alone. Tonight, I rest."

We watched him walk to his tent.

Baird turned to Coco. "Night watch?"

She nodded.

"I'll go first," he offered.

As I looked at the unwashed dishes, I considered how Boyo hadn't contributed to setting up the tents, preparing dinner, or cleaning up. Perhaps he was unaccustomed to thinking of such things, in his privileged role as an ambassador.

I lay staring up at the slate-colored fabric walls of the tent, as they swayed gently from an outside breeze. Coco lay quietly beside me. Since Boyo had my tent, I was sharing Coco's.

"You miss Joshua?"

"Yes."

"Do you think this will work?"

I presumed she referred to the magic cure rather than the blindfolded passage through The Waterlands.

"I've seen enough magic to believe." Magic thus far had never failed me. "Magic has rules and parameters that have to be followed, but it works. I seldom understand it fully, but it works."

"And what about the cost to Joshua?" Her tone was soft and delicate—out of character for the Coco I knew.

"If it works, then it will be worth the risk of weakening him. If it doesn't work, then he, too, will die of the disease. I'd rather take my chances with the magical cure."

"No matter the cost?"

I turned to stare at her. "What are you getting at?"

"Nothing." She bristled.

Silence settled over the moment.

Wonderful. Another unfinished conversation.

To change the subject, I asked, "What happened with you and Baird?"

"What do you mean?"

I barely suppressed a sigh. "You were courting each other at one point a few years ago. Why did it end?"

"You mean he didn't share those details with his beloved champion?"

"What? No. We may spend time sparring, but I know very little of his personal affairs."

She unleashed a great sigh that deflated her haughty tone. "We have different life objectives."

I waited for her to elaborate, but she didn't. "Are your objectives *so* incompatible?" I asked.

"My devotion is to the Queen. His passion is to travel and cultural studies."

I thought about Baird's books. He'd studied and written about almost every cultural group on Crithos. He said he wanted to explore other continents next.

"Is there no compromise? What if you became an ambassador like Boyo? Traveling to other countries?"

"I'm a warrior not a political figure."

I couldn't argue with her statement. Diplomacy was not a strength she possessed. I could relate.

"Is there anyone else?"

"Truthfully? Relationships within the castle walls are difficult. I never know if a suitor is interested in me, sleeping with the Captain of the Guard, or just gaining a closer audience with the court."

"That's awful."

She chuckled "Yes. Quite right."

"So, one of the few men who has no ulterior motives, Baird, is incompatible because he wants travel and immerse himself in foreign culture. You, meanwhile, must stay near Marrington to protect the Queen. Is that right?"

Coco didn't answer. The tent had grown dark, so I couldn't see her expression.

I continued, "He has a star. He could be with you most evenings, when he isn't sailing the ocean." Since a ship sailed in constant motion, there was no way to transport back to it if he left.

"He suggested as much."

"Then what's your hesitation?"

"You."

"Me?" I jerked my head toward her.

"He adores you, Abigail. You and he share a connection. I can't compete with that."

"You have nothing to compete with! We're friends. Dear *friends*. We have nothing romantic in our relationship, and I'd never be unfaithful to Joshua."

"You and Baird will outlive Joshua and I."

"And I can't stomach the thought of life without Joshua. I can't fathom how I'll survive that unhappy day. But, I assure you, I don't consider Baird a companion in the way *you* suggest."

"And your connection to him?"

She referred to our link, which allowed us to communicate across the world and without others knowing. "It's unusual, and intrusive, and we didn't want it at first, but it has been extraordinarily valuable in times of crisis. We once saved an entire island from a harbor wave because we could communicate with our minds. I couldn't have done it without him."

These days, we mostly used it so he and Joshua could coordinate fishing trips.

I continued, "I assure you, there's nothing romantic about the thoughts we communicate."

"Or the magic stone you gave him?"

"No, I—"

"Or the wolf you gave him?"

"I—" After stammering, I fell silent. I could see how my actions could be misconstrued by another woman.

She chuckled. "You did all of that out of friendship?"

"Yes. Strictly platonic."

"Perhaps I've been overly-jealous."

"You're a beautiful, intelligent woman. You've no reason to be jealous of *me*."

After several long moments, Coco said, "Perhaps I'll speak with Baird."

We let the conversation end there, and went to sleep.

. . .

I WALKED the corridor in my dream, the one with the curtained doors along either side.

Tonight I resolved to find Orrick, the bestower of my latest magical gift.

I pulled back curtain after curtain, trying not to voyeuristically linger too long in the privacy of other people's dreams. One room revealed two carefree teenagers running through a forest. The young man had unruly brown hair and the girl had flowing red hair.

Oh, Baird.

I recognized him in his youth from a prior vision we'd shared. The young girl was Mary—the love of his life, who'd died tragically young. So, it was true—a woman *did* stand between Baird and Coco; only it wasn't me.

I hoped Coco would try a relationship again, and help Baird heal from his loss.

I drew back from the curtain before young Baird could see me.

Continuing down the corridor, I heard a man's voice. "Oh, Abigail."

Puzzled, I pulled the curtain aside. It was Hans, sitting upright in a large bed with silk, cream-colored sheets, while a woman stripped before him. Her nightgown fell to the floor.

His green eyes gazed at her with raw hunger. "Yes, come to me."

The woman complied. I gaped at her—at *me*. Han's dream version of me was flawless, with glossy hair and perfect skin. As she climbed into his bed, I recoiled. I didn't need or *want* this insight into Hans, but now that I knew, there was no unknowing it.

Shuddering, I tried to shake the image of him half-naked and lusting for me out of my head. I'd need to be guarded in our interactions from now on.

I made my peeks into each room briefer and briefer. I didn't find Joshua tonight so I suspected he wasn't sleeping at this moment.

I found Orrick, laying in his bed in his forest home and thrashing. He appeared to be suffering from a nightmare. Small, vicious brownies swarmed over his body, as he twisted and writhed beneath them.

"Orrick?"

He sat up, the brownies tumbling off of him and vanishing into the floor. "Abigail?"

I lifted my palm, the moon tattoo shimmering in the dim light of the forest around us. "Moon magic?"

He grinned with boyish giddiness. "It worked! Yes, you are now a dreamwalker."

I pursed my lips. "Some people's dreams make me want to gouge my eyes out."

He chuckled.

"Any other surprises I need to know about?"

He shrugged. "Spontaneous can be fun."

"And disturbing." I rubbed my eyes.

"I'm experimenting with magic I know scant about, so I'm ill-equipped to fully inform you as to its benefits, dangers—and potential."

I blinked at him, "One might suggest you shouldn't meddle in magic you don't fully understand."

"Bah." He waved a hand at me. "Then there'd be no meddling at all, and the supernatural would go untapped."

"I'm an experiment for you?"

"In a good way—not the way your tone suggests."

I eyed him skeptically. "I can jump into anyone's dream?"

"Anyone you've met."

I thought about my children. I missed them, but wondered if entering their dreams would be something that would bring them joy or turmoil.

"Are you doing okay?" I asked the meddling magician, thinking of his nightmare swarm of brownies.

Orrick's eyes crinkled in amusement. "You have the fate of the world weighing you down and you stop to ask an old man how he is? You've seen the worst of my worries—harmless, well-intentioned brownies."

He clasped his hands together. "Tell me, young champion, are you close to the cure?"

I looked down at the dirt floor and kicked my toe against a root. "Hardly. There aren't an abundance of survivors on Kovia, and the remaining ones we've encountered are fanatics."

As he placed gentle hands on my shoulders, Orrick spoke, "Keep to the quest. I believe in you."

I swallowed, feeling his pale, blue eyes bore into me.

With small retreating steps, I exited his dream. "I want to check on Joshua."

When I entered the corridor again, soft sobs caught my attention. Hesitantly, I drew back another curtain. Goran Foal, warrior turned Kovian diplomat, knelt beside a small bed. A stuffed bear was its only occupant.

Merciful Monks.

Had he lost a child?

I started to turn to leave him to his grieving when his gaze caught mine. "Lady Cross."

"I'm sorry. I didn't mean to intrude."

He stood and walked toward me, wiping at his eyes. "Don't go." He reached for me, clasping my arm.

As his grip closed gently over my skin, his eyes widened. "Are you truly here?"

"I am. I'm a dreamwalker."

—Or so I just learned.

Glancing down at the bed, I felt my heart wrench. "I'm so sorry."

He shook his head. "Gwen is still alive. I was having a terrible nightmare." He squeezed my arm, as if assuring himself I was still here. "You need to be warned about a sickness spreading across Kovia."

I nodded. "I know. The Omega plague has already reached Crithos. All the way to Marrington."

He released me as his shoulders sagged. "Then, there is no hope. My family and I isolated ourselves outside Kovo, but we are ill. My wife is the most dire. We'll die together, as a family. Is your family ill?"

"My husband is ill, my children are safe."

"That is one blessing. Your health?"

I bit my lip, struggling with honesty and the risk of giving him false hope. "I'm in Kovia, between Billington and the Waterlands. A group of us are traveling to the salt mines in search of components for a magical cure."

"Magical cure?"

"This plague struck your continent hundreds of years ago. It was stopped with magic. We're hoping to replicate that."

With a contemplative gaze, Goran stared down at the empty bed in the room. He squeezed the stuffed animal in his hands. "I'm a practical man, but if the champion has magical powers to bring hope through my dreams, then I'll place that hope in a miracle. I will do anything for the life of my children and wife."

I took a step back and narrowed my eyes at him. "I require nothing from you. I'm not a profiteer who uses my skills for a price. I'll do the best I can—that's the only promise I make. I can't even promise this plan will work."

He lowered his hand. "I didn't intend to insult you."

I shook my head. "Don't worry about it."

"The train is the fastest way to the salt mines."

"The train is shut down. We're on horseback. We're cutting through the Waterlands next."

His face paled. "Be careful. Keep your wits about you."

"So, the rumors that they show the future are true?"

"They aren't rumors. The Waterlands show the future. The truth. I had a vision that I would see a woman with bleeding eyes and evacuate my family from Kovo ten years before it happened. The Waterlands are the reason we still live. The danger lies in segments of the future being subject to misinterpretation. Take the segments for the little insight they offer, but don't dwell on them."

His downtrodden spirits clutched at my heart. This once formidable warrior turned self-made diplomat was reduced to waiting for a magical cure, and hoping his family survived long enough to be healed by it.

I sat in a small wooden chair in the dream version of his child's bedroom. Although I couldn't promise I could save the lives of his family, I would at least ease his pain and let him share some stories about them. "Tell me more about your family, Goran."

16

The next morning I woke early and left the tent with my satchel in hand.

I pulled out Isabel's memory puzzle. Although it didn't belong to me, I felt a connection to her through her memories—as though they were in part meant for me. Isabel had been a mother and a wife, with both magic and obligations, and it made us seem so similar. If I was to learn anything from her in the brief time I had access to her memories, I needed to capitalize on it now.

I twisted the device.

I suddenly found myself in her memories.

Isabel sat in a chair, as an attendant wove ribbons through her satin brown hair and another selected the jewels she'd wear.

Her face remained impassive, but with an element of sorrow at the corners of her eyes and mouth. I heard her voice fill the room. "Dinner is with the Emperor of Kovia tonight. How do I face a man I know will be assassinated by the king of Bellos when he returns home? Sometimes, the expansion of my magic to seeing the future is more of a curse than a gift. I probed my options. If I warn the Emperor, and he takes his family into exile, I've seen his fate. He'll be tortured, and his family suffers greatly before their own deaths. If I offer refuge at our castle, he declines and doesn't become an ally owing to his own skepticism and distrust of my abilities. I have no course of action to save him. If I don't tell him, then at least his death will be swift and merciful."

Isabel blinked slowly, and her gaze dropped to her ring finger. "I don't think I'm the wife King Dallik wants me to be. I'm not a docile creature at his beck and call. Not an obedient dog at his heels. I have my own political agenda—one of peace. I sense his frustration at my impudence and my assertions that a road to peace exists. I want to explore magical opportunities while my husband insists on meeting might with might. Since his and his father's methodology hasn't succeeded in ending the war that has raged for nine decades, what delusion would lead him to believe fighting was still a logical solution?"

WHEN I FINISHED THE MEMORY, I returned to our campsite.

It was early morning, and I rekindled the fire and situated a pot of water over it. One by one, everyone woke up. We quietly ate oatmeal, watching the fire. I sipped warm orange spice tea, trying to rid my bones of the cool morning air. Although Coco and I had shared a tent, we hadn't shared much warmth.

I now knew why we'd never become friends. She was jealous of the relationship Baird and I shared. He and I were good friends—the type of friend in whom I'd trust my life and the lives of my children.

Our friendship was born of kinship, made malleable in the volcanic lava of Mulan, and then shaped by the hammers of battle. It was as unbreakable as a Ballik blade and as irreplaceable as a Che stone, but it was in no way, shape, or form *romantic*.

Boyo chucked the remainder of his unconsumed tea on the dying embers and set his cup on the ground. As he stretched, he said, "If we ride steady, we can be near the Waterlands by early afternoon. From there, I'll find my own transportation south to Sylvia."

He turned and walked toward Phobus. He lifted the saddle off a log and laid it across Phobus' back. My horse gave me a half-confused, half-pleading look.

Amused, I stood to help. "Have you never saddled a horse?"

Phobus sidestepped, tilted his back, and let the saddle slide off him and land with a thud on the ground.

I plucked the saddle blanket from inside my tent, where I'd stored it overnight to keep it dry from the morning dew.

Boyo gave an embarrassed smile and took a step back from the horse. "I usually take the carriage, or the stable boys prepare the saddle. I'll watch and learn."

I smoothed the hair on Phobus' back before applying the blanket. After picking up the leather saddle, I knocked the dirt off it and laid it on top of the blanket. I flipped the girth belt over and retrieved it under Phobus. Securing the belt, I looped the leather strap to the saddle.

As I worked, I explained, "You have to make it snug, but the horse knows what you're up to, so he'll puff his chest out. Wait a minute and cinch it a bit tighter when he's not expecting it." I patted Phobus' belly.

He snorted.

Boyo nodded and proceeded to study the belt and loops involved.

With the horse saddled, Hans and I cleaned dishes while Baird and Coco disassembled the tents. Soon, we were mounted, and we trekked east once again. Carrot opted to fly, while Raven rode Fury alongside us.

. . .

Without stopping for lunch, we rode until the horses needed a break. Then we walked further, eating dried berries and nuts while the horses grazed from the side of the road. Even resting, we made onward progress.

Boyo walked beside me. His gaze flickered to Coco ahead of us, and then back to me. "She is a captain, yet I sense you are leading this group as much as she is."

"I'm a servant to the Queen," I replied, aware that my words provided no answer to his unspoken questions. I had no desire to elaborate on my role as Avant Champion to a stranger.

He shook his head slowly. "Crithian culture is vastly different from that of Bellos. There are no women in our armies."

"That's your loss."

He chuckled. "Yes, I suppose so. I'd be intimidated to encounter someone like Captain DeFay on the battlefield. Most of our women stay home, bear children, and teach the next generation."

"I have three children, I teach at Marrington University, yet I can still serve my country on a quest."

His mouth gaped slightly, before the diplomat in him recovered. "You have children?"

Judging by the incredulity in his voice, I suspected he refrained from saying: 'You have children *you're neglecting*?'

I arched an eyebrow.

He gave me an apologetic, though not entirely sincere look. "We do have a warrior class of women, chosen for their prowess for certain tasks. But they don't breed."

Preoccupied, thinking about how absurd he sounded, I couldn't muster a reply. Prowess? Were these women spies? Were they assassins? As far as I knew, Crithos had no such warriors. Did these women warrior not have children because they *chose* not to? Or did someone else chose for them?

"Where are your children now? Who cares for them?"

"My parents."

Boyo fell quiet, his expression suggesting he thought that culturally acceptable. "And their father?"

"He's a healer in the castle."

He leaned closer. "I've heard some healers on Crithos use magic. Is it true?"

I listened to the sound of birds chirping, as I considered an answer to his question. "What does Bellos know of magic?"

He shrugged and added a casual saunter to his walk. "Rumors mostly. Talk of Crithos being a magical hub of sorts. Having magical rocks. Traders tell of a great battle against evil over a decade ago. Apparently, an evil destroyer was slain and magic was involved in vanquishing him."

Uh, yes and no. Magic was involved. Malos was evil, but technically I banished him and didn't slay him.

"And what is your impression of those rumors?" I asked, betraying nothing.

He gave a smirk, conveying to me that he saw truth in the tales—and also saw through my evasive questions. "Sounds fanciful. Stories told to children about an evil-doer named Malos, just so they behave. And yet," he made an odd, absent-minded gesture of tapping his belly, "this plague can only be the work of dark magic."

"Is that so?"

Dark magic? What in the name of Crithos was that supposed to be? The only dark magic I knew of belonged to Mal, and it was fueled by our own evil. Now who was telling scary bedtime stories? Yet, Mal and I both knew the world of man's suppressed evil was changing. Was it because of dark magic somewhere? If Crithos was the land of light magic, was Kovia the land of dark magic?

My mind dizzied with unanswered questions. I needed to consult with Wizard Oak.

"Yes," Boyo replied. "The evil in this land is palpable. Don't you think so?"

I looked at the greenery—trees, grass, and bushes—all around us, and frowned. The cities had been laid to waste and Moontown had been eerie with its ash and bones. However, a dark shroud of death and devastation didn't equate to the presence of dark magic.

"Thus far, I've seen dark deeds done by men. I don't know about any dark magic."

He brushed at his sleeves and straightened his tunic, as if ridding himself of the conversation. "Baird told me he and Hans are monks?"

"That's correct." *Mostly* correct. Hans was still in training. He'd accepted the vows of his order, but his order still needed to accept him.

"And they simply volunteer for quests? They are some sort of philanthropic group?"

"Monks dedicate their lives to helping others. Sometimes it's a quest, sometimes it's cultural studies, sometimes it's education. Sometimes, it's just helping others become monks themselves."

"Peculiar."

AFTER WE FINISHED EATING, we resumed riding at a fast walk. An hour later, when we slowed the horses to let them recover and drink from a small stream, I hopped off Prince from behind Coco and stretched.

I drank water from the stream and watched as Baird approached.

He clasped Boyo on the shoulder. "Tell us about Bellos."

Boyo smiled. "It's a big country. The crowning jewel is Victoria. The capital city has over two-hundred-thousand inhabitants. Traders from all across the world come to sell their wares in the market. The king's estate is made of alabaster stone, and bronze statues pay tribute to former kings. The white structure rises above the city as a beacon of magnificence."

As Boyo knelt to dust dirt off his boot, I wriggled my eyebrows at Baird.

Sounds fanciful, I told Baird. *Do you suppose there's a virgin for every man, and they dine nightly on gold plates?*

Baird didn't reply. I saw only the barest curve in the corner of his mouth acknowledging my comment.

I spoke to Boyo, "Baird has written several books on Crithian culture. Perhaps he could travel to Bellos and write a book about culture in Victoria."

"That would be splendid." Boyo beamed.

We mounted our horses again and set off a brisk pace.

TWO HOURS LATER, we reached the edge of the Waterlands—Boyo's departure point. The road veered north and south, but didn't continue into the Waterlands itself. We dismounted, and Boyo thanked everyone for the food, the company, and the hospitality. He may not know how to wash a dish or saddle a horse, but he'd mastered the art of gratitude.

Boyo handed me Phobus' reigns. "I'm trying to grasp how a group of your making comes together for the quest of finding this cure. Obviously, Captain DeFay is crucial as a warrior and leader. Baird Fox would have the cultural sensitivity for such an excursion, if the population had not been decimated. He brings an apprentice to learn —Hans Stallman. But you're a chemistry teacher, dressed as a warrior. What is Abigail Cross's role in all this?"

Coco stared forward; but from the slight tilting of her head she was keenly interested in my reply.

Hans stiffened. "Abigail is—"

"—a chemistry *professor*," I interrupted him with a smile. I wouldn't have Hans blurting my title out again in some misguided defense of my honor. "I offered to help. My husband tends to the sick as we speak. I hope to end the suffering and protect my family from the spread of the disease."

Boyo nodded, but I sensed disappointment to my response. Perhaps he would have been impressed to know I was the greatest warrior on the continent, with the strength of a giant and the ability to transport almost anywhere I pleased. However, I only trusted a handful of people with my secrets. The last stranger I'd helped in a time of crisis had betrayed me, and cut my stone necklace off my chest, stripping me of my magical strength. I'd not make that mistake again.

Most who knew of my abilities kept in quiet awe of them; but some saw me as either a threat or a challenge, while others revered me to the uncomfortable and inaccurate extent of declaring me a goddess. I'd discovered the hard way that life remained simpler if I ensured I was generally perceived as a mother, or wife, or teacher—nothing anyone might think of as extraordinary.

WE SET off at a run after Boyo departed.

Each day, with less food to carry, the horses' packs grew lighter, and we could stretch their exertion a little longer.

The landscape shifted around us. Trees vanished. Then grass. Soon, the ground became dry and the air moist. When we were within view of the edge of the Waterlands, geysers and ponds became visible in the distance. We pulled the horses to a halt. Carrot squawked seconds before landing on my arm.

"I can lead us," Baird offered. "I'm not afraid of whatever mysteries the future may reveal to me."

"I'm not afraid either," Hans retorted.

I gazed out over the misty land before us. My stomach pitched and rolled. I *was* afraid. I feared the future. Evil was spreading, and Mal and I didn't know why—only that it had began after the volcano erupted.

The only thing keeping me in a bubble of sanity was ignorance about the future of the decline of man. As long as I didn't know, I could pretend it would eventually take a turn for the better. If I learned it would get worse, I'd feel obligated to take action. What would that involve? Less time with my family? More frustrations on behalf of the university?

In addition, no one knew if our cure would work. What if I saw the future and saw that we'd failed? What hope did we have then?

Furthermore, everyone kept reminding me that I would outlive Joshua. I wanted a long life with my husband and my family; yet, I sensed my time with them was a precious, dwindling commodity. I didn't need to see the devastation ahead to know it existed. Mal had once told me Joshua and I had decade upon decade together—so at least I knew I had some time.

Yet, if I didn't offer to lead the group through treacherous land because of my own selfish fears, what was I exposing my friends to?

I can do it, I told Baird. *Mal may be able to protect me from visions of the future. If I haven't gone mad with Mal's company yet, what harm can a few glimpses into the future hold?*

He didn't answer, but I sensed his disapproval at my offer.

Coco stepped forward. "As Captain of the Guard, any information I glean may be helpful to the Queen."

I suspected she offered less to garner information for the Queen and more because her disciplined disposition and staunch sense of control wouldn't allow her to trust anybody else to get her safely through danger while she remained helpless and blindfolded.

"We all stand to gain or lose," Baird said. "We'll draw grass straws for it."

He dismounted and plucked four pieces of long, brittle grass and arranged them in his fist, with the bottom stalk sticking out. "One of these tips is bent at the end. Whoever draws the bent tip will lead us through the Waterlands."

"Apparently, I don't count?" Raven asked.

"My apologies." Baird began to reach for another strand. "Did you want to be part of the draw to see who leads the way?"

"No. I have no interest in the future. Good or bad."

He nodded and straightened. "You are right, though. I should have at least asked."

One by one we picked the grass straws, inspecting for the fine bend on the end.

Coco raised her piece for us to see.

"The captain leads the way," I remarked.

Raven climbed up from Fury's back to sit on Phobus' neck.

We tore off parts of a blanket—at least it wasn't my red cloak this time—to make blindfolds. As we sat on top of the horses, we secured our blindfolds and put our trust in Captain DeFay.

For the first twenty minutes, Coco described what she saw—pools of water and spritzes of moisture. Then, she grew silent.

The hairs on my neck stood on end as I resisted the urge to tear off my blindfold.

"Coco?" Baird called.

Only the sound of gushing water in the distance replied. Beneath me, Phobus continued to walk steadily onward, and I could feel the slight bob of his head and turn of his neck.

"Leave your blindfold on," Baird commanded.

I heard shuffling. Phobus continued walking, but his weight shifted uneasily. I placed a gentle hand on his neck.

"Baird, I'm coming with you," Hans called.

Brilliant.

More scuffling, followed by the sound of hoofbeats. Fury whined briefly and then fell silent.

Baird?

Nothing.

"I guess I'm going to be the last fool to take off my blindfold." I blinked against the bright sun. When my eyes focused, I sat alone on the horse with Raven. How had everyone else vanished?

Baird?

Still no response. As I dismounted Phobus, Carrot took flight. The strange silence was pierced by a distant scream.

"Abigail?" Raven's voice hung on the edge of fear.

"Whatever happens, stay on Phobus. He'll lead you to safety."

"Then why don't you get back on?"

She made a point, but from the ground I hoped to spot footprints or hoofprints to see in which direction everyone had dispersed.

A fierce stream of water suddenly emitted a meter away and tore ten meters into the air. Phobus startled at the sudden violent gush and took off at a gallop with Raven barely clutching at his mane.

The stream of water disappeared as quickly as it had appeared. I looked down at the hole in the ground. "Not particularly frightening."

What *did* frighten me was being able to see in every direction, yet my friends were nowhere in sight.

Phobus and Raven had vanished. The optical illusion reminded me of the Veil Stone, where objects within its magic remained unseen unless one stepped within its umbrella of magic.

I walked carefully, as the soft ground shifted under the weight of my feet. I chose my way between the pools of water and quiescent geysers, focusing on keeping my gaze fixed to the front of me. Around me, the landscape blazed in beautiful pinks and oranges intermixed with blue water reflecting the sky.

As a chemistry teacher, who'd also taken a geology class in college, I knew the colors around the pools of heated water comprised various types of thermophilic bacteria. However—subjectively—the landscape stole my breath. I wondered if Natalie would appreciate the majestic rainbow. She loved color and beauty. When we traveled to market, she was drawn to jewelry, dresses, and ribbons. But I could never bring her here; not with the threat of the dangerous visions.

Abigail, work your way out of the geysers. We can reconvene on the other side. I'm through.

Did you see this magnificent beauty? I asked Baird.

Eyes ahead. No distractions. Don't look at the water.

If Mal was here, he'd marvel in the beauty with me. Prior to his curse, in which he'd become a sponge for evil, he'd lived in confinement in his family castle in Karnelik; born in an age of constant war. He'd never seen a beach, or a waterfall, or a geyser growing up. He'd only known his castle walls and the towering icy mountains behind them.

A blast of water abruptly propelled toward the sky only a meter away from me. I tried to avert my eyes, but I saw Malakai.

"Mal!"

After several days of silence, he'd finally decided to visit me. I stepped my way closer, keeping my gaze on him as he appeared to be standing within the tower of water. Time slowed, causing the water to trickle rather than gushed upward.

Mal's figure was replaced by menacing-looking men in strange clothing, all with long hair. They stood on the shores of Mulan, wearing expressions of hunger and greed.

The scene shifted to Boyo as he sailed across the ocean. With relief, I realized he made his way home to Bellos—or *would* make his way home, as this was a vision of the future. We'd saved his life and freed him, giving him the chance for safe passage.

In the following image, Boyo was freshly bathed and slipping on a clean tunic. His hand caught the jagged edge of a candlestick holder. As blood welled on the surface, he cursed at the minuscule cut. A glow of soft light emitted from his abdomen, beneath his shirt and under the surface of his skin. As it illuminated his skin, the tiny wound healed. Then the smooth, round glow faded. My stomach soured. He had a Che Healing Stone. He'd kept healthy during the plague through magic. Magic he'd hoarded for himself.

Boyo hadn't healed any of the captives who'd been in the shed with him or any of the sick people he'd encountered on his travels. He'd hoarded the magic for himself.

Moments later, Boyo, dressed in fine silk garments, bowed his head before a large bearded man in crimson silk. He sat on a throne of black skulls, forged from iron. The king of Bellos, I presumed. His pale green eyes seemed to reflect a blanched soul, devoid of warmth, and color, and compassion.

"Crithos and Kovia are ripe for the taking," Boyo said, his voice deeper and more sinister compared to the friendly tone he'd used with our group. "They were weakened by something they're calling the Omega plague. But they have magic. Queen Rebekah sent magic bearers to harness a cure. Regardless of whether the cure worked, the continents are weak—we can conquer them."

"Patience Vinchenko. Emerald sees the time is drawing near, but first we must finish building our army and our ships. Our glory will come. We will reestablish the power and global reach once held by Ophelia Bornak."

With another shimmer of water, I saw their massive fleet of ships and legions of armies. I recognized the shores of Marrin beach. They were invading Crithos, in a vision representing the distant future. How distant? Years? Decades? How long would their army take to build? How prepared could Crithos be for such a battle to come?

I thought of my role in the battle. The Avant Champion wasn't created to fight people. Was I? The champion had been devised as a creation to fight Malos—to fight evil forces. While I had killed living beings—giants on southern Crithos, who had been corrupted by a greedy leader—I hated death. I hated considering it a solution to anything. But death would arrive on Crithos at the helm of these giant wooden ships.

I sucked in a deep breath as I stumbled back from the geyser. The world spun around me. As my stomach flipped, I looked at my surroundings. My mouth went dry. I stood alone and had lost all sense of direction.

I walked forward in a hurry, tripped, and plunged into a pool of water. Instead of falling into wetness, I fell through a rainbow tunnel. Bright colors swirled around me as I tumbled through the tunnel.

When I finally slowed to a stop, I saw Natalie, my daughter, kneeling in a shimmering blue and silver gown. Long curls of hair trailed down her back. She appeared older—in her early twenties, perhaps—and she wore an expression of both excitement and apprehension. A young man dressed as a page held out a crown on a red velvet pillow. Aman, Queen Rebekah's counsel, gently lifted the crown with his aged, trembling hands and placed it upon her head as she recited an oath to serve Crithos.

Mother Moon.

Not Natalie. Not my daughter! Not the lifelong commitment to the crown. Being the queen was not an honor—it was a life sentence with the castle as a prison. No mother who'd spent company in the presence of the queen would wish such confinement on her offspring.

This couldn't be true. It *couldn't* be the future.

I ran through the maze of the castle walls. Panic and claustrophobia caused me to hyperventilate. Stairs materialized before me. I took them two at a time. If I could get to the top of the watchtower and get some fresh air, maybe I could regain my wits.

At the top of the stairs, a wide balcony opened beneath a starry sky. I didn't recognize this location as any part of the castle I knew. At the opposite end of the balcony, I saw myself lying limp in Mal's arms. Someone else, someone I couldn't see clearly, lay in a heap on the floor—surrounded by shattered, multicolored glass.

I moved to take a step closer to my vision of myself.

Mal's apparition appeared in front of me, blocking my view. "Don't look, Abigail."

I tried to peer around him. "Why not? What's going on? Am I injured?"

He moved closer, continuing to obstruct my view. "It is your death."

"My—," I stammered.

I turned glaring eyes on him. "Where have you been?"

He looked down at me with a slight grin on his lips, as though my question implied I missed him.

"There were instances where your insight would have been helpful," I explained.

He arched an eyebrow.

I tried to look around him once more.

"Don't." His voice was gentle, with a depth of sorrow I seldom heard from him. "Please."

I stopped and stared at him. I tried to remember if I'd ever heard him say 'please' before. "Okay," I agreed.

"Let me help guide you out of this mirage."

I nodded.

Slowly, he placed his fingertips on my scalp. A tingling sensation spread warmth over my head. Our surroundings dimmed as the sound of gushing water grew louder. Rippling water appeared, as though I stood behind a waterfall looking outward.

As he stepped back from me, Mal jutted his chin toward the water. "Go through there to leave the geysers behind." His tone had turned dismissive.

"Wait. The images I saw. Are they all true?"

"Visions of the future are ... *complicated*. You may see truth but, without context, comprehension is difficult."

"I can comprehend that I saved Boyo's life only to have him encourage his king to invade us. I can comprehend that Natalie takes the crown one day." The images of what I had seen paraded through my head as I talked. "Was I dying in your arms?"

He didn't look at me. He kept his eyes averted to the ground and obscured by dark lashes.

"Mal, how is that even possible?"

"Stop." He barked the word as a command, before looking startled at his own outburst. "Stop," he repeated, in a softer, more pleading tone.

I scanned his face—sadness swirled with anger. "Have you seen my death before?"

He looked into my face, his doleful eyes filled with suffering. "Don't you understand how difficult this is for me?"

I wanted to ask him the same question. This was *my* death we were discussing. Well, attempting to discuss. The way he seemed in genuine pain stole any fury I might have previously summoned to unleash upon him.

"Mal—"

"We can consult Orrick on the matter later. He's better at interpreting the future than I am. Please, *go*."

I turned and walked through the sheet of falling water. Confusion and frustration burned through me. How was my death difficult *for him*? What about the terror it put *me* through? How could he deny my questions about what I'd seen?

Sunlight seared my eyes. After blinking several times, I focused on the surrounding grass.

Grass. Not rainbow-colored soil and pools of water. I had reached safety.

Thanks to Mal. Mal, who'd abandoned me, and then mysteriously reappeared. Mal, who'd nearly cried at a vision of my distant death. *How* distant?

Nope. *Don't make yourself insane thinking about it.*

Phobus trotted to me and gave me a nudge.

"I accept your apology for leaving me. Glad you made out, boy." I scratched an ear and nodded at Carrot and Raven, as both were perched on my saddle.

In the distance, I saw Baird riding toward me on Butterfly. His blindfold hung loosely around his neck like a bandana.

"Abigail, are you okay?"

"A little shaken, but no more or less crazy than when we went into the Waterlands."

"Butterfly went mad. All of my concentration focused on controlling her. I saw no visions."

"Lucky for you."

Fury nudged a wet nose into my palm until I petted him. Raven transferred from Phobus to Fury.

"You saw something. You're still pale from it," Baird said.

I pursed my lips.

"How bad?" he asked.

"Let's just say I wasn't parading through the castle while Marrington's subjects threw rose petals at my feet."

He dismounted and gently grasped my arms. "You want to discuss it?"

I shook my head. "We need to find the others."

I wanted to discuss it with someone who could help me make sense of it. I would have to wait until I could visit Orrick again.

"You don't actually." Coco's tone was brisk as she approached, staring at the scant distance between Baird and I with narrow, twitching eyes.

Hans, looking harried, ambled beside her with their horses in tow.

Baird released me and turned toward the other survivors.

"You can blame me." Coco looked down at us from atop Prince. "Now we're all burdened with images of our future."

"Do you suppose we all saw the same future?" Hans' ears burned red.

Baird gave him a reassuring pat on the shoulder.

Coco took sudden interest in stroking Prince's mane.

I climbed onto Phobus. "Did anyone else see the king of Bellos plotting an invasion of Crithos?"

All three of them stared at me, wide-eyed and open-mouthed in shock.

"I would venture to guess we did *not* all have the same visions."

Hans looked oddly relieved.

Coco's mouth still gaped. "An invasion?"

"An invasion." I leaned forward, signaling Phobus to break into a lope. We headed east.

After a hard, cathartic ride, I slowed Phobus. The setting sun indicated we needed to make camp. Behind us, the sky was turning deep shades of orange and magenta. As I dismounted, tiny crystals crunched beneath my boots. I knelt and scraped pale, pink crystals into my palm. I touched my tongue to the small particles—salt.

"Gross," Raven commented.

On a hunch, I tried to transport and failed.

Coco, Baird, and Hans arrived, pulling their horses to a halt.

"What's wrong?" Hans asked, kneeling beside me.

"Salt crystals. And I can't transport here."

Hans looked to Baird who shook his head. "Nor can I."

"We'll camp here," Coco declared as she dismounted.

"Why can't you transport?" Hans asked.

I stood, rolling the coarse crystals in my palm. "Must be the salt."

Coco rolled out a tent. "You've transported in and out of the ocean. That's salty."

"True. Some other compound or compounds must also be involved."

"And the Black Stag Forrest isn't made of salt," Raven added.

"Also true. But it isn't far from the ocean, and it may have salt layers in the bedrock."

Baird helped Coco setting up the tents. "So, salt and some other compound?"

As I stared at the pink crystals, I thought about the red soil of the Black Stag Forrest. "Iron. The crystals have a pinkish hue and the red soil of the forest is rich in iron. Perhaps the link is a chemical composition involving salt and iron."

"The chemist solves the mystery." Coco said. She stepped back from the assembled tent. "Right now, we need a fire—but we have no wood."

Baird began rummaging through bags for food. "We have a bigger problem. If we can't transport while on these grounds, we'll be delayed in getting the bat back to Marrington. We'll have to ride back toward the geysers before we can deliver the bat to the castle."

"Not *we*," Coco corrected. "Only you or Abigail, since you're the transporters. Abigail is the faster rider. As soon as we have the bat, we send her racing."

I brushed the salt from my hands. "I like the plan."

By nightfall, we'd consumed the last of our rations—salted fish and raw nuts for us, and grain for the horses.

I lay on my back staring up at the stars. They blanketed the sky, looking like thousands of Che stones lit in unison. I ran my hands through Fury's fur as he lay snuggled next to me.

"You want to talk about what you saw at the geysers?" Baird lay on the opposite side of his wolf.

Hans and Coco had already retired to their tents.

"We have no secrets, but it'll be an uncomfortable recounting."

"I don't need to pry. Tell me only if it helps you to do so."

I didn't know how helpful sharing what I'd seen would be, but I wanted Baird to know. "Well, I already mentioned Boyo convincing the Bellosian king to attack us. We have that to look forward to in ... I don't know how many years. Then, at some point, Natalie takes the crown."

"Natalie becomes queen? But that would mean—"

"Queen Rebekah dies? Yes. Well, she is in her seventies."

"But Natalie—"

"I know. She will have to activate the Leadership Stone to prove she's heir to the throne."

The corners of his mouth turned down. "I see you've given this a lot of thought."

"I might have been mentally digesting it when I galloped with Phobus earlier."

"Anything else?" He asked hesitantly.

"My death."

"You're certain? When?"

When? The big question everyone wants answered. How much longer do I have to live? The question no one gets answered—until the very end.

"Not when I'm old and gray—that much I *could* discern. I die in Malakai's arms."

Baird tensed. "Literally, or figuratively?"

"He was *literally* holding me in the vision I saw."

"Did he kill you?"

"No." I recalled the look of devastation on Mal's face. There'd also been a corpse on the ground—a man I didn't see enough of to recognize. "No, and I didn't see who does."

"How is it possible he holds you? I thought you only see him as an apparition."

"I do. I don't see *how* it's possible. We can't physically touch—which is a good thing given the number of times I've wanted to stab him, kick him, or throw rocks at him."

"Your relationship with him. Is it healthy?"

I wasn't sure about healthy, unless I took into account how I wouldn't be alive if it weren't for him. "It is *helpful*. If not for Mal—"

"I know. The volcano and the harbor wave."

"And saving Joshua and Coco from Windish. *And* letting me know of the Omega plague, so I didn't transport to Joshua's clinic and infect myself."

Baird scratched at some grayish brown stubble on his chin. "Definitely helpful. Did you ask him about the vision you saw?"

"Yes. He was ... evasive."

"Fascinating."

"Don't you mean infuriating?"

"Well, he's already demonstrated he'll save you at every opportunity. If Mal's avoiding this particular vision then perhaps he can't affect the outcome."

"Fascinating," I grumbled.

"Can you pin him down on *why* he's avoiding a discussion about this particular outcome?"

I couldn't pin Mal down on anything. "I'm planning to ask Orrick about it."

"Very well. Let's get some sleep. Final quest day tomorrow. The good news is you already know you'll live through it."

18

That night, I used my dreamwalking skills and found Joshua's dreams.

Peeling back the curtain of the doorway, I watched him sitting at the desk in his clinic—the one that no longer existed, burned to the ground—as he wrote in a journal by candlelight. His smooth jaw glowed tan and his eyes focused on his task.

"Even in your dreams you're working."

Joshua turned to me, and cocked his head to one side. "Aren't you a sight for sore eyes!"

The heat in his expression sent a thrill through my body. As he stood, I walked closer.

"I miss you, Joshua."

"Oh, Abbey." He pulled me into his arms. "I wish you were here. I wish this wasn't only a dream." He buried his face in the hair on my neck.

"I am here. As much as I can be. I'm intruding on your dream."

"You feel real." He crushed his body against mine, his erection pulsating into me.

I gasped as his warm hands slid under my shirt and caressed my back.

Looking into my eyes, he asked, "Are you really here?"

"It's a new skill I've acquired."

He kissed me, soft lips and tongue turning from gentle to exploratory to hungry.

"Please, Abbey, let me have you."

"You already do." In seconds, our clothing vanished, and I pressed against his hot, bare body.

His kisses grew passionate and fierce as his hunger turned Joshua savage. I missed him and missed his touch. I wanted him to take his fill of me and leave nothing left.

His touch and his lips caressed the skin at the nape of my neck until he worked his way to my breasts. I gasped as he licked.

When he lifted me up, I wrapped my legs around him and sank my fingers into his hair.

He released a throaty growl that danced along my spine. Our desire escalated as flesh on flesh created heated friction. At last, he drove into me, filling me with ecstasy. He thrust faster, encouraged by my groans of delight. The dream world we shared burst in a thousand brilliant colors as we climaxed together. I floated on waves of effervescent pleasure outside myself.

When I finally reassembled myself, I opened my eyes to the soft glow of bioluminescent light. I lay comfortably on warm furs inside a dim room smelling of cinnamon and sandalwood. Joshua lay on his side with his bare chest exposed, his mouth held in a slight smile. I tried to decipher his expression. Relief. Love. Arousal.

I smiled back at him as I took a long leisurely stretch. He reached out for me and heat rushed through my body at his touch. As he scooted closer, Joshua whispered my name, his breath warm on my neck. He brushed hair away from my throat, sending a tantalizing shiver down my spine.

"I miss you," I said.

"Will you be back soon?"

"We're at the salt mines. I hope to be back before dusk tomorrow."

"Stay with me tonight."

"All night," I promised.

He curled his body around me.

I jolted awake. The first rays of morning sun lit my dark, barren tent, streaming through the sewn slits in the fabric.

I sat up on the hard, unforgiving ground—still wearing the tunic and leggings I'd gone to bed in.

Fury whimpered and nuzzled into my tent.

"Come in, boy."

He crawled on his belly as he wormed his way in and over to me. I wondered why he wasn't with Baird, but was glad for the company. I ran my hands through his fur.

"Lucky wolf."

I looked up to see Mal had appeared in my tent.

He sat on the ground, regarding me with his dark eyes. "You're glowing."

"I am not." I looked down at my arms to see a gentle white glow illuminating from my skin. Okay, so I *was* glowing.

I turned my gaze back up to Mal. "To what do I owe the honor of the reappearance of my absent apparition?"

He cocked his head to one side. "Testy much?"

I glared at him. "Unless you've got a comfortable mattress and a spare blanket in your pocket, you may go."

His playful expression vanished. "I came to explain the visions. Well, I came to explain that I don't *have* an explanation. I don't know anything more about what you saw than you do. You were dying. I was holding you. I don't know when, or how, or why."

"Why didn't you say that in the Waterlands? Why shove me away?"

"Because it doesn't make sense."

"I can't make sense of half the things that happen in life, but I don't take it out on you."

His lips curled in a slight smile, but his eyes were still sad.

"Look. I'm grateful for all of the times you've helped me," I told him. "I don't expect you to have all of the answers, even though you like to act like you know everything."

He regarded me through dark lashes.

"Friends give reassurance to each other, not dismissive moodiness." I continued, "I don't want to die, and I certainly never wanted to see my own death, but death is inevitable for all of us. As deaths go, it didn't look terrible. I wasn't screaming in pain or falling into boiling lava. I'm not upset with you—unless you're the one that kills me. You're not, are you?"

"I am not."

"Then stop looking like you feel responsible." I shrugged. "I'll talk to Orrick about it and see if he has any insight."

"As you wish."

I changed the topic. "I want to show you something. I'd have done it sooner if you hadn't been off sulking for days." I pulled out Isabel's memory glass.

When I twisted it and aligned different symbols, a new memory flooded me. In this memory, I saw young Malakai dressed in fine silks of red and gold. His hair was a dark mop of curls and his face was smooth and bright. In the great hall around him, music played and people in lavish clothing danced. I could almost feel the merriment of the activity—like heat from the sun.

"My son." Isabel beamed. She took her husband's hand in hers. "My king has given me the greatest gifts of my life—my sons. Malakai celebrates his 16th birthday today. I'm amazed at how time has flown."

"Our wonderful sons," the king remarked, interrupting Isabel's narration briefly.

Isabel continued, "How many times over the years have I felt like an insufficient mother? As I struggled to balance royal duties with magical studies and raising children? Perhaps I've succeeded despite my own self-doubt and worries."

Malakai approached his mother with gleaming eyes. After a bow, he extended his hand. When his mother accepted, he led her to the dance floor where they began to waltz. The scene of the mother and son dancing looked so beautiful, I felt my eyes well with tears.

I emerged from the memory to the dim tent, Fury beside me. "You weren't with me?"

"I'm right here," Mal said.

"But you didn't join me in Isabel's memory."

"My mother's memory?"

"The cylinder holds her memories. A turn and alignment of symbols takes me into her memory."

"I saw you staring at it, but you didn't move or transport anywhere."

I frowned. "I hoped you'd be able to see her, hear her. This last one was your sixteenth birthday."

He looked at his hands and fidgeted.

"I'm sorry. I meant to share a memory with you, not torture you with it. She adored you. Maybe you have to be touching the glass for the memories to transmit."

His jaw tensed before he looked up at me, dark eyes glistening. "I adored her." His throat bobbed in a swallow. "We danced at that party."

"It looked wonderful." I knew what it was like to lose a parent. I had lost both for a decade until fate reunited me with my mother. My father was lost forever. My brother was lost forever.

Mal stood. "Well, your troops are stirring. Best get moving."

As Mal vanished, I threw off my covers to ready myself for the day. The last day of the quest.

I WATCHED Raven as she sat on Phobus' neck. The feathers in her hat captured the sun and shimmered a gleaming black and dark green.

"I'm glad you came."

She turned and blinked at me. "Me, too."

As Raven turned back, she added, "What happens when we get the bat?"

"We race back to the castle and become heroes."

She snorted.

"You don't want to be a hero?" I suffused my voice with incredulity.

Raven turned back around on the horse, situating herself to ride backward. She scowled contemplatively.

I waited for her snarky response.

"You're a legend among the brownies. Red Goddess. Hero of men. Slayer of Malos. Freer of Wizard Oak. I always thought—who wouldn't want to be Abigail Cross? But this trip has been a revelation. My eyes opened to the risk you take with your life and the pressure you're under to succeed. Too much expectation rides on the shoulders of the Avant Champion."

My expression softened. "The quests are hard and the demands can be crushing—emotionally and physically—, but I have a wonderful marriage and three wonderful children. I enjoy my university work. All of the challenges I've had make the other aspects of my life all the more precious."

She arched an eyebrow. "Your outlook is brighter today than it was at the beginning of this trip."

I thought about my night with Joshua and coughed to cover my blush. "That's because it's almost over. Before sunset, we'll have the quest complete." Then, I wouldn't have to invade Joshua's dream to make love to him.

Raven glanced at Coco as she rode Prince. "Seems Coco and Baird are reuniting."

"Are they?" I looked toward them. Their horses walked close, but they rode in silence.

"You apparently didn't hear the noises coming from their tent."

"Uh, no." I grinned. "That's good, though. They need each other."

Raven smirked. "They can need each other more quietly next time."

I stared at the cave entrance across the water. We had arrived.

I tried to smell and savor the salt on the air, but the humidity was so low that the scent was faint. We were one captive bat away from returning home.

I stood at the edge of the moat. The water's stillness crisply reflected the blue sky; and it was so flat it appeared as if I could have walked across the glassy, azure surface. A hundred meters south, a small boat with oars sat on the shore.

A ripple coursed through the water—something had moved within the depths of the moat. Taking a step back, I positioned my hand to the hilt of my sword. Probably a fish—but I was on edge after three days of travel, not to mention seeing a vision of my own death.

A large, pink, moist limb lashed toward me. Carrot took flight with a screech of alarm.

"Look out!" Coco shouted.

I watched as the rubbery tentacle sailed past me. A second one reared out of the water toward me, knocking me off my feet. As a third rose into the air and came crashing down. I rolled aside, barely out of reach. The ground shook as the great heap of slimy limb struck where I'd been lying a moment earlier.

Another tentacle had ensnared Hans. A scream emitted from his lips. As the beast tightened its hold, Hans's face and neck began to turn plum colored. With the tentacle cinching around his torso, his arms were trapped. His scream cut short.

Taking a running start, I pulled out my sword and leaped. I slashed at the flailing tentacle. As I brought my sword down, I sliced through the meaty, octopus-like arm.

Hans plummeted to the ground, but landed on his side on top of the tentacle as it loosened its hold. As he gasped for air on the ground, Coco and Baird battled other limbs. Fury snapped his canines, snarling at the slithering appendices. With the injury to one arm, the other squid-like limbs began writhing wildly.

As things stood, we were four against seven. I swung my blade at a tentacle, missing it. I tried to see the body of the beast in the water. The arms churned the water so ferociously I couldn't see a clear target. I wished I had more paralytic Black Marsh adder venom.

Can you talk to it? I asked Baird.

You don't want to know what it's thinking.

A blur of tanned skin and blond hair streaked past me and dove into the lake. With her sword leading the way, Coco plunged at the body of the octopus. She vanished beneath the gurgling surface.

As I gaped at where she'd disappeared, one of the tentacles grasped my waist and squeezed. I pierced the flesh with my sword, causing the limb to release me and flail spastically.

Suddenly, the chaotic motions subsided to small twitches and undulations and the many tentacles flopped flaccidly to the ground. The creature's arms rested limply, their rubbery undersides exposed, as though it died in prayer with open arms.

Coco emerged from the moat gasping for air. She was covered in salt water and thick yellow sludge that I could only assume was the giant octopus's blood. Baird and Han's helped her out of the water.

I sheathed my sword and smiled. "Well done. DeFay the Squid Slayer. No, that won't do. We'll need a more catchy title for when Baird writes about you in his narrative."

I took a step forward, but halted and raised my sleeve to my mouth. "*Mother Moon*, the stench." The creature's fluids smelled like a mixture of putrid fish, excrement, and sulfur.

After releasing Coco, Hans washed his hands in the water, trying not to let Coco see him gag.

Raven choked. "It's like someone wrapped a rotten egg in a rotten filet of fish and then partially digested it."

"You're welcome," Coco sneered.

"Hans and I will go fetch the bat."

"Splendid." Coco began peeling away layers of saturated clothing. "I'll be spending that time trying to get the smell out of my hair."

I glanced at Baird, whose silent nod conveyed he'd stay with Coco so no member of our team was left alone.

"Raven, can you watch the horses?"

From atop Phobus' back, Raven gave me a salute.

Be careful, Baird spoke in my mind.

You as well, she says with a wink.

He didn't reply, but I thought I heard a chuckle.

Hans and I walked along the edge of the moat until we reached the small boat. We climbed in and began to row across the shimmering blue water.

"Sometimes, I feel like you and Baird have unspoken communication."

"Is that so?"

Since being an unwitting viewer of Han's dream of me, I'd distanced myself from him. I was likely overreacting, since people surely had random dreams about those with whom they traveled. Dreams were not always the innermost reflections of a person's desires.

I watched the water for any unusual ripples, hoping that only one such enormous octopus occupied this area. We reached a small dock on the opposite side of the moat and tied off the boat to one of the posts.

Carrot swooped down and landed on my arm. I stroked her feathers. As we walked through the cave entrance, I was awestruck by the beauty. The white and gray salt had been ornately carved to make a rigged, dome ceiling. Carved steps led deeper into the cave. Along the right-hand wall, white figures in hooded cloaks had been carved to form a semi-circle of statues, all gathered around the carving of a man lying in bed. The background held the night sky, with the two moons carved into the surface—mother and infant moons.

"Mal," I whispered faintly, running my fingertips along the supine figure. My clever, infuriating friend.

"Do you love him?" Hans appeared beside me.

"What?" I lowered my hand and stepped back from the ornate decorative scene etched in salt and stone.

"Do you love Baird?"

I hadn't realized we were still on the topic of Baird. When I looked into Hans's dark green eyes, they were blended with a mixture of dread and anticipation.

"Of course. He's my friend. And he's been a mentor."

The tension in Hans' face eased. "What does the mural represent?" He turned to look at the wall.

"It's the transformation of Malakai to Malos. Legend says he was on his deathbed, with the forces of Bellos closing on Karnelik, when he took the mantle to be Malos—forever ending war."

Until the forces of Bellos march on Crithos again.

I found a stack of old crates and set Carrot down to perch on them. "I don't think you want to go any further, girl. We'll be back."

I'd crawled through orifices smaller than her wingspan in some caves, and I didn't know how small the paths we'd be expected to traverse might get.

As Hans and I walked deeper into the cave, our surroundings darkened.

Hans pulled out a jar of bioluminescent algae from his satchel. "When we find the bat, we're going directly back to the castle?"

Blue green light cascaded over the walls and floor.

"The sooner we get back, the more lives we save."

Further down the tunnel, the cave lost its sculptured appearance. The walls became rough-hewn, textured with coarse grains of solidified salt intermixed with stalactites and chandeliers.

"Will we see more of each other?"

I frowned at his odd question. "I visit the sanctuary all of the time, and you know where to find me at the university." I thought of Joshua and our lives returning to normal—well, as normal as possible with children and careers. As normal as possible with war coming.

Hans had fallen silent.

"There may be another adventure," I offered.

Or we may see each other in the battle to come.

He smirked. "Says the Avant Champion, who despises adventure."

"I love adventure." I gasped in feigned shock. "I hate the death and destruction that necessitates it. I like more contained adventures —climbing Mount Karn, spelunking in Optato, saving gypsies after an avalanche, tangling with jewel thieves in Ntajid. The more grandiose—fighting Malos, fighting Hunju giants, stopping a plague —are marred by devastation."

"You've done all of those things?"

"Yes."

I thought of the simplicity of a quest. When I performed each of those tasks, I had one objective and a narrow focus. Life required less juggling, fewer expectations. My efforts weren't divided among multiple facets vying for my time. When I wasn't on a quest, multiple obligations bled, overran, and distracted from each other to the point that each obligation was left wanting, and I was left feeling inadequate.

"You find love after Joshua."

I coughed and cleared my throat. "I beg your pardon?" This was not a conversation I wanted to have with any young man.

"In the geysers, I saw you with someone else."

"I don't like to think about my life when Joshua is gone. This is not an appropriate conversation for us."

His chattering would distract us from hearing any other lurking beasts. What if the squid was the first of more creatures guarding the cave?

"I'm sorry, Lady Cross. I thought the idea might give you some peace. Some hope." He lifted the jar of light higher.

"It doesn't." My tone was sharp enough to cut glass and, I hoped, to silence Hans.

"Do you know who—"

"Shhh." I strained to listen to the faint sound of running water.

As we walked deeper into the bowels of the cavern, the cave took on an appearance more like an abandoned tomb than a source of salt.

"Whoa!" Hans grabbed me by the shoulder, preventing me from walking farther.

The ground beneath us had suddenly vanished. I stood on the edge of a dark abyss.

A wave of sickening vertigo had me stumbling backwards. I wasn't afraid of heights, but as I'd nearly plunged to my death, I had to swallow back my terror.

"Thank you," I stammered.

Hans grinned.

I stared at the giant crevice in amazement. "It must have a been a cave-in."

Hans held is bioluminescent jar higher. "Do you suppose the cave-in unleashed the plague?"

"It's a good theory." An *excellent* theory. I thought about my dance with Goran at the spring festival in Marrington. He'd described an earthquake that had devastated eastern Kovia. The earthquake could have sent deep tremors as far south as the mines, and opened this crevice—unleashing the long-dormant plague.

"We'll have to climb along the ledge to the other side."

I assessed the sheer face of the rock as Hans held the light high. The tunnel continued on the opposite side, about ten meters below the level of our current platform. The distance between them was too far to jump, and the wall face looked jagged enough so that we could find holdings for fingers and boot tips.

It would be like climbing Mount Karn, and unlike the last rock face I clung to, at least there'd be no blizzards and wolves.

We started our descent. Hans led the way, trying to juggle the jar of glowing algae in one hand and grip the wall with the other.

Half way around the semicircle, Hans fumbled the jar. As it slipped from his fingertips, he extended his reach. His footing faltered, and he fell.

Hans screamed. I snatched out a hand and barely grasped his wrist. Grunting, he extended his other arm to clasp my outstretched hand.

I strained with the weight of him, using the power of the Warrior Stone to cling to the wall while hoisting Hans in mid-air.

When his jar of algae hit the floor below, it shattered, splattering blue green light across the bottom of the pit. A bed of skulls and long bones littered the floor. We hovered above a grave, or a crypt—one where bodies had been cast haphazardly into a pit. All that remained of the dead, after what I presumed to be hundreds of years, were brittle bones.

I squeezed my eyes shut and I focused on keeping my grip. The distance of the fall would likely break body parts, and I didn't have a rope to pull Hans back out again.

My muscles strained and my arm stretched. Any moment, Han's dangling weight would fully dislocate my shoulder. Shifting my weight, I brought my arm back and swung him like a pendulum.

On the third swing, I gave him warning through gritted teeth. "Brace yourself."

When I released him, he flew through the air and landed on the opposite side of the tunnel. He cried out, but I could faintly discern him rolling in the dark and standing uninjured.

I finished the climb, mostly by feel since our light lay sprawled at the bottom of the pit. At last, I reached the other side.

"Thank you." Hans placed a hand briefly on my shoulder.

"We're even." I rubbed at my shoulder. The hyperextension was going to result in a few days of pain.

He nodded with a lopsided grin, and we resumed walking, relying on the scant glow of my red stone.

As the cave opened into a cavern, I heard faint squeals and fluttering. Bat noises! The light from my stone couldn't reach the walls and ceiling of this enormous room.

"We need more light."

"You got any more magic tricks?" He asked.

"Magic." I looked at my hands and the moons on my palm. I remember the way I glowed in the tent last night and the catacombs of Karnelik. "Moon magic." As I focused on glowing, white light spread evenly over my skin and radiated outward. I rolled my sleeves to enable more light to glow from me.

Hans blinked. "You look amazing!"

The white glow illuminated the ceiling, looming five meters above us. Hundreds of small, black forms dangled from the ceiling. The sheen of their fine fur shimmered in the light of my glow, and the bat's eyes reflected light back to me like little red stars.

"We need to capture one, and I can't transport up and grab it."

"How do we lure them down?"

"Bats eat insects, but their cave has no vegetation, so we won't find any bugs around here for them. We'll have to have help." I whistled for Carrot.

The trip, which had taken Hans and I a half-hour, took the hawk two minutes. As she circled the room, her attention stayed focused on me.

I pointed to the ceiling. "Fetch."

As she flew higher, the bats panicked. The room burst with flapping wings. Carrot was a shark among a school of fish. The small animals swooped down from the ceiling and swarmed around in dizzying panic.

To his credit, Hans didn't cower but tried to capture one with his hands. The bats spun and dodged.

Carrot clutched a small animal as she made her approach.

I unclasped the cape from my shoulders. As she swooped, she released the captive animal. Quickly, I trapped the corners of the cape together and tied them off. The bat stuck inside hit the fabric repeatedly trying to escape.

Sorry. You're the unlucky one.

That they were harbingers of disease was no fault of their own.

"I've got one!" Hans cried.

"In the cape," I instructed him. I was ruining another red cape.

He shoved the small creature in the makeshift sack.

"Let's go." I held the sack closed as I dashed back up the incline and began the climb. My limbs burning from the effort, I pulled myself up the ledge. When I saw that Hans was safely up the ledge as well, I dashed up the steps of the mine.

The exit presented itself—glorious sunlight.

We were so close to finishing this mission. I needed to get free of the salted ground in order to transport.

We stumbled out of the mine and down towards the water. Hans and I reached the boat and shoved off the shore. We rowed as fast as we could, biceps and triceps burning with the effort.

"We've got a bat!" I called to Baird, when we neared the opposite shore.

He stood with horses ready. Coco was clean and sitting astride Prince. Carrot flew above us.

As I leaped out of the boat, my feet hit the ground with a crunch of rock and salt.

"Go," Hans instructed, as he pulled the boat to dry ground and secured the oars.

I ran to Phobus and mounted her in haste. As I took the reins from Baird, I held the makeshift sack containing the squirming bats close to my body.

Raven watched from Fury's back.

"Ride with the wind," Baird said. "If we fall behind, I'll transport everyone. Get to the castle."

I nodded, then spurred Phobus to a gallop. We thundered across the flat, dry ground, and as I clung to the reins, my thoughts turned to Joshua.

Four days. He'd still be alive, even if he was ill with the disease. The sooner he had the ingredients, the sooner he could heal himself. Heal the castle.

As my horse's hooves pounded like thunder, they churned the salty ground.

Bless you Phobus, for responding to my urgency.

Twenty minutes into the ride, I knew I was pushing my mount harder than I ever had. Sweat frothed on Phobus' neck and his nostrils flared.

The ground beneath us transformed from the alkaline salt and iron, sparse of vegetation, to fine strands of grass. After slowing Phobus to a halt, I dismounted.

"Rest, boy. I'll be back for you."

I transported and instantly appeared back in the deliberation room.

The room had been rearranged, with beds standing where benches had once been, to accommodate the Queen and several other sickly ministers. Guards were posted around the periphery, some looking strong and others as though they might collapse at any moment. To my relief, the Queen still lived. Joshua sat in a chair beside her, looking pale and ill with bloodshot eyes. My stomach lurched to see him so fragile.

On a small, round marble table in the center of the room, two stones sat—the beefy, red Blood Stone and Joshua's black and white

Healing Stone. No third stone. A porcelain bowl rested beside them. Everything appeared carefully arranged, waiting for this moment. Waiting for my arrival.

As two of the guards reached toward me, I relinquished the sack with the bats. Having exhausted themselves, the small animals curled in motionless balls.

"Where is the third stone?"

"They were unable to secure the Wind Stone," Tarik said grimly.

One of Captain DeFay's lieutenants stared at the floor.

If we didn't have the Wind Stone, we had no way to heal anyone beyond this room. Thousands—hundreds of thousands—would die.

"What was the problem?" I asked.

Lieutenant Jok looked up at me. His eyes shone bright against his dark skin. "Those guarding it were able to use the Wind Stone to fend us off. It's like trying to walk through a tornado. It's an impenetrable defensive wall of wind."

I couldn't blame the stone owners. If a raiding party arrived to steal my stone, I'd object as well. Judging by the dirt stains smeared on his clothing and armor, Lieutenant Jok had put up a fight—or at least been the equivalent of a tumbleweed in a tornado.

I placed a hand on Jok's arm. "Imagine the closest, safest place you were able to reach before you met resistance."

As I transported with him, I felt the instant humidity of a tropical climate. Around us, giant red cedar trees, banana trees, and rubber trees towered over us. Their thinly-barked trunks rose and then arched above us. Broad leaves formed a great, looming, green canopy. Beads of water pooled and fell from the leaves, evidence of a recent rain.

I swatted a mosquito that squatted on my arm before he could suck his fill. "The stone is here?"

Joe jutted his chin forward. "Through that patch of bamboo."

"Is this as close as you got?"

"Through the forest are ancient ruins atop a hill." He lowered his eyes. "We only made it a fourth of the way up the stairs before the winds hit."

We walked through the bamboo on a narrow, muddy path. As we walked, the wind blew above us. The hollow, pale-green stalks struck each other, creating an almost melodious sound.

After a short walk, the bamboo forest ended and a giant hill rose above us.

Jok halted. "The ruins and stone are at the top."

I squinted up. Dense foliage obscured the path. I couldn't transport to it if I couldn't see where to put my feet.

"I'll take it from here." I clasped a hand on his shoulder. "I'm going to take you back to the castle now, because once I have the stone, I'll transport from wherever I'm standing directly to the deliberation room."

Swiftly, I deposited Jok back to the castle and then transported instantly back to the forest. I circled the base of the hill, until I saw a small ledge several meters above ground. If I started there, then perhaps I could see where to transport next. Star traveling would be faster than climbing this beast of a hill one step at a time.

I transported and appeared on the face of the rock. I gripped the ledge with my fingertips and positioned the toes of my boots on another ledge, only centimeters wide. As soon as I completed that journey, my fingers slipped on the wet, mossy rocks. I fell backwards. Rather than plummet ten meters onto the ground, I transported two centimeters from it. As my back hit the hard surface, I released a grunt.

"*Crithos.*" I coughed and swore. "Fine. We do this the hard way."

I removed my boots, sword, vambraces and breastplate. I needed speed and agility more than protection—although I still kept the small dagger Hans had given me.

Then, I climbed. The trail was a slick mixture of mud, stone, and fallen branches. It wrapped around the hill, the turns preventing me from seeing my destination and transporting there.

"Abigail, why don't you go ahead and collect *all* of the stones? Easy as slicing pumpkin pie." I shook my head. Mal wasn't here, and yet I was still talking to myself. I decided to blame it on exhaustion.

Wind picked up pace and hurled in bursts from atop the hill, causing trees to sway and leafy plumage to smack against my skin relentlessly like a hundred tiny whips. On one side of the hill, I reached a ledge where the trail had washed out.

I gripped the slick rock with my fingertips and toes. I used the Warrior Stone to keep my grip against the fearsome wind trying to force me to fall. A delicate balance ensued. If I gripped too fiercely, the rock would crumble beneath the crushing grip of my strength-enhanced fingers. If I gripped too lightly, the wind would win and whip me straight off the side of the rocky outcrop.

I climbed, slowly but surely, and when I finally reached solid ground again, I took off at a sprint. My muscles protested and burned. I *definitely* needed more running in my conditioning routine. Did I even have a routine? I had a haphazard approach to training, which took place when I had time and wasn't exhausted from the children and work.

So, first, I *needed* a routine. Then, to add more running to it.

The path ahead of me cleared. Above, I could see more of the trail —as well as one rose-colored wall of what must be ancient, stone ruins. I transported up one level of stairs and froze, listening as I tried to catch my breath.

The wind ceased.

I walked forward the last few steps. A full view of the ruins emerged. They were a towering monstrosity of pinkish, golden stone, partially obscured by rogue vines. The ceiling had collapsed in several areas, and a large, gaping hole stood where the front entrance had once been.

Men wearing cotton dresses hollered in surprise at my appearance and scurried to block the entrance to the ruins. It was clearly a protective gesture on behalf of whoever wielded the Wind Stone. The men held short, broad swords in one hand and gold-painted shields in the other.

Behind them, a tall woman rose from a dilapidated throne and strode down the steps towards me. She barked at me in a language I didn't understand. Her gold jewelry glinted in the sunlight, and she wore the same brown dress as the men.

"I speak Crithian," I said, speaking between gasps of air, since I was still breathing hard from the climb. "Quite the summer home you have here."

One of the men translated for her.

The woman stared at me with a puzzled expression. I imagined I hardly looked like a threat—clothes smeared in mud, my feet bare and bleeding, and my wet hair clinging to my neck.

She spoke through her translator. "I am the Goddess of Wind, and you're trespassing on sacred ground."

Her men leveled their swords at me.

The air around her began to swirl, spinning her hair and leaves wildly. I saw the glowing stone in her hand.

I sighed. "I'm the goddess of I-don't-have-time-for-another-fanatic-with-delusions-of-grandeur." I transported, and instantly appeared behind her—the blade of my dagger pressed to her throat and my arm around her torso. She gasped in surprise.

I'd need to remember to thank Hans for the dagger.

"You want to play goddess?" I hissed. "Come with me and save some lives instead of hiding out here with a bunch of men who don't know what you really are—just a girl with a stone."

As her translator spoke the words, he reached to pull a short sword from his belt. I pressed the blade into her skin. Wind Goddess —as she dubbed herself—lashed out a hand and grasped his wrist, halting him.

"Now that we're all touching ..." I transported the three of us to the castle.

WHEN WE ARRIVED in the deliberation room, I introduced the latest arrival. "This is the self-proclaimed Wind Goddess and her translator."

The woman and her translator took one one look at the assembled group of armed and armored royal guards and meekly decided not to resist.

The two of them were ushered to the table with the bowl and

other stones. I took a few steps back and bumped into a chair. With rising relief, I sank into it. The guards took the Wind Stone and secured the woman and man, who still seemed stunned by being transported who-knew-how-many-kilometers to an unfamiliar room in an unfamiliar castle.

Baird, Coco, and Hans had arrived at some point while I was retrieving the Wind Stone. I didn't see Raven and suspected she was still back in Kovia, watching the animals.

Tarik took a bat out of a cage. He made a nick and drained blood into the bowl. I was surprised to see him get his hands dirty, and wondered who it was he loved that was ill ... other than himself.

After Joshua placed the Blood Stone in the bowl, he rested his hand on the Healing Stone. A woman, a gray-haired minister I hadn't formally met, stood beside him and activated the Wind Stone with her touch. All three of the stones began to glow.

I closed my eyes and prayed. I pleaded silently to the Unideit for this miracle to work. I prayed for my loved ones, my leaders, to be healed with the magic.

Baird, Coco, and Hans walked closer to me. Hans found an empty wall where he could see the room, leaning back and folding his arms. Baird sat beside me, and Coco stood on my other side.

"Well done, Abigail," Baird commented.

I felt too exhausted to do more than grunt.

The luminous stones grew brighter, bathing the room in yellow, red, and blue light. As they shone, wind spun in a circle around Joshua. Breathtakingly beautiful streams of healing rays fanned out, touching the people around Joshua. The Queen's pallor resolved almost instantly; the rash and weeping eyes clearing even as we watched. The rays of brilliant light twisted and spun out the windows, and far off into the distance.

My heart lifted. The magic was working, healing the kingdom. Joshua was succeeding. My gaze fell upon him. He appeared gaunt and pale. His sandy brown hair was turning white, streak by streak. My breath hitched and my chest tightened.

"Wait!" I pushed to my feet.

"Restrain her," Tarik snapped.

The guards descended upon me. The first man that tried to seize me took a shove with the full force of the Warrior Stone. He flew into two others, knocking them down. Joshua, focused on healing, seemed oblivious to the fighting.

"Stop! It's killing him!" I glowered at the other soldiers as they advanced. They were no match for me and the fury rising within me. How dare this room of people have no qualms in sacrificing Joshua.

Baird stood to one side, facing a group of soldiers and preparing to defend me.

I felt a cold blade against the back of my neck. It twisted against my skin, cutting my necklace. The stone fell to the wood floor with a sickening thud. As I reached for it, a black boot kicked it across the floor and out of my reach. Coco's boot. I felt the betrayal as solidly as if she'd plunged the knife between my shoulder blades.

Baird gasped. "Coco, what are you doing?"

"My job."

She tried to grab me, but I struck an elbow to her cheek. Coco stumbled back.

I'd deal with her later. Now, I needed to save Joshua. I turned back toward him. I'd have to transport to him and then transport the both of us to safety.

A hand clamped over my wrist, moist and gritty. I tried to transport and failed. I looked down in shock at Coco's grip. Salt. She'd coated her hand in salt from the salt mines!

A guard grabbed my shoulder. I brought a knee into his abdomen. As he stumbled back, I kicked, striking his jaw. He fell to the floor with a grunt.

"Wait!" Baird cried. He stepped between me and the other advancing guards.

As they unsheathed their swords, he raised his baton and prepared to fight. Hans shrugged up from the wall, to his mentor's aid.

I twisted in Coco's grasp, but she held firm. Even when I kicked a vicious blow to her ribs, she held firm.

In the distance, Joshua grew paler and weaker. White hair danced in the wind as his skin withered.

I rounded on Coco again, screaming in fury, and I punched her face directly on the red, swelling mark my elbow had left. She fell back, releasing me.

I tried to transport again and failed. Looking down at my red, inflamed wrist, I could see it was still coated in salt crystals.

Pain, as ferocious as my skull splitting open, suddenly shot through my head and the room went black. I fell to the floor. The last thing I saw was red brownie sleeping dust glittering before my eyes.

I woke on a cot and jerked upright. Cold shackles firmly secured my wrists together. As I cupped my hands to my throbbing head, I smelled a peculiar scent on the iron cuffs. I touched my tongue to them. Salt.

I was a prisoner in the castle. How quickly life unravels. How quickly friends become enemies. How quickly the mighty fall.

Just a girl without her stone.

Looking around the bedroom, I saw several aged men—Queen's healers, by their long white robes—tending to an elderly man with white hair.

Mount Kapri.

My heart thudded in painful beats. "Joshua." I yanked on the iron cuffs, but they remained secured to a bar on the wall. Without my stone, I couldn't free myself from my restraints.

Coco walked beside me, carefully just out of my reach.

"Let me see him," I snarled. "Let me help him."

"I will remove your restraints on the condition of your controlled behavior."

I glared at her. "I can help him."

She studied my expression, before withdrawing a set of keys and unlocking the shackles. They fell to the floor with a clatter as I raced toward Joshua.

His eyes were closed, but his skin still held warmth. A gleaming white mop replaced his usual brown hair, and his body seemed smaller, frailer.

"Joshua." I spoke his name in a sob, scooping his torso into my arms. Tears pricked my eyes. I transported us instantly to the one place which could heal him. The springs had never failed us.

Warm effervescent water engulfed us. I found my footing and held fast to Joshua. This would work. I needed to be patient and let the magic waters heal him. I remembered the first time I'd brought him here. During the battle against Malos and his forces, Joshua had been attacked by a Slasher. Before his last few breaths left him for dead, we made it to the springs, and he'd been healed. The second time I'd brought him here had been after his captivity and torture by the Dantajists, during the Hunju civil war.

His eyes flickered open.

"Joshua?"

His once golden-brown irises had turned a pale gray.

"Abbey." His voice sounded pitifully weak, as his body floated listlessly in my arms.

"You're going to be okay. We're at the springs."

The waters should have begun to heal him by now—they were already healing me. The throbbing blow to my head eased, cuts and scrapes on my skin closed, and the shoulder I'd nearly dislocated was already pain-free.

"It's too late," he said. "Too much of me is gone. I'm sorry."

"It's okay. You're going to be okay." I stroked a hand through his now-white hair.

"I couldn't see another way. I had to help them—*all* of them. Did it work?"

I nodded with lips trembling. "Yes. You did it. You saved everyone." I didn't know if that was entirely true, but I wouldn't tell a dying man otherwise.

He gave a faint smile mixed with relief and pride. "I knew I could do it."

My throat constricted. He must have suffered these last few days, with the weight of the world on his shoulders. He'd fought to live, hoping to have the strength and ability to perform the magic needed to cure thousands.

"Don't be mad at Coco. I told her she'd have to stop you if you tried to intervene."

I pursed my lips, tears falling from my eyes. I couldn't promise not to be angry with her.

Joshua closed his eyes.

"No. No. We have plans! We have a future together! Your children, Joshua! You have to live!"

"Too much of me is gone," he repeated. "I'm sorry. I wanted more for us, but not at the expense of everyone else. Tell the children I love them. I'll always be with them. With you."

I watched his breathing grow shallower, before stopping entirely. I stared in shock and disbelief. Even the healing springs, which had healed all manner of trauma, couldn't reverse the life force he'd lost using the Healing Stone.

I held him close, whispering over and over: "I love you. I love you. I love you."

Pain and anguish racked my body. Even though the waters had healed my physical wounds, I felt as though my heart had been ripped from my chest. The ache and despair crushed me like an iron fist.

Abigail, Baird's tone was delicate.

Healing springs, I replied.

Baird appeared. Wordlessly he stood on the opposite side of Joshua. As he pulled both of us into his arms, he wept with me. "I can only imagine the hurt you must feel."

I felt raw, like someone had scoured me from the inside out. More than bruised muscles and aching bones, I felt emotionally beaten. That pain seared me on a visceral level. That pain would take longer to heal than any physical wound.

"Abigail?"

I looked into Baird's eyes, red and weary.

"Let me take him to the castle."

I shook my head. "I can't go back there. I can't. They stole him from me."

"Let him have the hero's funeral he deserves. This was his choice. Give him the recognition he deserves." His soft, deep voice over-flowed with sorrow.

"I can't go there."

"You don't have to. Not yet. I'll take him."

I nodded and stepped back from them. After a final farewell kiss to my husband, I watched them vanish.

21

For several long minutes, I watched the spring water bubble around me. Twice the waters had saved Joshua's life for me. I wasn't granted a third time.

When I finally transported back to the field where I'd left Phobus, I found all three horses grazing. Raven sat atop Phobus, petting Carrot. My horse lifted his head as I approached. I buried my face in his neck.

"Did you succeed?" Raven asked. Her worried expression reflected how I must look.

"We succeeded. The kingdom is healed." I didn't add at what cost that victory came—to Joshua, to our children.

"So ... those are happy tears?" she asked doubtfully.

I sniffed. "I need to get the horses back to the ranch."

"Why are you wet?"

I grabbed all four sets of reins and transported us to the corral at my home. Prince and Butterfly jerked in startled surprise at the sudden change in their surroundings.

I set to work removing their bridals and saddles. My motions were slow and labored. Although the springs had healed the injuries from my quest and recent fight, I was still physically and emotionally defeated.

Baird appeared with Fury, and began helping me, starting with Butterfly. "I'll take care of this."

I continued to work. I needed to do something mundane and routine to keep moving. Once I stopped moving, I doubted I could begin again.

Raven paced the ledge of one of the stall doors. "Can someone enlighten me as to why you both look like you were beaten in a fight, and yet Abigail claims the magic worked?"

"The magic worked," Baird confirmed, "but it consumed a great deal of Joshua's life force. Abigail tried to stop the spell to save Joshua. I tried to keep the guards from hurting Abigail."

She turned to me in a wide-eyed stare. "Joshua is okay?"

My throat constricted, and all I could do was shake my head.

Raven scowled. "How were you defeated?" She looked at my injuries, my clothing, and my neck. "The stone is gone?"

"Taken."

Her face flushed with rage. "They betrayed you!"

"Coco did what she thought was right." Even as Baird spoke the words in Coco's defense, they sounded hollow.

Raven put her hands on her hips. "*She* bested the champion? She deceived Abigail. How can you defend her?"

My head throbbed. I scooped grain into buckets. The horse ate hungrily.

"Although I understand her actions, I'm still upset by them," Baird explained.

"What are you going to do?" Raven looked at me.

"I have to tell my family." I choked out the words before leaving to walk to my home.

I stood outside my mother's cabin, frozen.

The ocean breeze tugged at the black dress I wore. Although I'd washed myself clean, through automatic motions, and forced myself to arrive here to see my family, I didn't know how to go any farther.

Not even the power of the Warrior Stone could have given me enough strength to knock and open that door—not that I even had the stone anymore. Once the door opened, the children would learn the truth. Life would be different. Forever. I was the bearer of news that would cause agonizing pain.

I stood at the door, my feet heavy as if sunk in quicksand.

The door swung open. "Abigail! You're back." My mother held the door open for me. The sound of laughter resonated from the house.

I couldn't move. I could barely breathe.

"Abigail, what's wrong? Is it Joshua?"

My tongue felt thick and my throat constricted.

"Oh, honey." Her voice cracked.

The children rushed past her to greet me with enthusiasm. I fell to my knees, as I embraced them. As a tidal wave of tears and sobs erupted, I felt their mood shift from joy to sadness. At some point, I managed to say their father was gone and that he gave his life to save everyone.

They cried with me.

Bringing the children home and unpacking blurred with the preparations for Joshua's funeral, which blurred with the funeral itself several days later.

Baird had been kind enough to fetch Joshua's parents, who'd apparently been on their deathbeds before Joshua healed the kingdom. They stayed at the castle, so they could greet all the people coming to the funeral to give thanks to Joshua for saving their lives.

My mother stayed at my home and helped look after the children. Raven tended to the horses and Fury. Baird served as our communication link between my household and the castle.

ON THE DAY of the funeral, my mother helped me dress in a gown of black crow feathers. I took Joshua's Healing Stone and the leather wristband he'd made for it and wore it as a band on my upper arm. The brown leather had been worn until it was smooth and supple.

After arriving at the castle, I was led to the amphitheater and took a seat before Joshua's casket.

Hans approached and gave his condolences as he knelt before me. He looked older and paler since the beginning of the quest. Gone was the rosy-cheeked boy I'd met at the university. He'd been replaced by a man who appeared to carry the worry of someone twice his age, yet he still possessed the fragility of youth.

I searched for some kind words. "The dagger you gave me helped me secure the Wind Stone."

He lowered his head, avoiding direct eye contact with me. "I'm glad to hear it. If you ever need anything, milady ... " His voice trailed off, as he stood and left the stage.

Baird stood beside my chair. Although he remained silent, I felt both the reassurance of his presence and the weight of his sorrow. His thick, blue coat billowed under the slight breeze.

Beside him sat the Queen, grave and forlorn—but steadfast. Always steadfast. I could never bottle my emotions the way she did. Even now, days after Joshua's death, I felt like a mild breeze could have scattered the shattered pieces of me like a dandelion in the wind. If the heavy clouds above unleashed a shower, I'd dissolve into my chair, to be swept away across the marble before vanishing into the dirt.

The children huddled near my mother and stepfather off to one side, so they could mourn, but not be near the attention of the crowds who'd come to pay their respect to Joshua.

Joshua's parents huddled together off to one side, mourning the loss of their only child. We had hugged, but I'd had no words to offer them for the sacrifice he'd made.

Arturo approached, wearing loose-fitting black leggings and a tunic. He began to kneel, but we were too good of friends for that nonsense. I stood and let his enormous arms envelop me. Arturo had been a witness at Joshua's and my wedding—our first wedding, on the *Juniper*, out at sea. Much later, Arturo and I fought together in the Hunju civil war. Arturo was half-Hunju, half-human; and had fought for the rights of the mixed race. The civil war had brought them closer to equality, although thousands of years of cultural repression wouldn't change overnight.

"I don't have words meaningful enough, Ab'ay."

I sniffed. "It's enough that you came."

He gave me another great squeeze before easing me back into my chair.

Warmth crept into my hand as it lay on the armrest. The sensation soothed me, like drinking orange tea for a parched throat. I felt some of the tight sensation that had been around my chest for days ease, allowing for deeper breathing. When I looked to my right, Mal was kneeling beside me, watching the crowd of mourners and holding my hand.

Allis approached next, with a trail of children of varying ages behind him—all dressed in matching maroon-colored clothing.

Allis grasped my hand and kissed it. "Joshua's life will be sung in songs for hundreds of years, and his death will be mourned by all." With a bow of his head, he released my hand and stepped back. He turned and melted into the crowd.

I looked at Mal to my right, giving him a grateful nod. My eyes fell to the long-fingered hand he'd slipped into mine. After several seconds, I felt the contact pulse with warmth and energy—as though he was transmitting a steady stream of silent reassurance.

I realized that in our many years of friendship, our grazing touches had never lasted more than a second or two other than the moment Orrick had us touch. Apparently, with prolonged contact, I could actually *feel* his presence.

A long procession of people expressed their condolences and threw flowers at the foot of Joshua's casket. Layers and layers of flowers piled higher and higher, with their bright colors contrasting against the dark clothing of those who bore them. So many flowers. So many mourners. So many lives saved by Joshua's sacrifice. I thought of the Callabus funeral song.

My time to rest,
My place to nest.

Take my soul home,
End my weary roam.

Light a torch for me,
My body from sand to sea.

From the sea to the moon,
By the stars rests my tomb.

A small figure, no heavier than a rabbit, hopped up onto my bed.

"Go away," I told Raven.

"You've been in bed for three days." As she peeled the covers back, sunlight blinded me.

"Not long enough," I complained, pulling the covers back up.

She yanked them off and out of reach. "You have children, and a job, and a life to get back to."

I dropped a pillow over my head. "Everything hurts."

"That's because you haven't moved. You need to get up, get dressed, and *move*. Not to mention eat something." She tore off my pillow and threw it on the floor. "And bathe!"

I sat up and blinked.

"This is not the behavior befitting the Red Goddess."

"I hate that title."

"Well, right now, you don't deserve it."

"I'm mourning. Where's my mother?"

"You've mourned long enough in bed. You can finish mourning while you resume your daily routine. Your mother is with Rebekah. She's not going to save you from me. No one is. They've all pampered you long enough. Now, go take a bath. Your water's ready."

I swung my feet to the edge of the bed and touched them to the cool, wood surface.

"You have a whole list of things to do." Raven crossed her arms.

"That's not motivating me."

"You promised Orrick you'd bring him here. The poor wizard is languishing among brownies until you rescue him. And you haven't told the Queen about Bellos' army yet."

I sighed as I stood.

After pulling off my nightgown, I climbed into the bath. The water was comfortably warm and lavender scented. "Thank you," I said, before sinking my head under the water.

When I emerged, Raven sat on a nearby stool and handed me a bar of soap. We hadn't talked about taking her back to the forest, and she seemed careful to never bring up the topic.

"Would you like to stay here with me and my family? I'll take you home if you like, but we'd like you to stay."

Raven straightened her black-feathered hat and beamed. "I'd like to stay."

When I'd finished washing, I dried and pulled a clean nightgown over my head. I plucked an apple from a basket of fruit on my bedroom dresser and snacked on an apple.

I reached for the glass memory cylinder beside the basket. I needed to give this to Orrick. First, I'd watch one last memory—a farewell to Isabel Dallik, who seven-thousand-years after her death, still gave me strength.

I entered the memories and found myself watching Isabel work fervently in a library, surrounded by an array of open and closed books. She took notes and jumped sporadically from book to book.

As she worked, I heard her speaking—her voice filled with pain. "The king has left for Bellos to attempt diplomatic negotiations. Even knowing he'd ignore my request, I pleaded for him not to go. The Bellosian army is days away from invading Karnelik with forces ten times that of the Karnelik army. We can't win, and soon the kingdom will learn of my husband's death. The answer—the solution—lies somewhere in these books. Somewhere, peace can be bought through magic. Generations can be spared the heartache I've known. I have to find the correct concoction. I have to save people from themselves and save my sons."

I marveled at this woman's strength and determination. Knowing her husband died at the hands of their enemies, she still didn't cower —didn't sulk under her bed sheets for days—but continued her life's passion: Searching for a cure from the evil infecting men.

. . .

With Raven's encouragement, I managed to bathe, dress, and have dinner with my family. We talked about the horses, and Carrot, and the next planting of the garden. All of the conversation had a dreary edge to it.

"What will happen to father's clinic?" Natalie asked.

I mustered a smile. "The investors have agreed to build the hospital your father planned. They'll call it the Colt Center for Healing."

"Mama!" Natalie gasped. She left her dinner seat, came to me, and climbed into my arms. "He still gets his clinic. He still gets his dream." She buried her face in my neck and cried tears of joy.

"Yes, he does." I sniffed. I held her close, hoping we could stay this close as she grew older. So far, she hadn't accused me of not doing enough to keep him alive. So far, she hadn't blamed me as I blamed myself. One day—perhaps more than once—she would blame me in a fit of anger. She'd wish that I'd taken her father's place. When that unhappy day came, I'd bear the brunt of her pain. But today, in this moment, she let her love for me warm the cold that Joshua's absence had left.

That night, I dream walked into Goran's room. It was vacant, so I took a seat in the little chair by his bed, hoping that he hadn't died, but simply wasn't asleep yet.

"Lady Cross."

I looked up to see Goran standing over me. Despite the scar on his face, his expression held delight.

"I was hoping you'd come back." He beamed with a vibrancy that conveyed his gratitude.

To my surprise, he pulled me to my feet before twirling me

around the room. "You are my miracle." He kissed a cheek. "I owe you everything."

"They all live?"

"That they do."

My heart swelled to learn that he and his family had survived. Tears filled my eyes.

"Milady?" He stepped back from me.

"It's wonderful to know the magic saved you and your family." My throat felt tight.

"Oh, *by the Unideit*. Your husband was ill. Did he not—? Did he survive?"

"He did not." I couldn't get further words out of my mouth. I wanted to explain the hero he'd been, but I didn't want to give the wrong impression that I resented those who'd lived when Joshua hadn't.

Goran stepped closer, before tugging me into an embrace. "I'm deeply sorry. I'm pained for you. My family and I will travel to Crithos. We'll grieve with you, provide for you."

Composing myself, I stepped back from him. "No. Kovia has to rebuild, and I'm in no condition for company. Help your country—I have help available to me here."

"Very well. But, please, if you ever need anything—you know where to find me."

"I only needed the comfort of knowing you lived. I'll not haunt your dreams again."

"Unless I can be of assistance."

"Thank you."

22

I waited for the Queen in the courtyard.

I was dressed in black for mourning, with a black and silver breastplate and sword at my side. I'd left my hair down, and I'd omitted the red cape—especially since I hadn't replaced it yet, after converting it to a bat sack. Six alabaster statues of the prior Avant Champions towered over me. Fortunately, they hadn't yet commissioned funds to add the seventh champion. Besides, it would offset the balance of two rows of three champions. I wondered if the other champions had faced only the single hardship of slaying Malos—or if, like I'd found, that had only been the beginning of a lifetime of other challenges, expectations, and responsibilities.

The Queen approached, apparently recovered from her illness. She wore her gray hair woven in a tower above her head. A crimson, satin dress arched stiffly around her body. Her posture was as rigid as a plank, and her hands clasped firmly together.

She dismissed her guards, and we were alone.

"You requested to see me, Abigail?"

"My Queen." I bowed before her. "I—"

"How are the children?"

I swallowed. "Natalie is devastated. Paul is trying to grasp the calamity. Rebekah feeds off everyone else's mood even if she doesn't understand."

"How can I help?"

I eyed her warily. In the many years of our friendship—or my subservience—she'd never extended unsolicited help. I answered hesitantly, "I have help."

"Teachers? Cooks? Farm hands?"

"Yes. All of those."

"A head housekeeper?"

"No, mum."

"I will make a recommendation. You need someone to keep the others organized and manage schedules. She will also be trained in bookkeeping. She'll send our financiers records of all your employees' wages. Those will be paid for by the crown."

I felt my cheeks burn. I wasn't here for charity. "That is generous, my Queen, but—"

"No, it isn't," she snapped. "We cannot—will never be able to—repay Joshua for his sacrifice. This is a meager offering. Do not think of it as charity. Consider it payment of wages Joshua would have been able to make through his hospital work but can't because of what we did to him. "

The air felt tense with her barely suppressed anguish.

"What you're offering will help. Thank you."

"And the hospital?"

"We have all of the funds raised to build the hospital. I'll oversee it."

"What else?" Her question came out as a demand. Her gaze darted from my sword to my eyes.

I furrowed my brow in confusion and looked around the courtyard. "Nothing else, Queen Rebekah."

I added, "On another matter—"

"You've not come to kill me, then?"

I took a step back from her. "No!"

Her posture relaxed slightly. "We deceived you. Joshua knew you'd try to stop him when you saw the magic draining his life. He suggested the captain of guard may have to intervene. I gave Coco the order to do so if needed. In the deliberation room, you had an expression that you might kill us all one day. When you arrived, dressed as the Champion and armed, I thought perhaps today was when you meant to exact your revenge. I was prepared to let you."

I gaped at her. "You think I'm capable of executing you? I'm in mourning and miserable. I hate the events that happened, but I can't think of a different, better way for them to have unfolded." I began to pace. "Believe me, I've been angry enough at all of you to demand there must have been another way." I stopped and turned to her. "But I would *never* harm you. We don't always agree, and I don't always comprehend your motives, but don't fear me. I always have, and always *will*, defend you with my life."

She smiled weakly. "Then, I am sorry for doubting you. Oh, *for Crithos sake*, stop staring at me like that. I *do* apologize for my behavior on occasion. Now, you had some other news?"

I sucked in a deep breath. "The Waterlands of Kovia give the sight of the future. I don't know the validity of what they revealed, but it certainly *felt* real. It's concerning enough for me to bring it to your attention."

I paused to take a deep breath.

"Bellos will build an army—they may already be doing so. They will take Kovia, weakened by death and anarchy after the plague. Then they'll come for Crithos, probably on two fronts—west by sea, east by land. I don't know when—years in the future, I suspect—but you need to start building an army *now*."

The Queen rested a hand on her abdomen as though made ill by the news. "This sort of behavior is unprecedented. We haven't seen war in over seven-thousand-years. And yet, my sources suggest hostility brews across the globe. Malos' stone must be failing."

"Yes. I don't know why, but it is," I said.

"We will build an army," she confirmed.

"When they come, summon the Avant Champion. I'll be ready to help defend the kingdom side by side with your soldiers."

As I packed my belongings in my office at the university, Coco entered. Her ponytail was freshly smoothed back, and she wore a sparkling captain's uniform of blue and silver. I gave her the briefest glance as she set my Warrior Stone down on my desk.

Baird, who had been helping me fit books into chests, silently left the room.

The unspoken body language between him and Coco was frigid. She didn't make eye contact with him, and his shoulders and jaw were tense.

Coco walked over to the window. "Well, we know whose side Baird chose."

"We're all supposed to be friends. He shouldn't have to choose sides."

She looked around the room and the half-filled boxes. "You're leaving the university?"

"I am. At least, I'm taking a sabbatical long enough to get Joshua's hospital built. I may or may not come back."

She pursed her lips as she paced my office. "I had no choice. If I let you rescue Joshua from the magic destroying him, then the kingdom would have been destroyed."

I thought of how she'd planned everything. Coco's knife had been ready, and she'd brought salt with her back from Kovia. Her actions had been premeditated.

Yet, so much sorrow still filled me there was no room for anger. Joshua had given her instructions, the Queen reinforced them. Coco, ever the soldier, carried them out. As much as I wanted to blame her —because she was alive, and Joshua was not—Coco had just followed her orders.

She turned to look at me, her eyes filled with despair. "Do you want to know what I saw in the geysers? I stood before you like this, begging your forgiveness. Even though I hadn't betrayed your trust at that point, I'd been shown that I would. After Joshua ordered me to restrain you if necessary, I prepared for the worst." Her lips trembled. "I know a great deal about how the stones work from Baird. It was logical that a healing of this magnitude would severely drain Joshua, if not kill him. It was logical that when you saw the effect on your husband, you'd lose rational thought—choose his life over the lives of thousands. Even Joshua thought that."

I swallowed the lump in my throat. "I *do* forgive you, Coco. I wish Joshua had let me find a different solution, but his choice isn't your grief to bear."

She gaped at me.

Although I didn't think she'd enjoy me invading her personal space, I stepped in and hugged her.

Coco returned the embrace, sobbed once, and then stiffly stepped back. "Thank you."

I gave a weak smile. "We'd better stay friends now that I'm accepting my duties as Avant Champion."

"We're glad to have you."

"I hope so, because I'm officially unemployed now."

Coco's lips quirked.

When Coco left, Dean Lariat entered my doorway. Her gaze roamed around my office—at the books, boxes, and garbage. I'd given notice several days ago, so I guessed this would be her goodbye.

"We sure hate to lose our champion."

"No one is losing the champion. I'm still here on Crithos."

"Then why leave the university?"

I pursed my lips, before deciding to tell her the truth. "All I ever wanted at this university was to be valued as a chemistry professor—not the kingdom's heroine merely pretending to be one. I thought my moment of sacrifice and glory had been fulfilled thirteen years ago, and I could have the life I thought I wanted."

The Dean stiffened.

"You don't need to look sad for me," I told her. "Life didn't go as planned, but that doesn't make my important role any less crucial. For the things I need to do now—my family and my champion role—I have to narrow my focus and stop spreading myself so thin."

"You are a good chemistry professor. I didn't mean to imply—"

"You didn't mean to, but you *did* imply—and it's okay. I know where I belong now. Thank you for the career I had here. It will always mean a lot to me."

When I returned to packing, Dean Lariat lingered for a few more moments before leaving.

Baird returned to my office.

"Are you okay?"

I turned to my friend and mentor. He'd lost the woman he loved to a fatal illness, so I knew he understood my pain. "I'm not going to be okay for a long time, Baird. If you can wait at least a year before asking me that, then you'll spare me countless lies. I know you lost a dear friend when Joshua died, so I won't ask you that question either."

"I'm here if you ever need anything."

I began throwing away papers on my desk—lesson plans, formulas, unfinished notes. "I need you to be the friend you've always been. We need to keep sparring and keep preparing for Bellos' attack."

He nodded.

"And you need to forgive Coco."

He blinked at me.

"She acted as instructed, on orders from the Queen. She's going to feel miserable about her role in Joshua's death for a long time. She doesn't need to lose you as well."

He crossed his arms. "I believe you just gave me sage advice. That's supposed to be my role."

"Sometimes we judge the one's we love the hardest."

"Well stated."

I wrapped a beaker in thin paper, before placing it in a box. "How is Hans?"

"Undeterred from becoming a monk."

"Considering the quest opened his eyes to violence, devastation, and slimy man-eating squids, I'd say that's a good thing."

Baird ran a hand over one of my books before brushing the dust off the spine. "Perhaps."

"Perhaps what? What does that mean?"

"Zack and Luke and I shared the same concern over his killing Preacher Pinsky. The monk way is not murder—not of an unarmed man."

"He may have been unarmed, but he was still a monster. And that was Hans first fight. He was caught in the moment of battle." And why was I defending the young lad? Perhaps because I knew the crush he had on me, and irrationally felt responsible that Hans killed Pinsky defending my honor.

"Perhaps," Baird replied.

I arranged the boxes of books and supplies from my chemistry office against one wall in my study. As I did so, I looked at the book of magic I'd borrowed from Orrick. I ran my fingers along the stiff leather.

Magic.

Whatever invasion King Artemis schemed, might alone wouldn't drive his forces back. I needed to learn magic and not only stars and stone magic. I needed to learn from Orrick.

My gaze fell on the glass, cylindrical puzzle box of Isabel's memories. I needed to learn Isabel's type of magic—that of a sorceress powerful enough to create Malos and banish Orrick to a tree for seven thousand years.

I touched the cool, bluish contraption, careful not to touch the symbols that released her memories.

As I turned it over, there seemed to be a pattern of symbols on one end out of alignment. I hadn't noticed that before now. I turned the raised piece of attached glass. A clicking noise emitted and the small circular piece opened. A scroll tumbled out and onto the floor.

I set down the cylinder and picked up the rolled piece of paper. As I unrolled it, I sat near a window for more light.

The black ink on the parchment was in a language I didn't know. As I stared at it, wondering if it had been composed by Isabel Dallik, the black lettering moved and swirled as the ink reformed into letters in Crithian.

> *Dear Abigail,*
> *You have suffered heartbreaking loss and devastation. For*
> > *the role I played in setting events in motion so long ago,*
> > *I am deeply sorry. I hope you will believe my intentions*
> > *were to help the world in a time of crisis. My actions*
> > *saved thousands of lives, but it also damaged the lives of*
> > *others.*
> *You will never know the hope you have given me. Seeing*
> > *you arrive in my son's future, and how you set him free,*
> > *has given me peace and strength. You save my family,*
> > *Abigail.*
> *You will be the greatest Avant Champion the world has ever*
> > *known. Magic will help you achieve your destiny.*
> > *Learn from Orrick. In a few years, he'll bring you the*
> > *Spirit Stone and then you will learn from me directly.*
> *You are Crithos' strength and salvation.*

—Isabel

I reread the letter several times, dumbfounded. Isabel knew about me thousands of years ago. She referenced me saving Orrick. Had she known I'd release him before or after she banished him to the forest? My blood had released Orrick from the oak tree. *My* blood. Isabel's reference gave me hope that I truly would have the ability to harness the same power of magic that she'd mastered.

I knew now that I would fully embrace the mantle as Avant Champion as I never had before.

I knocked on Wizard Oak's door as a dozen brownies stared up at me. I probably looked underwhelming to them—dressed in my slacks, boots, and cotton shirt. I held Isabel Dallik's memory puzzle in one hand.

The old man opened his door and swept me into his arms in a crushing hug. "Abigail! Abigail, such a tragedy."

I swallowed the lump in my throat. How had he known? Had word of Joshua's death spread this far south? Or had the wizard simply divined the information?

"Come in for tea." He closed the door behind me.

He'd already poured two cups of steaming tea, as if he'd known I was coming.

I stared down at the object in my hands. "I came to give you this. It belonged to your mother. It holds her memories. I'd have returned it sooner but—"

"Don't fret champion. You've been a little preoccupied."

I thrust the glass cylinder forward. "I saw some of her memories. She was a remarkable woman."

"She was a force of nature."

"She loved you and Mal immensely."

"I believe she did. Perhaps I had my doubts when she turned me into a tree—but I came around. Life as a tree allows for a great deal of reflection." His eyes sparkled. "I know she loved us." He took the object and looked it over.

"You twist and align different symbols to trigger a memory."

"Wonderful. Many thanks for traveling out here to bring this to me." He set it down and handed me a cup of tea.

"I also came to let you know I'm having plans drawn up for a small house for you on our property. It'll be bigger than what you have here, but still modest. You can stay as long as you like—or make it temporary, until you find something, some*where*, you prefer." As I sipped the warm tea, the taste of vanilla and lavender soothed me.

"That's a generous offer." He stroked his white beard.

When his eyes softened, I felt he knew I meant every word. I loved this man as a friend and a mentor of all things magical. If I was to survive my life without Joshua, I needed to surround myself with love. If Orrick was to survive into his next decade, he needed to not be surrounded by an encampment of boisterous brownies.

With a bow of his head, he said, "I accept."

23

I looked out across the beautiful shore. The water began as emerald green, and then stretched to a light blue that transformed into deep sapphire. In the light blue sky above, the two crescent moons shone.

I sat on the beach of my dream world, feeling a cold numbness. In the blink of an eye, my life had been irrevocably changed—as had the lives of my children.

It wasn't their fault they'd been born from stone bearers, who held the responsibility to use their talents to help others. Nevertheless, they'd suffered the consequences.

Mal appeared beside me, wearing his usual black suit.

I continued to stare at the water. "Do you remember the time all four of us teamed up against the harbor wave? Well—first you had to show me what a harbor wave was, so I'd understand the terror of it. You did that right here. Then we rescued the villagers. Every last one of them." I stared down at the sand and caressed the grains with my fingers. "We came back later and helped them rebuild."

"I am so deeply sorry about Joshua."

I felt the depth of pain and truth in his words.

"Did you know?" I asked. There was no trace of accusation in my voice.

"No."

"Interesting the geysers chose *not* to show me that piece of information. I saw my own death, but not Joshua's. Do you remember when you and I first met in a dream? Do you remember when you told me Joshua and I had decade upon decade together?" Despite my words, my voice was fraught with despair rather than anger. I still had no spirit left for anger.

"I saw him dying of old age. I didn't know it was because the stone magic took his youth."

I remembered Goran's warning about how the Waterlands showed pieces of the future and that they were subject to misinterpretation. Even Mal had misread a glimpse of the future, when he'd seen an aged Joshua die in my arms. Because I'd never have aged at the same rate as Joshua, Mal had assumed that Joshua and I had spent a lifetime together; not realizing the Healing Stone had zapped the years from him prematurely.

I listened to gentle lapping of the waves.

I pulled my knees up to my chest and hugged my legs to my body. "I'm lost without him." My voice was a hollow whisper.

"Understandable. But you won't always be. You'll find your way— your strength. You'll continue to be an amazing mother."

I blinked at him. "You think I'm an amazing mother?" I don't know why his opinion on the subject mattered, but I felt the reassuring weight of it. He'd never expressed such a sentiment.

"Of course you are. You provide their needs, education, and

enrichment—and you've managed not to strangle Rebekah, the little spitfire."

I chuckled.

"Apparently, you are also raising a future queen."

I grunted. "It places a little more pressure on parenthood."

"You'll do fine."

I laid back on the sand, looking at the perfect blue sky. "And us?"

Mal took a quick intake of breath. "We need to separate."

I felt the words slice through me, even though I'd suspected they were coming. Mal had already begun the process by distancing himself from me during this quest.

I didn't understand one thing. "Why?"

"You've seen man is back in possession of his evil. You saw the devastation of this plague—the death toll was higher because man's evil let fear and brutality win against compassion and benevolence. We still don't know why evil had returned to nest in individuals. The only thing different about this millennia, compared to every other, is *you*."

A cold shiver coursed through me, which had nothing to do with the ambient temperature. I couldn't argue with his logic, and I refused to be weak and ask him to stay. A rogue dream tear streamed down my cheek. I was losing my husband and my friend in one terrible week.

"I've stayed with you longer than I should have out of my own selfishness. I've ignored my responsibility these last few years because I've had the pleasure of your family to distract me. I can't ignore it any longer."

"You'd been isolated for seven-thousand-years. One might expect you'd want to enjoy the opportunity to see parts of the world you never had."

He gave me a sidelong glance through his thick, dark lashes.

"We're friends," I added.

He looked up at me with a hard stare. "And I've let our friendship successfully distract me from my obligations."

I clenched my fist, knowing and hating where the conversation was taking us. "No."

"I think our friendship is only making the world worse."

"You don't *know* that."

"It's the one thing that's changed. I'm only in existence because of this link we share. I should be on Mulan, nonexistent, until enough evil is absorbed."

"You think our relationship is the reason human evil is not being absorbed?"

"I've no other explanation."

"And your solution is separation?" I spoke the words through clenched teeth. I felt a stab of irrational betrayal. After everything we'd been through together, he was content to disappear? He was leaving me?

Mal gave a subtle nod.

"Fine," I said.

"Fine?"

"Yes, *fine*. We'll separate. We'll save the world from our damaging friendship."

"Abigail."

"No, you're right. The prince of darkness shouldn't be amiable with the Avant Champion. The continent cannot be simultaneously bathed in summer sun and coated in winter snow. Perhaps we've violated some rule of nature. We'll end it."

He eyed me skeptically, seeing through my veiled attempt to appear agreeable to his suggestion.

I sniffed. "So, if your theory holds true, we'll start to see evil recede from humans the longer we're apart?"

He nodded.

"How do we know if it isn't working, and your theory is wrong? How much time is enough?"

"I suppose, theoretically, if the flow of evil is the same to and fro, the damage could be reversed in eight years."

"Then, in eight years I'll either see you again, if you're wrong, or never again, if you're right."

He let silence take a few beats before saying, "Yes. Goodbye, Abigail."

I closed my eyes. "As you wish."

He dissolved into the breeze, taking a piece of me with him. Although we'd settled on a plan, I knew I would see Mal again.

I knew I'd die in his arms someday.

The next day, I transported to a small, unoccupied area of land to the north—somewhat southwest of Karnelik. I watched the lake water ripple and listened to the birds. Joshua and I had been to this spot many times. I'd seen him naked for the first time in that water, touched his warm, bare skin. I remembered the heart-stopping look of desire in his rich, brown eyes. I remembered the feel of his muscles and tender embrace.

Raven was right. I had months and years of mourning to do, but I couldn't stop living while I did it.

I had always known the stone would take Joshua from me prematurely, since it stole energy from its user in order to function. But I never imagined it would take him so soon, so suddenly.

I'd been the one to give him that stone. I'd relinquished it as a bribe during college, so he wouldn't tell my brother, Paul, about the scuffle I'd been in during my studies in Karnelik.

The Healing Stone had defined who Joshua was. He unselfishly gave his strength—his life force—to heal others. He'd intended to spend a lifetime doing so. He'd be proud to know his legacy had been to save thousands of lives—to save the kingdom.

Paul, Natalie, and Rebekah would grow up knowing their father had been a hero. I would have preferred they grew up knowing *him*, but I couldn't see a way for events to have unfolded differently in the face of that devastating plague.

Joshua embraced who he was—who magic and destiny declared him to be.

I had fulfilled one destiny as the Avant Champion and set any further acts of greatness aside. I felt the singe of my selfishness. Coco had been right, years ago, when she'd accused me of leaving my obligations unfulfilled. I wanted a family and a teaching career. In those pursuits, I'd turned my back on my country. Now, hostile forces surrounded Crithos. Chaos and anarchy gripped Kovia, while Bellosian forces plotted against us.

My gifts, and the loss of Joshua, meant that I couldn't continue the life I'd built for myself. The cocoon I'd woven around myself was an illusion, and now it was forever shattered. A new life beckoned me.

Joshua had the fortitude to embrace his fate as a powerful healer. I needed to embrace my fate as a powerful warrior. I had to prepare to defend Crithos.

<<THE END>>

DEAR READER

You can find a map of Crithos and a map of the world at http://www. cbsamet.com/epic-fantasy.html. There is also a link to download Malakai, an Avant Champion story of Malos, for free, as well as The Book of Stones on pdf.

If you enjoyed this book and want to know about future releases by CB Samet you can CLICK HERE to sign up for my mailing list! I promise I won't spam you (I only send an email when I have a new book release, giveaways, or special discounts), and I'll never sell your info. You can also unsubscribe at any time.

I also wanted to take a moment to thank you for reading this story. As an independent author, I rely heavily on readers to spread the word about books they've read. If you enjoyed this novel and are looking forward to reading more, consider leaving a review or let someone know.

Thanks for reading,
CB Samet

ALSO BY CB SAMET

The Avant Champion Series

Rising, Book 1

Honor, Book 2

Malakai, a story of Malos (prequel)

Ashes, Book 3

Brothers Bond, Book 3.5 (novelette)

Conquest, Book 4

Book 5 (coming 2020)

Paranormal Romantic Suspense Novella Series

Romancing the Spirit

Sadie's Spirit

Willow's Windfall

Cassie's Chase

Phoebe's Pharaoh

Vanessa's Valentine (coming 2019)

Carol's Christmas (coming 2019)

MODERN ACTION AND THRILLER BOOKS

BY CB SAMET

The Rider Files:

Meridian File, Book 1

Masters File, Book 2

McMillan File, Book 3

Maltese File, Book 4 (coming 2019)

The Dr. Whyte Series:

Black Gold

Whyte Knight

Gray Horizon

The Avant Champion ~Conquest~
Sample Chapter 1

The outline of a massive ship broke through the fog. I watched the gray mist swirl around the great bow, with its bronze horse head. The fog and smoke around the volcano island coated the air so densely that the ship appeared to be floating on a sea of mist. It stilled on the ocean surface, presumably dropping anchor. My children followed my gaze to see the big vessel.

"That's not from Crithos," Baird commented. His blue cloak billowed around him as he stood to get a better view of the ship.

My long-standing friend and mentor, Baird Fox, was right. We had a port on Crithos at Waterton, but it serviced mostly fishing boats. This horse-headed beast had been built to sail the open ocean —to bridge continents.

But why come to Mulan—the barren island of the serpent volcano? The captain must've been lost. Mulan was a small, volcano island devoid of life—except for the sea serpent dwelling in the caverns below. Most people knew the island as a place of death. Many terrible shipwrecks had occurred on these shores. Individuals who'd survived to reach the black and rocky beach found a desolate island without so much as a tree or shrub.

I squinted to watch as a small boat was lowered to the ocean surface. Figures aboard began rowing their way toward shore.

Toward the resting place of evil.

This island had once terrified me. It had separated my parents from me and taken the life of my father. It had sheltered the powerful scepter belonging to my greatest enemy—who had subsequently become an ally and then disappeared from my life. This place of so many memories and so many mixed emotions was now an island I enjoyed visiting with my children. Here, we could picnic, and I could share their heritage with them.

Baird knelt back down on the blanket where the children sat by the food. "Well, they'll be a while making it ashore. Might as well finish lunch."

I nodded uneasily. My children took their cue and resumed eating. Rebekah, the youngest at five, found it difficult to sit still as she watched the small boat approach.

"It's getting close," she declared. Her unruly black hair, not unlike my own, whipped around her small face as she bobbed up and down with excitement.

"Settle down," snapped Natalie, obviously annoyed at Rebekah disrupting the meal.

Paul sat calmly, always drifting in a sea of his own thoughts—much like his namesake, my brother, had done. Abruptly, he stood. "I'm going to warn Andi to stay hidden, since we don't know these stranger's intentions."

Ever the protector, just like his father.

When lunch was finished, I packed up the blanket and basket. Paul returned from the island cave as Natalie and Rebecca watched the small boat row ever closer.

"Let's get everyone back to the house." Anxiety swelled and clawed at my stomach.

"I want to stay and meet them," Natalie said.

"If she's staying, I'm staying." Paul straightened and tensed slightly—as though showing he wasn't afraid. Although he had strength and courage at the tender age of seven, I didn't think he'd ever been in a fight. The physical contact of the rough-housing on the farm wasn't equivalent to fighting with sharp, penetrating objects.

"*Everyone* is leaving. Baird and I will meet the sailors with all of you safely at home." Until I knew these traveler's intentions, I wasn't exposing my children to them.

My family's safety was my priority.

I took Paul's hand and gave him an arched eyebrow of warning. He frowned but took Natalie's hand, and Natalie then took Rebekah's. They knew my Traveler's Star worked by contact.

Although our home was an ocean away, I didn't use conventional means of travel. Many years ago, I'd been gifted with the Traveler's

Star. A large, blue tattoo on my palm enabled me to transport anywhere I could see or had been before. As such, I brought my family several times a year to picnic on the island of the serpent volcano. Other days, we'd travel to the beach of Misty Isles, or to Karnelik to climb mountains, or to Marrin Beach to cliff dive.

Baird was the only other person I knew of with the Traveler's Star. Years ago, we'd made the mistake of holding hands, stars touching, while attempting to transport a large army together. That interaction had created a permanent connection between us. We could communicate covertly and sense where the other was if we concentrated.

I'll be back, I told Baird.

He nodded.

Using my Traveler's Star, I shifted, taking the children and myself home.

"But Baird!" Paul protested.

I released his hand once we stood safely inside the lounge of our estate.

"I'm going back to help him. I'll return as soon as I can." I handed the blanket to Natalie and the picnic basket to Paul. I bent down and kissed Rebekah on the cheek, but it didn't remove the worry on her face.

In an instant, I stood back on the beach.

Baird had his arms crossed, watching the men row through the surf before pulling the boat ashore. Twelve men arrived—all human. Their attire was as foreign as their ship. Their pants consisted of leather hide, laced along the outside of their legs the way we laced our boots. Their tunics were a thin, light material that probably dried quickly, providing an advantage on a ship. Short blades hung at their sides, along with small iron clubs that I didn't recognize.

By all appearances, and the scowls on their faces, they don't appear friendly, Baird said silently.

Twelve against two. We've had worse odds, I replied.

"I'm Abigail Cross and this is my friend, Baird Fox."

Baird, with his salt and pepper gray hair, probably looked old enough to be my father or an uncle. We'd been friends long enough for me to consider him family.

The lead sailor appraised my blue cotton dress and casual, comfortable attire. Perhaps he was surprised to encounter two people on Mulan, especially if he knew anything about the history of the island.

"I'm Porter Stout, son of King Artemis Stout." His accent betrayed that Crithian was not his native tongue.

His men began maneuvering around us. Porter glanced around as though looking for a ship, or any hidden threat. He'd find no tangible means of transportation.

"You're from Bellos," Baird said, stepping closer to my side. He held his wooden baton vertically, like a walking stick rather than the weapon I knew it to be.

"I was told this is an evil island, desolate and deserted," Porter said.

Most days, he'd have been correct about the deserted part. His statement betrayed his knowledge of the island and suggested he had intentionally come here. But why?

"As you can see, it's neither deserted nor evil," I said.

Prince Stout's lip curled as his shifty eyes glared at me. His long, dark hair ringed his shoulders. His high cheekbones accentuated a long, crooked nose.

"Insolent woman! Bow before the Prince of Bellos," one of the men commanded.

I turned my gaze on what was presumably Prince Stout's second in command—a stocky man with an abundance of facial hair. A hand rested on his iron club, ready to attack.

"I bow to those who earn my respect through their actions. So far, you have only demonstrated your ability to attempt intimidation."

Porter's first mate drew his club and pointed one end at my chest. I inspected the iron contraption. It had a hollow barrel like the Hunju blow darts I'd seen, but an odd, closed handle. It was obviously capable of launching some type of projectile. I was evidently supposed to cower in its presence and do its owner's bidding—but, for better or for worse, I'd never been one to yield when confronted with danger. Nevertheless, I did recognize the contraption as a danger —an unknown weapon. The Hunju blow darts contained a paralytic neurotoxin. If this were anything similar, a conflict with these men would be challenging.

Porter spoke again. "You will bow to me, and then you will take me to the scepter of Malos."

I arched an eyebrow.

So, he seeks the scepter.

I could practically feel the anger rolling off Baird like heat from a fire. We'd fought side by side over the years, and I knew he would step in and fight as soon as I made the first move.

There were many things I might have said to our aggressors that could have had some element of diplomacy. I could have introduced myself as the Avant Champion. I could have explained my relationship with the Queen of Crithos. I could have invited them to further peaceful discussions.

Yet, at that very instant, they were threatening my friend and me. Words and diplomacy were not my weapons of choice to diffuse the situation.

Using my Traveler's Star, I repositioned myself beside the man with the weapon in his hand rather than in front of him. With my left hand, I grabbed his wrist and forced his arm skyward. With my right fist, I punched his jaw. He released a grunt of pain and surprise as his head snapped to one side. Pulling the weapon from his grip, I hit him with the hefty handle.

Baird, with baton in hand, began fighting a group of three men.

Prince Stout reacted quickly. He reached for his weapon, but Baird was already lunging at him.

I moved to a short, stocky man, kicking him in the chest. I followed my kick with another to the man's legs.

A lanky Bellosian swung his short sword at me, murderous intent in his eyes. I vanished before he could strike, appearing behind him and clobbering the iron weapon I still held against the man's head. He crumpled to the ground, grabbing his bleeding brow.

Baird was still battling Porter, who seemed to be a formidable younger opponent.

Seven left.

Am I fast enough?

I needed my wooden baton. With it, I could disable the men faster than with my fists—and with less pain to my hands.

I attacked the next man—a bald, foul-smelling sailor. He screamed as his knee buckled under the weight of my kick.

Two other men seemed to have gained an understanding of the situation—that they weren't confronting normal adversaries. They took defensive steps backward from the fighting.

I made quick work of two other attackers. They were soon splayed on the ground, clutching at arms and legs.

A deafening noise erupted, and Baird fell to the black sand. My stomach sunk into a pit of fear. I snapped my gaze to the source of the noise. One of the men I'd knocked to the ground had his weapon in his hand. A thin stream of smoke swirled up from the hollow, iron barrel. Whatever had emerged from that contraption had severely wounded and incapacitated Baird.

"Baird!" I screamed.

I transported to the armed man, kicked my heel into his jaw and stole his weapon. Now, each of my hands held a weapon. I turned them around, so that I gripped them the same way these men had been holding them. I noticed a small trigger. The trigger seemed similar to the releasing mechanism of the crossbows used by the Caballus Clans.

I pointed the open end of the barrel at Porter, who struggled on his hands and knees as blood gushed from his nose. The threat to their Prince was effective—as the men not already injured on the ground stilled.

I held absolute conviction in my gaze and posture. I'd killed before—not recently, but blood stained my hands nonetheless, thick and crimson.

I glanced at Baird, who lay on the ground, red blood staining his blue cloak.

I'm going to the springs. I'll be back, he told me.

I nodded. Fear and worry escalated my heart rate. I'd never forgive myself if Baird were in some way severely injured.

He vanished.

I suddenly felt unworthy to have such a friend. Without question or hesitation, he'd come to my aid—head-long into danger. With the flash of an exploding weapon, he'd nearly lost his life. Guilt pressed into me, making me want to sink into obsidian quicksand. I assured myself that the healing springs would mend his wound.

What could have inflicted so much damage? I stared at the weapons in my hands. Whatever projectiles they emitted, they were clearly small enough to fit inside these contraptions.

I'd have to examine them later. These foreigners needed to be presented to Queen Rebekah, and their intentions to steal Malos' scepter revealed.

What had they hoped to accomplish in stealing it? The scepter held massive power—needed to achieve its duty of accumulating evil over the millennia. In doing so, humans were prevented from lapsing into the cycle of war and devastation that our kind had once been trapped in—before the scepter's creation over seven-thousand-years-ago. Yet, as far as I knew, only Malos could activate it—so was their motive to destroy it? That would only serve to unleash evil.

Admittedly, in my youth, the same thought had occurred to me. I'd wondered: Were we *ourselves* if part of us was missing? Even if that part was evil?

The concept of stealing the scepter for personal gain puzzled me. Later, I'd have to consult my friend, Mal, about other potential uses for the scepter.

Except I hadn't seen Mal in over a year.

"What use have you for the scepter of Mulan?" I asked Porter.

The man glowered at me. "I don't converse with underlings."

"That's a haughty disposition, given that I'm the one with the weapon."

"You'll be hanged for this."

Baird materialized back at my side. His blood-stained clothes testified to his recent injury, and his face looked pale, but he appeared healed.

"Are you okay?"

"That wasn't a survivable wound—not without the spring water." He took one of the weapons from me and turned it over in his hands.

"Give us your weapons," he demanded. "You'll be presented to the Queen of Crithos for your invasion."

When the Prince nodded, his men complied—despite their malicious glares.

I kept the gun aimed at Porter, while Baird collected the men's swords and metal clubs. He piled them several meters away from the cluster of Bellosian sailors.

"Can you manage for a few minutes? I'll go collect something to restrain them and return shortly." I handed Baird the other weapon I held.

He held the weapons high and aimed them down at our captives. "I can manage."

<<<BUY BOOK 4 TODAY>>>

9 781732 452503